GEMINI MAN

GEMINI MAN

THE OFFICIAL MOVIE NOVELIZATION

NOVELIZATION BY **TITAN BOOKS**

BASED ON THE FILM BY **ANG LEE**
STORY BY **DARREN LEMKE** AND **DAVID BENIOFF**
SCREENPLAY BY **DAVID BENIOFF** AND **BILLY RAY** AND **DARREN LEMKE**

TITAN BOOKS

GEMINI MAN – THE OFFICIAL MOVIE NOVELIZATION
Print edition ISBN: 9781789093018
E-book edition ISBN: 9781789093025

Published by Titan Books
A division of Titan Publishing Group Ltd
144 Southwark Street, London SE1 0UP

First edition: October 2019
1 2 3 4 5 6 7 8 9 10

A CIP catalogue record for this title is available from the British Library.

Printed and bound in the United States of America.

GEMINI MAN

CHAPTER 1

The train route from Liège, Belgium, to Budapest, Hungary, is a crooked line, passing through Germany and Austria, then skirting the southwestern border of Slovakia before it finally reaches its destination in north-central Hungary. Travel times can be as little as thirteen hours or an entire day, depending on how many stops there are and how many times you have to change trains. There is no way to get from Liège to Budapest without changing trains. Four or five transfers are most common, although on some itineraries there are seven or even ten changes.

All things considered, this made Valery Dormov's itinerary a minor miracle. It required only two changes—the first in Frankfurt, the second in Vienna, and a total of eleven stops altogether, twelve if you counted Budapest—for an estimated travel time of not quite thirteen hours.

This extraordinary bit of scheduling had not been devised by Dormov himself but by some faceless *rabotnik* with a gift for seeing timetables in three dimensions rather than merely columns of numbers that most people would find almost impossible to coordinate. Dormov imagined that when the *rabotnik* came up from their basement office and presented this amazing bit of work to their superiors they'd had to withstand a chorus of bitching about the number of stops, rather than applause or even a pat on the back. But the stops couldn't be helped—there weren't any non-stop trains. On European railways there was no such thing as flyover cities.

Valery Dormov didn't care about the number of stops but his bodyguards did. Every stop left them open to possible attack, or was at least an opportunity for an assassin to board the train, and transfers were even more dangerous. The bodyguards had gone over with him step by step how they were going to keep him alive in the Frankfurt and Vienna stations, emphasizing how important it was that he do *exactly* as he was told.

Dormov had been tempted to tell them that any putative assassin had probably boarded with them here in Liège but he knew they weren't going to welcome him telling them how to do their job and instead simply nodded. He was a Russian in his sixties and he was just glad there were only two transfers, which meant he wouldn't have to get up every few hours to run through train stations with three large, tense bodyguards. Not because he was disabled in any way—at his last check-up in the US, the forty-year-old doctor had actually said he envied Dormov's blood pressure and muscle tone—but simply because he had been traveling nonstop for several days and he was tired. He could spend most of the next thirteen hours sitting down. Anything he could do sitting down wasn't even an inconvenience.

It had been Dormov's idea to go by train. Flying would have gotten him home more quickly but he had pointed out to his contacts that if the Americans were looking for him they would have already staked out the airports and even enlisted the security staff to help. No doubt they were watching the train stations, too, but it would be easier for him to blend in among the other travelers, even with bodyguards. In truth, Dormov had always hated air travel; on a train, you could get up and go to the bathroom any time you needed to, which at his age was an important consideration.

He suspected that if he *had* wanted to fly to Moscow, the bureaucrats would have turned him down. Not because airline passengers were easier to track but merely to put him in his place—Russia was happy he was coming home but that didn't mean he could just snap his fingers and get whatever he wanted. Bureaucrats had to posture to compensate for their otherwise colorless jobs. Dormov didn't mind. He could posture, too, and show them that after thirty-five years in the US, he wasn't spoiled and demanding.

In fact, Dormov had mellowed about many things as he'd grown older. Even just twenty years ago, he'd have been highly annoyed at the little girl running up and down the aisle, chattering in softly accented Belgian French. These days, he was content to let children be children and do all the things children did, like being excited about going on a train ride. Too soon they would grow up and be browbeaten into the dullness and mediocrity that in too many places passed for good citizenship. Or they'd turn cynical and bad-tempered, finding fault with everyone and everything in the mistaken belief that this made them discriminating or insightful.

The train had yet to leave the station but the bodyguard sitting beside him asked for what seemed like the thousandth time if he wanted coffee or tea or something to eat. Dormov waved him off with one hand, shaking his head as he turned to look out the window. The other two bodyguards sitting on the other side of the small table were the usual kind of Russian muscle—stoic, stone-faced, and far more alert than they might appear to the other passengers.

His seat-mate, however, was somewhat younger and less experienced. Dormov wondered if this could be his very first field assignment because he didn't seem to know he was supposed to just sit quietly and look intimidating, or at the very least unapproachable. He kept asking Dormov if he wanted something to eat or drink or read, was he comfortable, did he want a blanket.

Well, Yuri had said that quite a number of people were eagerly anticipating the return of the prodigal scientist to the bosom of Mother Russia. Typical Yuri—he'd never met a sentence he couldn't embellish. Dormov thought it had something to do with the fact that the nature of Yuri's work meant he had spent so many years oscillating between East and West. That sort of thing made operatives quirky.

East and West had many similarities but their differences weren't complementary: Madonna's bustier wasn't a good fit for the bosom of Mother Russia. Dormov had always been secretly convinced that the fall of the Berlin Wall and the subsequent end of the Soviet regime was directly attributable to three things: Madonna, MTV, and scented toilet paper. And the Internet had made sure no one looked back.

He had seen it coming back in the evocative year of 1984, when the Americans had first wooed him with the promise of a high-tech paradise without the threat of secret police watching him to make sure he toed the party line. Dormov had thought that sounded great. Over the next three and a half decades, however, he had learned that secret police came in many different forms, and just because you weren't in a Siberian gulag didn't mean you weren't in a prison (albeit with softer toilet paper).

And then there was the matter of ethics. *Bozhe moy!*

He had always tried to be an ethical and moral man, a man of integrity. These were complex matters in an overcrowded world. He had been born the year Joseph Stalin had died and in those days there was less ambiguity about such matters. Stalin had outdone Hitler's death toll, all of them Russians. Surviving under the Soviet regime was complex but ethics and morals were quite clear.

Dormov had gone to the US not for MTV or toilet paper but because he'd been certain that sooner or later, his scientific research would somehow come into conflict with the party. He didn't want to wake up one morning and find himself in a gulag where the best thing he could hope for was a good tattoo of a cathedral on his back.

The decision to leave the US had been much harder.

Again, the young, eager-to-please bodyguard on his left asked if he wanted a pillow and again Dormov shook his head. The two men sitting opposite didn't change expression but Dormov caught them trading furtive glances. Maybe they were wondering why he put up with all the pestering. Dormov chuckled inwardly. The guy was just a kid; this was his version of running up and down the aisle, chattering. After thirty-five years in exile, Dormov enjoyed hearing his own language spoken by another Russian rather than an American with a pretty good accent.

The other two bodyguards had barely spoken to him at all, except to map out the plans for changing trains and to check him for bugs or GPS trackers. They made those devices so small these days, a person could hang one on you just by casually brushing past you in the street—or in a train station, or even while you were sitting in your seat on the train—and you'd be none the wiser.

Dormov knew all the tricks—the Americans had given him a thorough education in surveillance, though not always intentionally. From time to time, someone who was absolutely, positively *not* in any way a spy had tried to bug his laboratory, or even his home. He always knew because they came from vaguely named government departments he'd never heard of. When that happened, he would refuse to work until his lab was swept clean—the *whole* lab, including the bathrooms. Anyone curious about what he and his assistants were up to could watch the feeds from the bugs that were already in place.

Surveillance wasn't the reason Dormov had decided to go home. He knew damned well he would be monitored even more closely in Moscow—the Soviet state was no more, but old habits died hard. Even so, the Russian government had never been as coy about surveillance as the Americans. In Russia, you had to assume somebody, somewhere, was watching. In the US, they made a lot of noise about privacy, how everyone was entitled to it and the government had no right to violate it, so they made the bugs smaller and hid them better.

Then 9/11 had happened and even the average US citizen was conflicted about the choice between personal privacy vs. public safety. Not that the American government hadn't already been wiretapping and bugging and just generally poking its nose into the private affairs of people they considered threats to national security. 'National security' was one of those vague terms intelligence agencies found so very useful as a way to avoid having to explain their actions, or even admitting to them.

Still, government surveillance was one thing; this latest thing they had asked of him was something else, completely unacceptable. Dormov had never been a fan of Soviet-style communism but letting capitalism run riot was just as bad, maybe even worse. He had always suspected that someday he would reach his limit and then he would have to leave the West altogether. Finally he had understood that the Americans would never even allow him to retire, not with all that knowledge in his head—he was a risk to national security. He'd known then that he had to get the hell out and go home.

Russia was no utopia of enlightenment and he had no illusions about why they were so happy to take him back— getting all the knowledge in his head would be a real coup. Plus, it would upset the Americans. It was nothing personal, but at least he'd be able to get a decent bowl of solyanka. Which he could enjoy with a pint of kvass—the real thing, not the bottled sugar-water sold in US gourmet shops.

Dormov looked out the window at the swooping curved lines of the canopy roof. The Liège station was breathtaking. When he had first seen it, he'd thought it looked like an enormous white wave that had somehow been captured and frozen in transit, an enormous white wave with grooves. It was all steel, glass, and white cement, *sans* facade, or grand front door, just that swooping roof. The grooves were actually white concrete beams that threw geometric shadow patterns in the sunlight.

According to his helpful bodyguard, this was a trademark of the architect, Santiago Calatrava Valls. Dormov admired the design—he thought he would enjoy meeting a man who could see something like this in his head. At the same time, however, the station looked so utterly *strange*, like something from another planet. Except it wasn't; the train station was right where it was supposed to be. *He* was out of place.

But that was just his homesickness, Dormov thought. As his journey eastward had progressed, he had come to realize he had been homesick for over thirty years, and the closer he got to the bosom of Mother Russia, the more intense the feeling became.

It would be a relief when they reached Budapest and made contact with Yuri. Hungary wasn't home, but it wasn't the West, either. If he couldn't get solyanka and kvass yet, he'd happily settle for kettle-made goulash and vodka.

Several miles southeast of the city, on a desolate hilltop overlooking a valley untouched by development, a man named Henry Brogan sat in an SUV. One dark brown, well-muscled arm was stretched out, his hand resting on the steering wheel as he gazed into the distance. A casual observer might have thought he had come to that deserted place for some solitary introspection, maybe to take stock of his life and consider the circumstances that had led up to this moment, with an eye to deciding what he might do next.

A more careful observer, however, would have noticed how straight he sat in the driver's seat and attributed his posture to military service. Henry had been a Marine but those days were long behind him. The only thing he'd taken with him from that time besides a skill set he had since enhanced and improved to an incredible degree was a small tattoo on his right wrist, a green spade. He might have jettisoned that along with his uniforms and the rest of the military trappings except it meant more to him than all the commendations and medals he'd received put together. It was an icon; when he looked at it he saw the deepest and most significant part of himself, what other people might call the soul, a concept he had never felt comfortable talking about. Fortunately, he didn't have to; it was all contained in that little green spade, nice and neat, the way he liked things to be in his life.

Right now, his attention was focused on a set of tracks 800 yards away waiting for the train from Liège on the first leg of its long journey to Budapest. Occasionally, he glanced at the photo taped to the rearview mirror; it was slightly fuzzy, copied from a passport or a driver's license or maybe an employee ID badge, but clear enough to be recognizable. The name VALERY DORMOV was printed across the bottom in clear block letters.

Monroe Reed enjoyed taking the train anywhere on the Continent. The Europeans really knew how to travel at ground level. This was something he had learned to appreciate as travel by plane had become more complicated and less comfortable. It was bad enough that you had to wait in line for a godawful amount of time to walk through a metal detector and then maybe get felt up by some bored worker bee in a uniform. But to add insult to injury, airlines now had two or even *three* levels of coach and they all sucked.

Usually he didn't have to suffer commercial air travel when he was working with Henry. But on occasion the DIA would give him an extra assignment or they would tell him to stay behind and do some clean-up. The agency didn't send out jets for anyone as low as he was on the totem pole. Then he would be stuck listening to the screaming baby chorus while the kid in the row behind him kicked his seat for six hours—a kid he thought was probably very much like the one who kept running up and down the aisle right now, mouth going a mile a minute. Monroe wasn't sure how old she was—six, maybe seven? Too young to travel alone but he was damned if he could tell which of the other adults in the car she belonged to. None of them seemed inclined to rein her in. His own parents hadn't been big on corporal punishment but if he'd behaved like this at the same age, he wouldn't have been able to sit down for a week.

He should probably just lighten up, Monroe thought; nobody else seemed to find her annoying, not even Dormov, and he'd have expected the old man to be a prize grouch. Not that it would have occurred to Monroe to think any defector could be good-natured or likeable. On the other hand, Dormov was originally from Russia, so maybe the old man didn't feel like he was defecting so much as he was simply going home to retire. Maybe he still missed the place even after thirty-five years in the US. Now that the old Soviet regime was no more, he didn't have to worry about the KGB taking him away in the middle of the night and sending him to a gulag in Siberia.

Still, Monroe doubted Dormov would find retirement in Russia to be as cushy as it would have been in the US. And if he wasn't retiring, if he was going to carry on with his so-called 'work', he would discover that despite all the classified information he had brought with him from the US, the Russians would never be able to give him a lab as good as the state-of-the-art facilities and tech he'd taken for granted in America. Hell, he'd be lucky to get a chair with good lumbar support. Old guys were always complaining their chairs didn't have good lumbar support, or at least all the old guys Monroe knew.

Well, Dormov wouldn't have to worry about that, nor would he be spilling his guts. And Monroe would only have to tolerate the hyperactive kid until the next stop, where he'd be getting off if everything went according to plan. He was certain it would. He was working with Henry Brogan and Henry never failed to come through. When Henry was on a job, he was like a machine. Nothing rattled him or distracted him; he had focus like a laser and a sense of timing that was practically supernatural. The jumpiness Monroe always felt at the start of a mission was, in fact, sheer anticipation.

Today, however, that kid running up and down the aisle chattering away with her little-girl curls bouncing around her face was driving him crazy. *Was* she six? He wasn't good at guessing kids' ages.

Or any ages, he thought, remembering how he'd assumed Henry was in his late thirties. When Henry told him he was fifty-one, his jaw had dropped. How could *anyone* look that good in their *fifties*?

Dammit, where *were* that kid's parents? The train would be pulling out any minute, why hadn't they corralled her already? Oh, right—everything was different in Europe, including methods of parenting. Monroe had heard somewhere the French started giving their kids wine with dinner when they were three years old. The practice probably extended to every country where they spoke French, like here in the Liège province. He looked at his watch as the girl pattered past him for the millionth time, her mouth running like a motor. Too bad dinnertime was still hours away—a little wine would calm her down. She might even sleep all the way to wherever. Which, now that he was thinking of it, might have been why the French gave their kids wine in the first place.

Across the aisle and three rows down from him, one of Valery Dormov's bodyguards was fussing over him, had been ever since they'd boarded the train. Maybe he'd been a nursemaid in a previous incarnation. He wouldn't let up even though Dormov kept waving him off and telling him he was fine.

The bodyguard's unrelenting solicitude was getting on Monroe's nerves as much as the girl was. It was torment just having to listen to him asking him over and over if Dormov wanted something to eat or drink or read, did he need a pillow, was his seat okay. *Nyet, nyet, nyet,* the old man said, waving one hand. If it had been anyone else, Monroe might have actually gotten up and told them to leave the poor guy in peace. Dormov was hardly a *poor guy*, and he would rest in peace soon. The thought put a smile on Monroe's face.

The little girl ran past Monroe again going the other way. If the train didn't get underway soon, he thought, he'd have to start running up and down the aisle himself just to blow off steam. Still, it didn't really matter if they ran late, just as long as Henry was on time. And he would be.

As if in response to his thoughts, the train gave a jerk and began to move forward. At the same moment, a female voice came over the PA system, making an announcement about travel times, destinations, and passenger safety and, since it was all in French, it sounded enchanting and a bit seductive. Monroe had been told that Belgians had a softer accent than they did in France. His ear wasn't good enough to tell the difference. Henry's probably was, though; he was that kind of precise.

He looked out the window. "Car number six," he said, his voice quiet and clear. "We're moving. Four alpha. Repeat: four alpha. Window seat, his team on all sides."

Some miles to the south and east, Henry replied, "Copy that."

His eyes were still on the tracks in the distance, specifically on the spot where they disappeared into a tunnel cut into a hill. The entrance to the tunnel was somewhat lower than his vantage point. Moving quickly but without hurrying, Henry got out of the driver's seat and went around to the rear to raise the hatch before pausing a moment to check the time on his wristwatch. He'd bought it on base when he was still in boot camp because it looked right to him, like the kind of watch a Marine would wear. It was still working and he still liked seeing it on his wrist. Then he opened the hard case in the back of the SUV.

The Remington 700 sniper rifle was old and sturdy, like his watch, like himself, and they were all still going. The moment he began assembling the Remington, a sensation of calm control bloomed inside him and flowed outward from his core into his head and his hands, into the air around him so that he breathed the same imperturbable, perfect balance that made up his mind and body. And the Remington.

Henry calibrated the Remington's telescopic sight, attached it to the bipod on the barrel, then lay down on his stomach enjoying the way his body warmed to the position. It felt like coming home; it always did.

"Speed?" he asked.

"238 kilometers per hour and holding steady," said Monroe's voice in his ear. Henry smiled.

Monroe shifted in his seat. It was as if his skin were on too tight. He transferred the book he'd been pretending to read—or trying to pretend to read—from one hand to the other and back again.

"You sound excited," Henry said, as calm and matter-of-fact as ever.

"I *do* love capping bad guys," Monroe said, shifting again. If Henry had seen him, he might have knocked him out with the butt of the Remington. *Had to, for your own good,* he'd say later when Monroe came to. *You were going to give the whole thing away.*

Monroe forced himself to stare down at the book instead of stealing another look at Dormov and his bodyguards. This wasn't his first rodeo; he knew damned well you had to be careful not to look at the target too much. They would notice and get the idea something was up. Then he looked anyway.

Dormov was finally starting to show a little impatience with the helpful bodyguard, waving him off without bothering to turn away from the window. It wouldn't be much longer now. Knowing that made Monroe even jumpier.

The train appeared on the track eight hundred yards from the hilltop where Henry lay on his belly.

He loaded a single bullet into the Remington. One shot was all he'd get. If he couldn't do it in one shot… but he always had.

He tapped the stock twice and took aim.

"Wait. *Wait.*"

Henry could practically *hear* Monroe's knuckles whiten. He was about to tell him to unbunch his panties when Monroe said the magic words:

"Civilian in play."

Henry froze and the universe froze with him. Except for the goddam train speeding toward the tunnel as if it were desperate to reach safe haven.

The good news was the little girl had finally stopped running up and down the aisle. The bad news was she was now standing in the aisle right beside Dormov and his party, staring at them as if transfixed. Dormov stared back at her, apparently disconcerted by her unabashed curiosity.

She's going to stand there and save his life, Monroe thought, horrified. *The little shit's going to save this bastard's life. She's going to blow our only chance to prevent a foreign power from getting hold of classified material, and she's going to do it just by being a goddam little kid.*

Monroe was about to get up and find some pretense to make her move even if he had to knock her down, when her mother finally materialized to take charge of her. There was a strong resemblance between the little girl and the pretty young woman dressed in a white blouse and blue skirt but somehow her mother had managed to remain invisible until now. She took her daughter by the shoulders and ushered her away, admonishing her gently in French that sounded musical to Monroe.

Monroe's sigh of relief cut off sharply when the two of them took seats in the next row, the girl sitting directly behind Dormov. She was far too close for Monroe's comfort but it didn't matter as long as she was outside the kill box.

"Clear," Monroe said under his breath.

Looking through the scope, Henry felt himself dare to resume breathing. "Confirm that," he said as the first car entered the tunnel. *And do it fucking now,* he added silently.

"Confirmed. Clear. Go to green," Monroe said, his voice tight and urgent.

"Copy." Henry's finger curled around the trigger and squeezed.

The moment of the shot was always *the moment*, The One True Moment when the universe was finally in order, when it finally made sense. All cause was aligned with effect, everything was in the right place, and every place was in the right position in relation to his own. He knew when the bullet left the barrel and visualized the path it took through the softly sunlit air all the way to the train, where, like everything else in the universe, it would be exactly where it was supposed to be.

Except it wasn't.

Henry took his eye from the scope. The immutable calm, clarity, and conviction that always enveloped him on a job had vanished. Everything in the perfectly ordered universe had slipped out of alignment; The One True Moment had not come together. There was no calm around him. He was only a guy holding a rifle, lying on his belly in the dirt below an uncaring sky somewhere in northwestern Europe.

He'd missed the shot.

He didn't know how he knew, he just did.

Monroe was unaware of Henry's frame of mind. The entire carriage was in an uproar. The little girl's mother was screaming as she held her daughter in her arms, one hand over her eyes even though the child couldn't see anything, not even the hole in the window beside Dormov. Dormov himself sat with his head cocked at a rather inelegant angle while blood dribbled down onto his shirt from the gunshot wound in his throat.

The bodyguards sat frozen in place as if the shot had turned them all into statues, even the one who had been so attentive, and they were still frozen when the train emerged from the tunnel. There was going to be hell to pay when they reported to their superiors. They'd had one job and they'd failed spectacularly.

Tant pis—for them. A bad guy had been capped. Now Dormov would never spill his guts about everything he'd gained from thirty-five years of government-funded research in America. Everything Dormov knew about chemical-biological warfare had died with him. Disaster averted, everything was as it should be. All was right with the world.

"Alpha, mike, foxtrot," Monroe said cheerfully.

Henry removed the tiny earpiece without responding. Normally Monroe's sign-off was the cherry on top but he wasn't feeling it today. He was on automatic pilot as he disassembled the rifle, without the satisfaction he should have felt after eliminating a terrorist—and a bioterrorist at that, thus making the world a safer place. Something had gone wrong, and for now, he and Monroe had nothing more to talk about.

CHAPTER 2

Henry had been around the world more times than he could count, first as a Marine and later for his current employer, but unlike many other well-travelled people, he did not subscribe to the belief that one place was pretty much like another. Anyone who did, in his opinion, wasn't paying attention. Every place he'd ever visited had characteristics and features found nowhere else, with one exception: abandoned buildings.

If someone had blindfolded him and taken him to an abandoned building anywhere in the world, then put a gun to his head and told him to guess where he was without looking out a (broken) window, he'd have been dead. There always seemed to be the same detritus on the floor, the same wood fragments from stairs or railings, the same scattering of shattered glass, and the same trash indicating it had been the site of more than one underage drinking party as well as shelter for someone in transit from nowhere to nowhere else. The abandoned building where he was now was no exception.

Abruptly he realized he had been standing over the crate marked FISH OIL like a man in a trance, holding the components of the Remington as if he didn't know what to do with them. Maybe he should take a few of those tins home with him, boost his brainpower with omega-3, instead of just using them to camouflage a weapon. Probably wouldn't help his aim, though, he thought ruefully as he stuffed the Remington's parts into the packing material.

"Shipping to the same place?" Monroe asked cheerfully from behind him.

"Yup." In spite of everything, Henry couldn't help grinning. Monroe had that effect on him. The guy was like a beagle—always glad to see him, full of good spirits. He was young, of course, but not *that* young. Most DIA agents his age had already begun to have their shiny-happy worn off but not Monroe, not yet. Henry wanted to believe that Monroe might be tougher in that respect than the average twenty-something. In which case, the agency would only work that much harder to wear down his spirit. You just couldn't win.

"Gotta say, that was your best *ever*." Monroe had a look of ineffable happiness on his young face as he joined Henry next to the open crate. Yeah, a human beagle. "Windage, minute-of-angle, redirection from the window. I was—"

Henry hated to burst his bubble but he had to. "Where'd I hit him?"

"Neck. On a *moving* train." Monroe showed him his iPhone.

Henry drew back, horrified. "You took a *picture*?"

"Me and everybody else," Monroe assured him.

An image popped into Henry's head of a crowd of people who were so busy jockeying for position around the dead man that none of them, including the conductor, called for help, and felt even more revolted. What the hell was *wrong* with people? Bunch of *ghouls*.

"Delete it," he ordered Monroe. "Jesus."

"Henry, *four* shooters whiffed on this guy before you got the call and they were all studs. Then *you* ring him up on the first try." He put a hand over his heart, pretending to sniff back a tear. "It got me kind of emotional."

"*Delete it*," Henry said again, growling.

"Okay, okay, I'll delete it." Monroe showed him the iPhone screen. Now there was a photo of a cat with a word balloon over its head asking ungrammatically for a misspelled cheeseburger. "There, it's all gone. Happy now?"

Happy wasn't the word Henry would have chosen—not even close—but knowing that Monroe wouldn't be walking around with death porn on his cell phone didn't make him *un*happy. It was just too bad that he was about to bum the kid out completely. He didn't want to but it couldn't be helped. When you knew the truth, you knew it, and it was no good trying to deny it.

Henry stuck out his hand. Looking surprised, Monroe hesitated, then shook it. "Just want to say it was great working with you and good luck." He turned to the backpack sitting beside the crate and zipped it closed as the beagle went from oh-boy-oh-boy-I'm-so-happy to confused apprehension.

"Wait a second," Monroe said. "'Good luck'? As in 'bye'?"

Henry shouldered the backpack. "Yeah. I'm going out of business."

For a second or two, Monroe was actually speechless. "But *why*?"

The mental image of Dormov slumped in his seat with a hole in his neck flashed through Henry's mind. "'Cuz I was aiming for his *head*."

Henry could practically feel Monroe's dumbfounded stare on his back as he walked away. He had really hated doing that to the beagle but he'd had no choice. As soon as he'd pulled the trigger, he'd felt it in his bones that it had gone wrong and the revolting photo Monroe had showed him proved the feeling hadn't been some kind of neurotic, I'm-getting-old brain fart. Way back in the beginning, he'd promised himself that the day he missed would be the day he quit and he could not, would not, break that promise. The next miss might not be close enough for government work.

But damn, he was going to miss that beagle something fierce.

CHAPTER 3

If one place wasn't pretty much like another (except for abandoned buildings), then it followed as the night follows the day that there was no place like home. And even if he was wrong about that and everything else, Henry was absolutely sure there was no place like Buttermilk Sound in the Georgia estuaries.

Henry ambled down the long dock to the boathouse, careful as always to keep to the center of the weathered boards. Now that he was no longer with the agency, he was going to spend a lot more time enjoying the pleasures of living near water. At the moment, however, there was one last thing he had to do before the mission in Liège was well and truly over.

Inside the boathouse, he pulled the photo of Valery Dormov out of one pocket and a Zippo out of the other. The lighter gave Henry a flame as soon as he thumbed the wheel. He touched it to the photo, watching for a second as it consumed the Russian's image before dropping the burning paper into a fishbowl on a shelf, where it joined the ashes of photos from previous missions.

And that was that. *Now* he was retired.

Henry turned to go back to the house and then paused. A goldfish bowl a little over half full of ashes. Was that *really* what his entire life's work amounted to?

Somewhere, a retiring office drone was being presented with a gold watch—or more likely a gold-*colored* watch—to commemorate the decades he'd spent achieving inertia at his desk. He would take it home and have a heart attack in front of the TV, passing away from the world as if he had never passed into it. At least he would leave a watch behind, something functional; by contrast, the ashes in that goldfish bowl wouldn't even make good confetti.

Henry shook his head as if to clear it. What was he *thinking*? Screw that—he *had* a watch and it was still running after a lifetime of use. And *his* watch wasn't just counting off the hours until he died.

He went back up the dock to the house. Dammit; missing that shot had taken the shine off everything.

The bright daylight in the living room lifted Henry's spirits and chased away much of the residual gloom from Liège. It was open and airy, with a lot more window space than solid wall. He liked being able to see so much of the outside from indoors; even more than that, he liked to let in as much daylight as possible, especially after a job. Unlike the mission in Liège, a lot of his work was done under cover of darkness and he knew all too well what a lack of daylight could do to a person.

This was the heart of the house, where he spent most of his time off the job, so it had a few unconventional features. Against the wall it shared with the kitchen, he had set up a cabinet with almost all of his tools, arranged in a way that appealed to his aesthetic sense while satisfying his need for order and efficiency. Screwdrivers, wrenches, wood chisels, reamers, pliers, sockets, screws, nails and everything else were arranged not only by size but for convenience, depending on frequency of use. He'd had an absolute *blast* organizing them, using the 20/80 rule—twenty percent of the tools were used eighty percent of the time, and vice versa. Maybe now that he'd retired from assassination, he could consider a new career designing displays of tools in hardware stores. He loved hardware stores, always had, even as a kid. Hardware stores followed the 100 rule—one hundred percent of the stock was useful for getting things done.

Nearby was the workbench with a large magnifier lamp. He had positioned it so he could see the TV easily and wouldn't have to miss any Phillies games while getting things done. He had been keeping an eye on his beloved Phillies while he had been working on the birdhouse. He turned to look at it hanging outside the window behind him and his mood lightened even more.

He had built the birdhouse on a whim. Or maybe it was more like a private joke with himself, at least when he'd started out. Building a birdhouse was the kind of thing a nine-year-old would do to get a scout badge, not how a trained government sniper relaxed between assassinations. But to his surprise, Henry had found the act of construction—cutting the wood, gluing it together, sanding it, and applying weatherproofing and varnish—to be unexpectedly gratifying. When he was done, he felt as if he had discovered something new about himself. Who knew that a hitman could have that kind of experience in his fifties (*very early* fifties; *barely* into his fifties, and dammit, how had *that* happened?).

When Henry had finally hung the thing up, his sense of accomplishment had deepened. He had actually built a house with his own two hands. Yeah, okay, it was a *little* house, not a boathouse or even a garden shed—he had hired someone to build both those things. Still, he had created a shelter for *living* creatures that would settle in and make it their home, at least until they migrated. How many other snipers were that constructive when they were off the clock? Probably none.

He watched the birdhouse stirring a little in the breeze then frowned. Something wasn't right. Maybe he was just having some residual bad feeling from Liège. After missing the shot, he had felt like the whole world was ten degrees out of true.

No, that wasn't it. There really *was* something off.

It took another moment before he spotted the problem—two splinters sticking out from the upper left junction of the roof and wall. Henry knew most people wouldn't have seen them, and even if they had it wouldn't have bothered them much, if at all.

But they weren't birds looking for a place to nest. On the birds' level, those splinters must have looked like a couple of sharpened stakes. A prospective resident who got caught in a sudden gust of wind and didn't stick the landing could get stuck. Maybe that was why it had remained empty since he had hung it up. The devil was always in the details, even for birds.

Henry went to the tool cabinet and opened the drawer where he kept small squares of sandpaper, organized in order of coarseness. He chose a square from the middle, then swapped it for the next finer grain and went out to repair the birdhouse.

He finished and looked around for prospective tenants—*Okay, I fixed up the fixer-upper. Better move in fast before some nasty-ass kingfisher snaps it up and you have to raise your chicks in an open-air nest above a thorn bush,* he announced silently. But instead of bird calls, he heard the alarm on his cell phone, telling him a car was approaching the house.

Henry knew who it was. He had been bracing himself for this visit, had actually expected it to have come sooner. Maybe traffic had been especially heavy. He started to walk around to the front of the house, then remembered the sandpaper and went back into the living room, ignoring the honking horn. If the entire company of archangels came to his door to tell him it was Judgment Day, his ass was grass, and the good Lord Himself was the lawnmower; they would have to wait till Henry put everything back where it belonged. There was a place for everything and he made damned sure everything was in its place before he did anything else. His house, his rules.

The car horn honked again. He went out to see Del Patterson finish parking his land yacht (badly, as usual) before he leaped out of the driver's seat and rushed at Henry brandishing the resignation letter he'd sent the day before.

"You can't *do* this!" Patterson said by way of hello.

"Yeah, good to see you, too, Del," Henry replied. "Come on in, sit down, make yourself at home while I get you something to drink."

Moments later, Patterson was perched on the edge of the sofa in the living room. The cheerful daylight was lost on him. He was still clutching the letter when Henry came in from the kitchen with a beer and a Coke.

"I *have* to quit," Henry said. "In almost any other line of work, you can lose a step. Not this one."

"You're *still* the best we've got—the best *anyone's* got," Patterson said. "And believe me, I keep track."

Henry put the Coke on the coffee table in front of him. Patterson glared up at him with the expression of a man who had been pushed to his absolute limit and wasn't taking any more shit. The black-framed glasses would have made another man seem bookish, like an absentminded professor; they gave Patterson the look of a no-nonsense authority whose decisions were final.

"Not a soda. Not today." Patterson crumpled the letter into a ball, dropped it on the table, then batted it away.

Henry's eyebrows went up. "You sure?"

"Are you really retiring?" Patterson said evenly. Henry nodded. "Then I'm sure."

Henry moved the Coke aside and gave him the beer. When he had first met Patterson, it had been obvious the man was fond of a drink and as time went on, he had grown even fonder. For a while, it had looked as if Patterson was going to take up drinking as a lifestyle. And then one day, without fanfare, explanation, or apology, his drink of choice had become Coca-Cola.

Everyone including Henry had wondered how long it would last, waited for Patterson to say something about it, but no one wanted to come right out and ask him. An agent who had suffered with the same problem inquired as to whether he was now a friend of Bill W., and reported that Patterson seemed genuinely mystified by the question.

Henry finally decided he had to know; his life could depend on it. Patterson told him that his job required him to be on call 24/7. Therefore, he had to stay clean and sober for the sake of his agents. And that was all he was ever going to say about it, Patterson added; talk was cheap, actions spoke louder than words, and the subject was now closed.

Henry had been satisfied. Everybody had their own reasons for doing whatever they did. If this was how Patterson managed to avoid going down a very dark path to destruction, then it was what it was and Henry was glad he didn't have to think about it any more.

Now Patterson would probably claim he had driven him to drink, Henry thought. He sat down next to him on the sofa, refusing to flinch from the other man's death-ray glare.

"Lots of guys can shoot," Henry said. "Marine STAs, Army Rangers, Navy SEALs—"

"They aren't *you*." Patterson made it an accusation, as if this was yet another way in which Henry had failed him. "They don't have the history you do."

"Yeah, I think the history might be the problem," said Henry. "I've got *too much* of it. We both know shooters don't get better with age, they just get older."

"Then who's going to finish training Monroe?" Patterson demanded, his expression pained. "Guy's called me three times already asking me to talk you back in."

Henry sighed and shook his head again. "I wish he hadn't done that."

Patterson sat forward, his face urgent. "Henry, we've been through a lot together, you and me. We made the world safer. If we hadn't done the things we did, good people would have suffered and bad ones would have profited, good things would have gone bad and bad shit would have gotten worse. What we do is *important*—it *matters*. But *I* can't do anything unless I'm working with someone I trust and I'm not going to trust a new guy the way I trust you."

Henry shook his head again, more emphatically this time. "I'm telling you, Del, something felt *different* on this one. That's why the shot was off—even the ground beneath me didn't feel right."

Patterson looked around as if there might be something in the room to support his counter-arguments, then spotted the birdhouse outside the window.

"So, what now—you're just going to build *birdhouses*?" he asked Henry.

"*Del*. There was a *kid* right next to him. If I'm off by six inches, she's dead," Henry said, talking over him. "I'm *done*."

Patterson's expression said he had finally heard him and he was devastated. Henry had known this wasn't going to be an easy conversation. In their line of work, there was no wiggle room, no time or space for socializing. Your focus had to be on the job, the whole job, and nothing but the job, not the people on your team. You had to be able to take it for granted everyone would be in the right place at the right time doing the right thing. It was all planning, nothing left to chance, no wasted movement, no nonsense, no slip-ups, so that nobody died who wasn't supposed to. Every time Henry thought about how it was only by virtue of sheer luck that he hadn't killed a child—a *child*—he felt shaky inside.

"You know, when I started in the Corps, it all made sense all the time," Henry went on. "My job was to take out bad guys. Art of the Kill—whatever worked. But in Liège—" he shook his head. "The truth is, in Liège, there *was* no Art of the Kill. I just got lucky. I didn't *feel* the shot, not like I should have." He paused, took a breath.

Patterson was starting to look more resigned than hurt. He was a pro; he understood.

"It's more than being older. I've made seventy-two kills," Henry said. "That many, it messes with you deep down. It's like my soul hurts. I think I've reached my limit of lives to take. Now I just want peace."

Patterson gave a heavy sigh. "So what do *I* do now?"

The question threw Henry completely. *Patterson* was the handler—*he* made the plans and called the shots. Patterson was supposed to tell *him* what to do, not the other way around.

Henry spread his hands and shrugged. "Wish me well?"

CHAPTER 4

There were bigger, fancier, more powerful boats moored at the Buttermilk Sound marina but as far as Henry was concerned, none of them was as classy as the *Ella Mae*.

Made in 1959, she was one of the smallest vessels at the marina, but her hull was polished wood. In Henry's opinion, this put her several levels above the fiberglass bath toys anchored here, no matter how big or fancy or expensive they were. Her wood hull meant she was higher maintenance, too, but in Henry's experience, that was true of anything worth having.

Henry steered *Ella Mae* over to the dock with the fuel pumps and filled the tank. When he was finished, he straightened his Phillies cap and headed for the booth in front of the marina office. To his surprise, there was someone new on duty today, a pleasant, smiling woman, dark-haired, pink-cheeked, and heart-wrenchingly young, wearing a Buttermilk Sound polo shirt. She removed her earbuds as he approached.

"Good morning!" she said in a cheerful, sincere voice that made Henry think she actually believed that.

"Hey," Henry replied. "What happened to Jerry?"

"Retired." She beamed. "He couldn't take any more of this bustling place. I'm Danny."

"Henry." He wasn't sure he'd ever been this young, even when he'd been this young. "I owe you $23.46."

"So what are you fishing for?" Her eyes widened as he handed her a hundred dollar bill.

"Peace and quiet. And mackerel."

She kept smiling as she made change. "So I guess you'll be heading to Beecher's Point?"

Jerry had never been so nosy. Maybe she thought getting acquainted was part of good customer service. "Is that what *you'd* recommend?" he asked, a bit archly.

"Seems like a nice enough day for it," she said.

Before Henry could respond, a bee flew past him. Reflexively, he took off his hat and snapped it sharply, catching the bee in mid-buzz. It fell to the deck.

"Wow," Danny said as she got up to peer over the counter at the dead insect. "Not much of a live-and-let-live guy, I take it?"

"I'm deathly allergic to bees," Henry told her. "So, are you a student? Or just a fish-whisperer?" He jerked his chin at the textbook on the counter; the cover photo was one of those arty shots that made jellyfish look ethereally beautiful.

"Working my way through grad school," she said. "Marine biology."

"UGA, Darien?" he asked.

She made a small fist-pump. "Go Dogs."

"Well, be careful," Henry chuckled. "There are some dogs on *these* docks, too."

"Nothing I can't handle," she assured him, her voice brisk, as she put her earbuds back in. Henry loped back to the *Ella Mae*, feeling like a prize fool. *There are some dogs on these docks, too*—what the hell was *that*? If he was going to go around giving fatherly advice to young women, he should get some felt slippers, a cardigan with leather elbow patches, and a goddam pipe. Maybe he'd better run back and tell her to look both ways before crossing the street on her way home. She might need the reminder, being so young and all.

He glanced at his watch. Nope, there wasn't any more time for making a fool of himself; he had somewhere to be.

An hour or so of solitude listening to Thelonious Monk while the *Ella Mae* swayed on the calm water smoothed out Henry's disposition considerably. Out here there was no age or retirement, no missed shots or saying dumb-ass shit to pretty young women at the marina office. Just the hard-salt cool air, the ever-so-gentle rocking motion of the boat, and the unique sound of Monk at the piano. The way Monk played, you didn't just *hear* the music, you *felt* it. The man *attacked* the keys, producing something that was more than music—music-plus. Only Monk could do it.

Out here, Henry was able to relax in a way he never could on land. He didn't care to be *in* the water at all, not one little bit. Being *on* the water, however—that was a whole 'nother story; Henry thought it had to be as close to heaven as a living person could get. He pulled his Phillies cap down low and let himself fall into a light doze—or what he thought was a light doze. When he heard the sound of engines approaching and sat up, he saw the sun had climbed a little higher in the sky.

The engine noise grew louder, a deep, full sound; something big was in the vicinity. Henry leaned over the starboard side of the *Ella Mae* and splashed his face with seawater to wake himself up. As he turned to reach for a small towel on the passenger seat, he saw the yacht coming toward him on the port side.

Henry recognized the make if not the exact model of the craft. It was favored by millionaires who were blessed with a sense of style as well as money. The small, canopied upper deck where the helm was located was just large enough to accommodate the pilot and a companion. Some pilots, however, preferred to have the helm all to themselves, like the man Henry could see up there now, throttling down the engines. He maneuvered the vessel alongside the *Ella Mae*, making it bob around like a cork on an incoming tide.

The man cut the engines and smiled down at Henry. Henry recognized him even though he hadn't seen him in over two decades and grinned back at him.

The lower deck of the *Scratched Eight* was downright elegant; wide, cushioned seating ran along the polished wood walls on either side, drawing Henry's eyes to the wet bar, which was also polished wood. The bar seemed to preside over everything; next to it on the starboard side, a set of stairs spiraled down below deck. Henry thought it looked like a mansion that had been converted into an ocean-going home-away-from-home. For all he knew, it could be—it was the sort of thing Jack Willis would do.

Jack looked every bit the lord of the floating manor in an open white shirt, floral board shorts, and boat shoes. While the years hadn't been as unkind to him as they'd been to others Henry knew, Jack had definitely aged. He was still as quick to smile as he'd been back in the day but the lines around his eyes were from worry, not laughter. His jawline had softened and he was thicker through the middle but he hadn't lost all his muscle; he moved with the unconscious, easy physicality of a man who hadn't spent most of his life sitting down.

Henry felt a surge of awkward self-consciousness and wasn't sure why. Jack had the same green spade on his wrist, so it wasn't like either of them had to pretend with each other. Maybe it was knowing Jack would also be taking note of how *he'd* changed over the years.

He had been astonished when he'd answered the phone the night before and heard Jack's voice on the other end. He had disappeared from Henry's radar when he had decided to go into business in the private sector. Jack had wanted him to come along but Henry had declined. Every now and then, Jack would send him a postcard, usually of some gorgeous beach resort with a short message scrawled on the back: *Wish you were here—don't you? Sure you won't reconsider?*

After a while the postcards stopped coming and Henry figured Jack had finally decided to take no for an answer. The last thing he had expected was a phone call with a request to meet. Not that he'd been unhappy about it—as soon as Jack had given him the coordinates he had been looking forward to seeing him again. And now all of a sudden he was like some clueless boot who didn't know what to do with his hands or where to look.

"I guess I don't have to ask how business is," Henry said with a laugh as he looked around.

"It could have been yours. I only asked you ten times." Jack's laugh was a bit sheepish and Henry realized he was on edge as well. "Good to see you, Henry."

"Yeah, you, too," Henry replied, meaning it.

They hugged, and that was an awkward moment for both of them. But after what they'd been through together, a little awkwardness was no big deal.

"What are you doing now? Feelin' sexy?" Henry nodded at the open shirt.

Jack laughed again as they moved into the cabin. "Thanks for coming so quickly."

"Still married?" Henry asked.

"Yeah," Jack said. "My wife's on a shopping trip in Paris and my son is in a Swiss boarding school. You?"

Henry shook his head. "No wife. No son. No Paris."

Jack went behind a polished wooden bar and took a couple of beers from a small fridge. He opened them, handed one to Henry, and they raised their bottles in a familiar toast.

"Here's to the next war," Jack said. "Which is *no* war."

"No war," Henry agreed. They clinked bottles and drank. It had been over twenty years since the last time they had done this. Henry wished he could take more time to savor the moment but neither of them had come out here just to have a few beers and catch up on each other's domestic status. "Okay, so what have you got?"

Jack laughed. "Still not one for smelling the roses, are you?"

Henry dipped his head to one side noncommittally. "I'm trying, brother. But you *did* say it was urgent."

Jack nodded and led him out to the stern, grabbing a laptop from a built-in shelf on the way. They sat down with their backs to the cabin and Jack opened the laptop. The screen came to life immediately. "Recognize him?" he asked.

Henry did; he had seen the photo only yesterday, when he had set fire to it and left the ashes in a fishbowl. He was careful to keep his expression neutral as he turned from the screen to Jack. "Who's asking?"

"Your old friend who's afraid you're in trouble." Jack's weathered face wore the kind of serious expression Henry hadn't seen for many years, and had hoped he would never have to see again. "So, do you? Recognize him?"

"Yeah. I AMF'ed him in Liège a few days ago."

"Did they tell you who he was?"

Henry frowned. Of course they had—the agency always told you who the target was. Jack knew that. "Valery Dormov, terrorist."

Jack's expression was pained. "No, Valery Dormov, molecular biologist," he said, his voice heavy. "Who worked here *in the States* for over thirty years." He tapped the touchpad with one finger; the image shrank and became the photo on Dormov's driver's license, issued in Georgia and not yet expired.

"But I *read* his file," Henry said. He felt as if he had a large, icy lump in his stomach. "It said he was a bioterrorist."

"The file was spiked," Jack told him. "I don't know by whom."

The yacht was barely moving in the calm waters of Buttermilk Sound but Henry felt as if the world were tilting sideways. He half-expected to see the horizon was now on a slant but everything looked normal. Except it wasn't, not if Del Patterson had lied to him.

For two and a half decades, Henry had put his life in Patterson's hands without a second thought, never less than a hundred percent certain that he could trust him, that the information Patterson gave him was solid, that he and Patterson and everyone else on the team were all doing the same job for the same side.

If he had heard this from anyone other than Jack Willis, Henry wouldn't have even considered the possibility. But Jack was his brother; he wouldn't have come to Henry after so many years to drop this on him unless he was more than solid on the facts.

"Why?" Henry managed after a bit.

Jack shrugged, looking apologetic. "Don't know that either, I'm afraid. But a lot of alarms went off when Dormov switched teams."

Henry's thoughts were racing now. What if Patterson *hadn't* lied? Maybe *he* had been deceived by someone higher up. Was Patterson a cunning traitor or a clueless dupe? Neither option fit the man Henry knew.

"Who told you all this?" he asked.

Jack hesitated, like he had to choose his words carefully. "A friend from the other side."

A 'friend.' Henry had a pretty good idea of who that might be and unfortunately, it wasn't someone he had ever been in direct contact with. He was going to have to rectify that in order to get to the bottom of this mess. Also, to rule out the possibility that *Jack* had been lied to. That didn't seem at all likely—Jack had always been able to spot a liar a mile away even in bad weather—but the only way Henry could be absolutely sure was to meet Jack's source face-to-face. Jack would understand; if their situations had been reversed, Jack would have felt the same.

"I want to talk to this friend," he said.

Jack choked on a sip of beer. "Oh, *sure*, no problem! What do you prefer, Skype or FaceTime?"

Henry kept his expression neutral. "I *want* to *talk* to him. I *have* to."

He could practically see Jack's mind shift into overdrive, coming up with all the reasons why such a thing was completely impossible and balancing them against the knowledge that Henry would never let it go.

"What the hell—the guy owes me," Jack said. He put his beer in the cup holder on his left and typed rapidly on the laptop keyboard. Then he turned the screen toward Henry, showing him large black letters on a white background:

YURI KOVAC
BUDAPEST

Henry was about to thank him when he heard something behind him. He turned to see an extraordinarily beautiful woman had come up the stairs from below deck. As she came out of the cabin, Henry saw that she had a headful of miraculously thick, honey-colored hair and an equally miraculous body not even slightly obscured by the filmy wrap she wore over a bikini that seemed to have been made for her.

She paused for a moment and peered at Jack over the top of her sunglasses with an expression that somehow managed to be both coolly reserved and possessive. Then she turned away and floated gracefully up the ladder to the next deck, a feat Henry wouldn't have thought possible. He turned to look at Jack; whatever her story was, it had to be fascinating.

Jack grinned and gave a small shrug. "Kitty. To make up for all the things I *didn't* do in my DIA years."

"You think you didn't do that in your DIA years?" Henry laughed. He considered pointing out that when he and Jack had started working together, this vision of loveliness would have been learning how to color inside the lines with her first set of crayons, but decided against it. It wasn't like he'd be telling Jack anything he didn't already know.

Jack showed him around his floating mansion, which was nicer than a few land mansions Henry had been in. The beautiful Kitty didn't reappear and join them for a drink. As far as Henry could tell, she had vanished without a trace, which was something beautiful ladies often did. It seemed to be their super-power. Jack didn't mention her again so Henry didn't, either. When you had shed blood together, you didn't make an issue out of anyone's coping strategies, even if it had been two and a half decades since the bleeding had stopped.

They went back to the stern to have another beer together, looking out at the water and enjoying the fact that there was no one and nothing else around them for as far as the eye could see; Henry certainly enjoyed it, anyway. He looked up at the smooth blue bowl of the sky.

Except it *wasn't* perfectly smooth. Henry saw a small spark, sunlight on metal. It was like a metal splinter ruining the otherwise flawless blue and for some reason, it gave him a bad feeling. But after what Jack had told him, he thought, there wasn't much to feel good about.

"You took a big risk contacting me," Henry said, turning away from the glint far above them. "I wish you hadn't."

"I know but what else was I supposed to do? I love you, brother." Jack's voice broke on the last four words.

"Love you, too, man," Henry replied, now thoroughly disconcerted. Sometimes when you were in the field together, your emotions could blindside you. But Jack had always been one of the steadier guys, good at keeping a lid on his feelings and staying focused on the immediate situation.

But then, this wasn't the field. Or rather, it wasn't supposed to be. That glint in the sky, however, suggested otherwise.

CHAPTER 5

"...they tell you who he was?" said Jack's voice.

"Valery Dormov, terrorist," said Henry.

"No, Valery Dormov, molecular biologist, who worked here *in the States* for over thirty years."

Jack Willis's voice was as clear as if he'd been right there in Janet Lassiter's office with her and Clay Verris, and not actually coming in via a live feed from a drone four thousand feet above the yacht and the tiny boat tethered to it in Buttermilk Sound. The camera was zoomed in close enough to give Lassiter and Verris a perfect view of whoever came out on deck.

Willis and Brogan were still talking when the woman appeared. Lassiter grimaced; she had almost forgotten Willis hadn't come to see Brogan alone. It was probably too much to hope that his lady friend would decide to spend the afternoon shopping in Savannah and follow that up with a leisurely, expensive dinner.

The woman climbed to the top deck, removed her cover-up, and settled into a small whirlpool right behind the helm, folding her long legs and fanning her shiny gold hair out on the deck to keep it glamorously dry. Lassiter herself was bewildered as to why anyone would put a whirlpool *there* of all places.

Well, to show what money could buy, of course. Anyone with enough money could buy a big expensive boat, but why bother if it looked like every other big expensive boat in the catalog? It wasn't about buying a big expensive boat—it was about buying a big expensive statement. Regular people had to settle for bumper stickers or tattoos.

In any case, Lassiter felt sorry for the woman. She must have taken one look at Jack on that yacht and thought she knew exactly what she was signing up for. But then, she had probably thought she knew who Jack Willis was. She'd had no idea what she was getting herself into, which Lassiter thought was an experience common to a great many women, if not most. Lassiter, however, didn't consider herself one of them.

She'd had no illusions about the line of work she had chosen. Intelligence had always been a boys' club and the DIA was no exception. From the outset, Lassiter had known that if she wanted to get anywhere, she would have to claw, push, and punch her way up through the ranks, and she had spent her career doing exactly that. There hadn't been *a* glass ceiling—there had been a whole *series* of them, one after another. The only thing you could do was bang your head against each one until either the ceiling broke, or you did.

The higher you went, the thicker the glass became, and the harder your head had to be, because no one was going to help you. No one—which was to say, no *man*—was going to weaken the glass for you by giving it a couple of hard whacks, or slip you a glass-cutter on the sly, or show you a secret passageway to get around it, not even your own father. Just as well—then she would never have been anything but Daddy's Girl.

If any of your male colleagues did actually step up for you, of course, everyone else would say you'd slept your way to the top. Which was ridiculous—Lassiter had seen with her own eyes that women couldn't sleep their way to the top in the agency. Some managed to sleep their way to the middle, but Lassiter's goals had always been much loftier.

After a great deal of punching, pushing, and clawing, she was now in the stratosphere, where the air was a whole lot colder and thinner. But she was damned if she'd let anyone see her shivering or gasping for breath. Every morning she got up, put on her game face, and headed into work an hour earlier than everyone else, telling herself that yes, it absolutely, positively, and without a doubt had been worth it; she had no second thoughts, no feelings of disappointment or letdown, none whatsoever. She had made it. She was a *director*. That was *godhood*, not a dead end or a sinecure or a hamster wheel designed to make the average, the shortsighted, and the uninspired worker bee believe they were getting somewhere until they keeled over and died.

And if she really was a 'soulless bitch-demon from the ninth circle of hell,' as someone had described her to a co-worker in a ladies' room that hadn't been as empty as either of them had thought, it was still a lot better than being a gossipy, glorified secretary who called herself an executive assistant.

But the one thing the jumped-up wage slaves from the steno pool had going for them was, none of them ever had to deal with the man who was currently sitting in her office and breathing her air.

When Lassiter had met Clay Verris, it had been enmity at first sight. Repeated contact over the years had deepened her animosity into a profound, unshakable loathing. But she didn't have to like him. Clay Verris loved himself, no doubt a hell of a lot more than she detested him. He saw himself as a visionary—a Steve Jobs of the military. A *weaponized* Steve Jobs, locked and loaded, minus the whimsy.

People in intelligence tended to be dispassionate but Clay Verris was cold-blooded on a level that made a python look like a puppy. He could also turn it on and off at will; in a line of work filled with dangerous people, it made him lethal. Lassiter knew she had to tread carefully around him but she refused to be afraid.

"It's a pity," Verris said, abrupt but casual, as if he were engaging in a conversation only he could hear. Lassiter wouldn't have been surprised; she imagined the voices in his head got pretty loud. She waited to see what else was going to come out of him.

"I always liked Henry," he added.

For a moment, Lassiter wasn't sure she'd heard him right, then realized she only wished she hadn't.

"Henry is DIA, Clay," she said sharply. "He's one of *mine*."

Verris glanced at her, annoyed. "He knows you lied to him."

"We have a tail on him," Lassiter replied. "That's standard protocol for a retiring agent. He'll be contained."

"*Contained?*" Verris gave a short derisive laugh. "*Henry Brogan?* Did you hear the same conversation *I* did? He's got Dormov's contact now and he's going to pull that thread until he ends up pointing a gun in our faces."

Lassiter shook her head. "Still—"

"What about his handler—the bald guy?" Verris asked.

"Patterson?" Lassiter shrugged. "He won't be happy but he won't cross me. He'll fall in line." She wasn't actually sure that was true but it would keep Verris from planning Patterson's death for the time being. At least, she hoped it would.

"*I'll* tie this off," Verris told her. "I can make it look like a Russian op."

Lassiter felt a surge of anger. "*You* will do *nothing*," she said. "I can handle this. I'll tell my team that Henry's gone rogue."

Verris blew out a contemptuous breath. "After you whiffed four times on Dormov? Forget it. You need Gemini for this."

Anger surged in her again, more intensely this time. "I will *not* let you do hits on American soil—"

"You don't have anyone who can take out Henry Brogan," Verris said, talking over her loudly. "*I do*."

This was one of those times when Lassiter understood the atavistic impulse to take a swing at someone. Verris had a way of bringing it out in her. "We'll clean up our own messes, thank you," she said in full-on bitch-demon-from-hell mode.

All expression drained from Verris's face as he stalked over to her desk and leaned his fists on it. "Everything we've worked for is at risk—thanks to *your* failures." His gaze bored into hers as if he were willing her to shrivel but the bitch-demon held her ground. "You have *one* chance to not screw this up. Please surprise me."

He straightened, still giving her his death-ray look, and then left. She stared after him. The bitch-demon still wasn't scared of him—not yet, at least. But Janet Lassiter was nervous.

After tying the *Ella Mae* to the piling on the dock, Henry decided to let Monk finish his solo before he set foot on land again. At some point between the time he had untethered from the *Scratched Eight* with Jack Willis smiling hopelessly as he waved goodbye and when he'd reached the marina, the glint in the sky had vanished, but that was hardly a positive sign. As glad as Henry had been to see his old friend, Jack's visit was like that glint—a harbinger of the turbulence to come, after which nothing would be the same. It was all the more reason to steal a few quiet moments while he could.

Henry leaned back, stretching his long legs out on the seat beside him. Monk was working his way up to the finish of 'Misterioso' when his gaze fell on the dashboard.

The rudder angle gauge was slightly out of position, as if someone had pried it out of the dash and put it back in a hurry. Henry felt a surge of anger. This was a custom-fitted dash—you weren't supposed to pop things in and out like Lego. The *Ella Mae* was a classy lady who wouldn't be caught dead with a hair—or a dial—out of place, and Henry had always treated her with the respect she deserved, making sure she looked her best. So who had been taking liberties with her, and why?

He worked the gauge out of the polished wood dash, being careful not to rip out the connections, and saw the problem immediately. Son of a *bitch*, he thought as he disentangled the fiber-optic line from the other wires.

Damn, he should have known better than to think that after twenty-five years with the DIA they would just let him go without pulling some kind of shit. This was one of the tiniest bugs he'd ever seen. It would be sound-only, and he found it hard to believe that it would hear anything other than engine noise, wind, and water, but these days surveillance tech was insanely good. For all he knew, the thing was picking up his pulse and respiration. Which should tell whoever was listening that he was furious.

The agency must have put this in while he was on his way home from Liège, right after Monroe told them he was retiring. Jerry would never have allowed anyone to touch the *Ella Mae*, so the DIA had gotten rid of him. Henry fervently hoped they had made him a retirement offer too good to pass up. Jerry was a nice guy who deserved a piece of the good life; emphasis on *life*.

Henry shut the music off and marched up the dock to the booth outside the marina office. Yeah, Ms. Marine Biology was still on duty. She probably thought she was pretty slick, looking oh-so-innocent as she took out her earbuds and smiled like there was nothing going on. Maybe she was so young she really didn't know what a pissed-off retired assassin looked like.

"Any luck?" she said brightly as he put the fiber-optic mic down on the counter in front of her. She stared at it for a moment, then looked up at him again, her smile tentative now. "Okay, most guys try flowers, or a playlist they think I'll find romantic. But—"

Did she practice that 'who, me?' expression in the mirror? "Are you DIA?" he snapped.

"Um…that depends," she said, still doing pleasant-but-bewildered. "What's DIA?"

"Dance Instructors of America," Henry told her. "Who sent you to surveil me? Was it Patterson?"

"'Patterson?'" she said, frowning a little, like it was a word in a language she had never heard before.

The guileless child act was starting to get on his nerves. "Listen, you seem like a decent person," Henry said, "but you're burned. Your cover's blown."

She tilted her head to one side. "I was in the middle of a Marvin Gaye song, so I think I'll just—"

"Name three buildings on the Darien Campus," Henry said. "Come on, marine biologist, any three. Go ahead."

"Really?" She looked at him dubiously.

"Really."

She sighed. "Rhodes Hall, McWhorter Hall, Rooker Hall."

"Now I *know* you're DIA," Henry said. "A *civilian* would have told me to piss off."

"Not a *polite* civilian," she said evenly.

"*Damn*, you're good," Henry said. "Keep it up, keep charming me—that's straight out of the DIA playbook. Do you live near here?"

She blinked at him. "What?"

"Because I want to see your place—"

"Excuse me?" She drew back from him in alarm.

"—where I bet I won't find a single textbook about marine biology, just a big ol' file on Henry Brogan," he finished, talking over her.

Suddenly she found her smile again, but not for him. Two fishermen were now standing behind Henry, patiently waiting their turn.

"This has been fun, really," she said, "but I kinda have to do my *job* now. So if you don't mind—"

"Okay, how about a drink, then?" Henry said. "Pelican Point?"

Her mouth fell open in genuine surprise. "Why? So you can keep interrogating me?"

"Maybe. Or maybe I'll spend the whole time apologizing. Either way, they've got a great band on Mondays."

Henry could almost see the wheels turning in her head like they had in Jack Willis. Should she say yes and then stand him up, should she drop the act and call for backup, were those two fishermen behind him going to start complaining, why the hell had she even gotten out of bed this morning.

"Seven o'clock," she said finally. Her smile was hesitant and a bit wary. "But how about you leave the crazy at home? Please?"

Henry grinned without agreeing to anything.

* * *

Danny made a quick stop at her apartment to change into jeans and a UGA Darien t-shirt before going over to Pelican Point, getting there a little bit early so she could sit at the patio bar with a boilermaker and collect her thoughts. A couple of guys on the prowl tried their luck one after the other, a couple of minutes apart; to her relief, they didn't try to change her mind when she made it clear she wasn't interested. Some guys automatically approached any woman sitting alone in a bar; at least these two had taken no for an answer.

She was less certain about what she would say to Henry when he got here... *if* he got here. No, *when*, definitely. Henry wouldn't stand her up, if for no other reason than to continue interrogating her. Or to apologize, although she had a feeling Henry didn't do that a whole lot. Some people would not, others could not and they'd do anything to avoid it. Even ask someone out for a drink.

By contrast, she had seriously considered standing *him* up. She still wasn't sure that having a drink with him was a good idea, not after the way he had treated her. What kind of person talked that way to someone they'd just met— especially a grad student on minimum wage? She knew what her father would have had to say about that. The two fishermen waiting behind Henry hadn't heard the whole conversation, just enough that they had both given him a funny look as he walked away. They had given her a funny look, too. She'd just shrugged and said, "The customer's always right," and distracted them by getting right down to their business.

Flowers suddenly appeared on the bar in front of her, a colorful mix of blossoms not overly elaborate but more than something you'd grab at the last minute from a convenience store; definitely suitable for an apology. Henry Brogan sure knew how to do things, she had to give him that. As she turned to smile at him, she felt her face suddenly grow warm. Dear God, she was blushing like a kid, she thought, mortified, which only made her face grow even warmer.

"Aw," she said, trying to think of some way to cover.

"Sorry about today," Henry said, taking the stool on her right. "Old habit. I don't trust easily. You probably don't, either."

Her heart sank; so much for her hopes that he was done being paranoid. "Why would you say that?"

He put a blank 8x11 sheet of white paper on the bar beside the flowers. She looked from it to him, shaking her head a little. "I don't—"

Henry turned the paper over and there it was—her own face staring up at her from a color photocopy of her Defense Intelligence Agency ID badge. It was blown up to five times its normal size, so her full name—Danielle Zakarewski—was easily readable. So was her signature.

Danny slumped on her stool as all the energy she had marshaled for the evening drained out of her. She leaned an elbow on the bar, rested her forehead on her hand for a moment. "Where did you get that?"

"After twenty-five years of faithful service, you make a few friends," Henry said. But his voice sounded gentle, not triumphant. He wasn't gloating. It was one more way in which Henry Brogan had surprised her. Although maybe it shouldn't have—all the information she had on him indicated he was a decent guy.

Danny finished her drink in one long pull and didn't quite bang the mug down on the bar. "Well, *now* I'm burned," she said, feeling herself sag a little more. "I'm *toast*. I'm *burned* toast."

"Not your fault," Henry assured her in the same kindly tone. "You were good. Buy you another boilermaker?"

She nodded glumly. A fine development this was, she thought. In the space of one day, her career had gone from on the rise with no end in sight to something you'd scoop up and bag while walking your dog.

"That's a *cop's* drink," Henry said as the bartender put the mug and shot in front of her. "You got cops in your family?"

"My father was FBI." In spite of everything, she couldn't keep the pride out of her voice. "And pretty big on serving your country."

"'Was?'" Henry asked.

Nothing got by *him*, Danny thought. Whereas *she* hadn't even noticed when he had taken the photocopy of her ID off the bar. This day just kept on getting better.

"He died off-duty," she replied. "Trying to stop a bank robbery."

"I'm sorry," Henry said, and she could tell he meant it.

Before she could do something stupid like start choking up, Danny poured the whisky into the beer and picked up her mug. Henry picked up his own drink and clinked it against hers before having a sip.

"Your file says you were Navy," he said. "Four years with the Fifth Fleet in Bahrain."

"I did like the sea," she told him. "What I *didn't* love was living in a tin can with a couple hundred sailors."

"That still beats a bunker in Mogadishu," Henry said drily.

"Yeah, I'll give you that one," she chuckled.

"After the Navy, you opted for the DIA, defense clandestine services," Henry went on. "Recruiting and running assets. Not a single demerit. And then Internal Affairs put you on a dock to watch a guy who just wants to retire." He gave her a sideways look. "That didn't bother you?"

Danny smiled. Every agency had a lot of status-jockeying; it was as much a part of intelligence work as it was in the civilian corporate world. She decided to change the subject.

"You know what he loved most about the Bureau, my father?" she said, taking another sip of her boilermaker. "The letters: FBI. He said they stood for Fidelity, Bravery, Integrity. He talked about that a lot—in between boilermakers—" she lifted her mug slightly. "How the very name of the place reminded him every day how to behave. 'Live up to these words,' he'd say, 'and I don't care *what* you do for a living, I'll be proud of you.' I hope he is."

"I don't doubt it," Henry said, as if he were actually in a position to know.

In spite of everything, Danny felt surprised and touched. For a moment, she wanted to tell him that meant a lot coming from him, and then caught herself. She was still on the job even if she was toast, and she had to behave accordingly. She was *professional* toast.

But that didn't mean she couldn't have another boilermaker.

Night had fallen by the time she and Henry left Pelican Point. Despite the less-than-optimal circumstances, she had found herself enjoying the evening immensely, trading stories with a man who was pretty much a DIA legend. Of course, she had been careful to edit what she told him and she knew he must have done the same. Still, this had been more fun than the last few dates she'd had. Maybe most of the dates she'd had. Or all of them.

"Well, I guess this is goodbye, Henry," she said, hoping she didn't sound quite as sorry about it as she felt. "It was nice surveilling you. And thanks for the flowers." She held them up. "But I'll probably be off to somewhere else tomorrow."

"Need a lift home?" he asked.

Danny shook her head. "My building's right here." She gestured at the apartment house barely fifty yards from where they were standing. She liked Savannah with its Historic District and riverboat cruises and the lively City Market, and she loved living near the ocean. But she sure wasn't going to miss this place. The agency had insisted that she live there—it was so close to the marina she could see the parking lot from her living room—but the paper-thin walls and the lousy Wi-Fi had been the bane of her existence.

She offered him her hand for a goodbye shake, then held onto him for a few extra moments. "Henry...why *are* you retiring?"

He hesitated and she knew he wasn't deciding which lie to tell.

"I found myself avoiding mirrors lately. I decided to take that as a sign."

That would be Integrity, Danny thought; it went with his Fidelity and Bravery.

"You watch your six out there," Henry told her.

"You too," she said, laughing a little, turning toward her apartment house.

"Goodnight, Toast," he added.

She laughed again but she couldn't help feeling a little melancholy, too, as she headed for her front door. Every so often, she had one of those moments of clarity when she realized what a lonely way of life this was. The job required her to be *among* people but never as one of them, never *with* them. Not even other agents, not really; you always had to keep a bit of a remove between yourself and your co-workers, not get too attached to anyone emotionally. If they got killed, if they changed sides or turned out to be a double agent, an emotional reaction could screw up your thinking, make you hesitate or do the wrong thing. That was a great way to get yourself and everyone else on the job killed, or worse.

When you were off the clock, it wasn't like you could just reset yourself to start connecting with other people the way a civilian would. And if you *were* connecting and enjoying the kind of social life regular people had, you couldn't just flip a switch and turn it off when your handler called to say you were going to Savannah to keep a legendary agent under surveillance because he wanted to quit killing people. So you lived a separate life, kept yourself apart from everyone else. It was like being an air-gapped computer in a world where everyone else was online.

But once in a while—not often, almost never—you met someone and despite your best intentions, you couldn't help connecting with them. You would get a glimpse of what it was like to have a relationship with another human being—a *personal* relationship of *any* kind, romantic or not. It happened to civilians all the time. They had the luxury of taking that stuff for granted; agents had to shake it off like a hangover.

And that was why this evening with Henry had definitely *not* been a date.

"Hey, Jack, you ever think about history?" Kitty asked from where she was standing outside at the rail.

Behind the bar, Jack Willis glanced up from the drinks he was mixing and laughed a little, not unkindly. He was a lifelong admirer of beautiful women; his wife was one of the most beautiful women he had ever met. In recent years, however, he had discovered that a woman who wanted to talk to him more than she wanted to go shopping had an extra special loveliness that went beyond big bright eyes, exquisite bone structure, or a killer body, all of which Kitty was also blessed with.

"That's what I think about when I look up at the stars," Kitty went on. "I think, *cavemen* looked up at those stars. *Cleopatra* looked up at them. *Shakespeare.* And they were the *same stars.* I mean, a couple hundred years is *nothing* to a star. That comforts me. I don't know why."

Jack didn't know why, either. It was hard for him to imagine why a beautiful woman would need comforting unless she was in an accident or a war zone. He glanced out at her again and started slicing up a lime.

"The people in the past, they were looking up at the sky just like I am," Kitty was saying. "And they felt just what I'm feeling—wonder. Which is the same thing people a hundred years from now are going to feel. It—"

Jack waited; the silence stretched and he knew even before he looked that Kitty was no longer at the rail feeling wonder about the stars. He drew his gun from the back of his waistband and moved out onto the deck, careful not to make a sound. Still no Kitty. He remembered what Henry Brogan had said once about how disappearing without a trace was a super-power all beautiful women shared. *It's how they ditch us for the cool rich guys.*

If only that were true this time, Jack thought, his heart sinking. He had not reckoned anyone would dare take a run at him while he was still in US waters. There should have been enough time for him to offload Kitty at some safe haven, dammit—

He spotted the scuba tanks and swim fins on the deck just as a shadow in his peripheral vision moved toward him, becoming a figure with a gun. Jack lunged forward to meet him and the two of them struggled together, each trying to get the upper hand. It had been some years since Jack had gone hand-to-hand with anyone and he could feel the other man was stronger and probably younger. He had to finish this quickly or be overpowered.

Jack was still trying to force the barrel of his gun against his opponent's chest when a shot rang out right beside his ear. Deafened, he fought harder, not knowing if he was hit, relying on adrenaline to keep him going. He almost had the gun against the other guy's belly when an arm reached around from behind and put him in a headlock.

Damn, he'd have heard a second attacker sneaking up on him if that damned gun hadn't gone off, he thought, and then everything went black.

The team of two worked quickly, moving in a deadly choreography that ended with the bodies of the primary target and his female companion trussed up, weighted down, and dumped off the stern. Neither of them had expected the job to be so easy; the woman was nobody but Willis was supposed to be a black ops badass. Obviously retirement hadn't done him any favors because he'd gone down so fast, it was anticlimactic—disappointing, even.

They really hoped the rest of the jobs weren't as easy. How were they supposed to maintain the high level of skill expected of them if the targets barely put up a fight?

CHAPTER 6

Henry Brogan was in a municipal outdoor pool in Philadelphia and he was drowning.

All around him, kids were kicking their legs, stirring the water into a bubbling froth, laughing like this was actually *fun*. And it was—for *them*. They weren't drowning. Why? Why was he the only one drowning and everyone else who jumped into the water had *fun*?

Just when he was sure he was going to die, two strong hands grabbed him under the arms and pulled him out of the water into the bright, chlorine-scented air. Henry blinked the water out of his eyes, choking and gasping while his father grinned at him. His face was so enormous that it blocked out the whole world, even the sky. It was all Henry could see, that big grinning face and the mirrored sunglasses his father always wore; the lenses showed him twin reflections of his terrified five-year-old self, skinny in a pair of oversized trunks that needed extra ties to keep them from slipping off, gasping and squirming, desperate to get away because he knew what was coming next, what always came next.

We have to work on your kick! his father laughed, his voice bigger than the sound of kids shrieking and splashing. *Concentrate, Henry! You're* five *now—this isn't hard! Now try again!*

The two Henrys in the mirrored lenses flailed helplessly, then shrank as his father tossed him back, like a fish that was too small. His father's shimmering shadow loomed over the water while Henry sank and kept on sinking down, down, down. The sound of that big booming laugh became muffled.

Panic hit Henry like an electric shock. He tried to scream and managed only a muted, high-pitched burble he could barely hear. Above him, the bright rectangle of the surface receded. No matter how hard he tried to kick and wave his arms, he couldn't push his way upward; the water wouldn't let him. His legs had become so heavy, *too* heavy, like there were enormous weights attached to them. He could feel them on his ankles, pulling him farther down, deeper than he had ever been, so deep he would never, never, never be able to reach the surface. Darkness was closing in now. The sound of his father's laughter, of kids yelling and splashing and playing had died away, and soon he would, too.

Please, he begged, raising his eyes to the distant, dimming surface. *Please.*

Suddenly, a dark silhouette crashed through the fading rectangle above, a person diving down to him. He recognized the shape—it was his mother. Now he did concentrate, willing the darkness to draw back as he reached out to her. She always came to save him... but she didn't always make it.

The darkness fought him, overpowered him, held him. The water was very cold, much too cold for a pool. He tasted salt not chlorine because this was the ocean and his mother wasn't coming. She wasn't around any more; neither was his father. This wasn't Philadelphia, this was a different place and time where he had discovered worse things lying in wait for him. His arms and legs were so heavy he couldn't even flail, couldn't scream, not even in his head. He could only keep sinking into the cold and dark.

A high-pitched, continuous whine cut through the silence. Henry knew it was a machine and the noise meant he had flatlined. Not for long, though—he was about to come back. He had been saved but not by his mother. This next part was going to hurt like hell. Just as the defibrillator paddles touched his skin, he woke with a start. His relief at finding himself in his own bed was short-lived; he could still hear that high-pitched whine.

Henry grabbed the iPad on the nightstand and shut off the breach alarm. Someone had set off one of laser tripwires at the edge of his property. If he didn't get his ass in gear, he was going to flatline for real.

There was a flicker in the mirror on the wall facing the bed, a shadowy movement reflected from the window to Henry's left. A tiny red light appeared, floating in the dark in search of a target.

Without making a sound, he grabbed his cell phone and dialed as he slid out of bed onto the floor. *Please,* he begged silently, opening the trapdoor beside the bed and slipping down into the crawl space under the house. The burn bag was right where he'd left it—dusty on the outside but (he hoped) still nice and dry on the inside. The number was still ringing. *Please. Please. Please—*

"*Please* tell me this means we're back in business," Monroe said by way of hello.

"Where are you?" Henry whispered.

"Surveilling a goddam *car*," the beagle said, very unhappy about it.

"Listen to me. Get away from there," Henry told him, still whispering as he pushed himself over the ground. He had ignored the funny look the builder had given him when he had said he wanted the house two feet above the ground on concrete pillars; builders didn't have to be ready to make a fast getaway in the middle of the night. "*Don't* go home, *don't* go to your girl's house. Get to a bus station and pay for a ticket in *cash. Only* use cash, nothing else. Steal it if you have to but *don't* take any money out of an ATM. Then go some place where nobody knows you."

"*Shit,*" Monroe said, shaken. "You're sure?"

"They're outside my window," Henry said. "Sorry, man. I made you a loose end."

"I'll be fine," Monroe replied, trying to cover the fear in his voice with bravado and failing utterly. "But how do I get in touch with you?"

"You *don't,*" Henry told him. "Don't call me if you want to live. In fact, you don't call anyone. *Ever.* Least of all the DIA. Just dump your phone. You copy that?"

For a moment, Henry was afraid Monroe might try to give him an argument but he didn't. Monroe said nothing at all. Instead, there were two loud bangs followed by the sound of a cell phone hitting the ground. Henry squeezed his eyes shut as images of the human beagle whirled through his mind: Monroe as he'd been when Henry had first met him, Monroe showing him that awful photo of Dormov on his phone, Monroe young, happy, and full of himself, sure that he'd live forever and never get old.

Henry rolled his grief up into a tiny ball and shoved it into a deep distant place in his mind. There was no time to mourn. Right now he had to concentrate on staying alive. He opened the burn bag and took a quick inventory: clothes and shoes, check—good thing, because no self-respecting agent would be caught dead shirtless and barefoot in pajama bottoms, not even in retirement. Nestled among the clothes were a few bundles of currency, a passport, a Glock, and best of all, two IWI ACEs. You had to love those Israelis—if you were in need of an assault weapon that would fit in a burn bag without any suspicious bulges, the Israelis had you covered.

He took out one of the rifles, made sure it was loaded, then elbow-crawled his way through the dirt until he was under the deck. *Okay, you assholes, come and get me,* he thought.

As if on cue, there was a barely audible footstep above him. Henry rolled onto his back and fired upward. The body fell heavily onto the splintered wood; at the same moment, he caught a motion in his peripheral vision, rolled over onto his belly again, and found another attacker through the sight. He fired; the guy fell to his knees. Henry took the head shot, then rolled out from under the house.

Immediately he spotted a third guy on the roof of the garden shed, aiming a sniper rifle at him. Henry fired and saw the scope explode along with his face. *You snooze, you lose,* he said silently, holding very still as he scanned the area directly in front of him. Was it over now?

Nope—there was a fourth guy, several feet away from the shed, almost invisible in the shadow of one of the larger trees. *Almost* invisible but not to Henry; he took careful aim and fired. The guy went down, leaving most of his head dripping down the bark.

Again, Henry scanned his surroundings but instinct told him he'd gotten them all. *Now* it was over.

Only four guys, he thought, dressing quickly, but as always, without rushing. Like four guys had a chance against him. Not even a week since he'd retired and the agency had already forgotten what he was capable of. What *was* the assassin industry coming to?

Henry jumped into his SUV and headed for the apartment building near Pelican Point.

At first, he thought he was too late, that a hit squad had already been and gone, tossing the place for good measure. Then he heard Danny sigh in her sleep and realized that, no, Agent Zakarewski was simply messy on a world-class level. Her one-bedroom apartment looked more like a dorm room. If he had seen this before he'd gotten the photocopy of her ID, he might have believed she really was a college student. Or maybe not—weren't grad students more organized?

He went to the kitchen, where the coffeemaker was sitting on the counter. The half-full carafe was still slightly warm. Coffee before going to bed? Oh, right—she would have had to email the agency a report about the evening to tell them her new status was toast. Writing reports was one more thing he wasn't going to miss.

Henry poured some coffee into a mug, then picked his way through the various things strewn on the floor to her bedroom. The cup made only a small noise when he put it down on the nightstand but her eyes flew open immediately. In the next moment, she was standing on the mattress, pointing a Beretta at his head.

"It's not *gun* time," Henry told her matter-of-factly. "It's *coffee* time. Where's your burn bag?"

"First, tell me what you're *doing* here." Her tone suggested his life depended on the answer.

"Someone just sent a team to kill me," he said in the same conversational voice. "Since you were too busy being asleep and *not* skipping town, that means you didn't know. Right?"

She frowned but didn't lower the gun. "Of *course* I didn't. I would have told you."

"Which means you're next." He looked around, spotted a pair of jeans lying at the foot of the bed and tossed them to her. "Get dressed," he ordered, turning his back to give her privacy. Or to give her a chance to shoot him in the back of the head, but he was betting she wouldn't. "You're a pretty sound sleeper," he added after a moment.

"Clear conscience, I guess," she told him.

Henry gave a short laugh. "That would explain my insomnia."

He was about to say something else when he heard the sound of metal rattling. He turned to her, putting a finger to his lips; she nodded at the front door. They moved soundlessly out of the bedroom together, weapons drawn.

The doorknob was twisting back and forth slightly.

Again Henry looked at Danny and she nodded. He threw the door open, surprising the hell out of the guy on his knees in the hallway, so much so that the lockpicks he'd been using were still stuck in the knob. Henry put him to sleep with the butt of the Glock.

"This *can't* be an agency-sanctioned op," Danny said, her voice small and toneless. She followed Henry as he went to the patio window. "These guys have *got* to be rogues."

If it had just been the clown with the lockpick Henry might have been tempted to agree, except for what had happened at his place. Even if those guys hadn't had much chance against him, they hadn't been amateurs, either. But there wasn't time to debate pros and cons. He had to get Danny onboard quickly or neither of them would get out of this alive. "Fine. Either way, they're rogues with agency assault rifles."

Now he saw a black SUV cruise slowly through the marina parking lot, lights off.

The marina…

"All the boats have dupe keys in the office, right?" Henry asked. Danny nodded. "Are any of them especially speedy?"

Danny nodded just as the guy in the doorway groaned and began to stir. Henry gave him a kick to the head that put him out for the night. He didn't so much as twitch when Danny stepped on his back as they left.

Danny had a quick look through the marina office's windows; the sky was only beginning to lighten and she couldn't see very much. But the office wasn't very large and offered little in the way of places to hide. As near as she could tell, no one had tossed it. To her relief, no one had jimmied the back door lock, either. She would just have to trust Henry to secure the perimeter, she thought as she let herself in.

The cabinet with the rack of spare keys was still padlocked; that had to be a good sign. She unlocked it and found the keys she wanted almost immediately. But just as she took them off the hook, someone behind her cleared his throat and said, "Feeling the call of the sea?"

Mentally kicking herself for not checking the bathroom, Danny turned around slowly. Her heartbeat went into high gear; the man who had come up behind her was dangerously close and the gun pointed at her chest was even closer. She took a breath and, still moving slowly, raised her hands, holding them just far enough apart to make it difficult for him to see both of them at once.

"Where is he?" the man asked.

Danny looked downcast and sighed unhappily, the way she had as a kid whenever her father caught her red-handed and she had no choice but to give up. The man with the gun bought it; she could tell by the smug look on his face. The moment she saw him relax his guard, she went for him, grabbing his gun with one hand and throwing a punch at his throat with the other.

He twisted out of her grip and backhanded her with the pistol. The explosion of pain filled her head with bright flashing light as she flew backwards, one hand automatically going for her own gun. The man knocked it out of her grasp and she heard a distant clatter as it hit the floor. When her vision cleared, she looked up to find him standing over her, aiming his gun at her face. Blood was flowing from her nose, running down her mouth and chin. Face and head wounds bled copiously because of all the capillaries; she'd learned that in first-aid class. The damnedest things crossed your mind at the damnedest times, she thought as she inched her hand toward her ankle.

"You can tell me where Brogan is *now*," the man said in a reprehensibly smug tone, "or you can tell me in five minutes minus your teeth. But you're *going to* tell me."

In one smooth motion, Danny drew the knife from her ankle sheath and swung at his knees. Or tried to—he blocked the movement, caught her wrist, and twisted it till she had to open her fingers. The knife landed on the floor; at the same moment, there was a rifle shot from outside. Two more followed; then silence. The man froze, still holding onto her.

"Well, *I* counted three," Danny said chattily. "How many guys did you bring?"

The question confused him, kept him immobilized just long enough to let her sweep-kick his legs out from under him. He went down with a grunt, and for a few seconds they grappled on the floor. He was a fist-fighter, a brawler, used to punching his problems into submission. But he wasn't as quick *off* his feet as he was *on* them and not terribly agile, either—Danny managed to wriggle around behind him and applied a chokehold until he went limp. Shoving him aside, she grabbed his gun as well as her own and when he came to, she was standing over him, giving him a good view of the barrel of her Beretta.

"Okay, let's hear it." Her blood was salty and warm in her mouth. "Who sent you?"

He didn't answer.

"You can tell me *now*," she informed him, "or you can tell me in five minutes minus your teeth." She gave him a red smile. "But you *are* going to tell me."

Waiting on the dock with their burn bags, rifle in hand, Henry was just starting to wonder if he should go after Danny when she came out of the marina office. In the early morning light, he could see she was roughed up, a little bloody, and more than a little freaked out, but not seriously injured.

"It's Lassiter," she said flatly.

Henry had already come to that conclusion but he had to ask. "How do you know?"

She was shaking with adrenaline as she took his hand and dropped something on his palm—four broken and bloody front teeth. Henry looked from them to her, showing his own teeth in a wry smile.

He almost expected her to say something like *He started it*, but she only strode past him down the dock. Impressed, Henry followed with the rifle and their burn bags to slip number seventeen. The thirty-four-foot Corsair moored there was brand new and whoever owned it had gone with the full package of options—which meant they weren't going to be terribly happy when they found out someone had taken their baby for a joyride.

We'll treat her only with the utmost respect and we'll try like hell to bring her home safe and sound as soon as we can—I give you my word, Henry promised the owner silently. Whether the owner would have thought the word of a retired government assassin counted for much was a different argument, and one that Henry didn't imagine would go his way. But what the hell—Grand Theft Nautical was pretty tame compared to what he'd been doing for the last twenty-five years.

Danny climbed aboard and motioned for him to load the bags, wiping away the blood from her nose with the back of her hand. Henry did so and untied the Corsair from the piling on the dock before joining her.

He cleared his throat and she turned to look at him. "Before we do this, there's something you should keep in mind—stepping on this boat is saying goodbye to everything you know. You understand that?"

Danny wiped the back of her hand across her mouth again. "Almost all the people I've come into contact with since I got out of bed tried to end my life. Only one decided to save it." She took out her cell phone and tossed it overboard. Henry couldn't help smiling as he went to the helm and started the engine.

She took the passenger seat and he saw that, despite her bravado, she was still shaking. Danny noticed him noticing; her face reddened as she folded her arms tightly against her body, trying to still herself.

"Hey, there's nothing wrong with being scared. Scared is *good*," Henry told her. "Scared means you're alert and alert means alive."

"It's just—" she cut off, took a breath. "I never had anyone try to kill me before." She sounded as if she were admitting to something embarrassing or shameful. Like she was afraid if the cool agents found out this was her first time as a target, they wouldn't let her eat lunch with them in the agency cafeteria.

"The important thing is, he *didn't* kill you. *You* whipped *his* ass—bad enough that he'll never forget it."

Danny's face brightened as if that hadn't even occurred to her. "I did, didn't I?" Pause. "So what scares *you*? Other than bees."

"Drowning."

Henry could feel her staring at him incredulously as he pulled the Corsair away from the dock and into the sound.

Lassiter seldom took special note of the weather. Rainy days never got her down because she was too busy to notice them. She wouldn't have noticed this one, either, if she hadn't been forced to spend part of it sitting on a bench next to Clay Verris. At least he had brought his own umbrella so she didn't have to share hers with him like they were a couple of furtive lovers. The park was practically on the other side of Savannah from her office, which meant she hadn't been able to stop at her usual coffee shop for her morning latte. Going without her standard morning pick-me-up was bad enough, even before the son of a bitch opened his mouth. And he was taking his sweet time about that.

"So," the son of a bitch said finally, "this is you cleaning up your messes."

Lassiter took a breath and listened to the raindrops pattering on her umbrella. "Spare me the lecture."

"It's like watching the Hindenberg crash into the Titanic." Verris made it sound like something he would have enjoyed seeing. Well, he was that kind of sadistic bastard, Lassiter thought. Although she might have enjoyed it herself if Verris was a passenger on one of them.

"I haven't decided what to do next," she said stiffly.

"Henry Brogan is like any other soldier," Verris said, going into full pontification mode. "When they're young and stupid, they believe anything you tell them. Then they get older. They start to wear out and grow a conscience.

This is why we need a new breed of soldier. Gemini will handle this."

Lassiter had a fleeting mental image of thrusting the point of her umbrella into Verris's eye. "I'm sorry," she said in an even stiffer tone. "I can't allow that."

"I'm not asking your permission," Verris said, and the edge in his voice was the vocal version of a lethal weapon. "You want to go to your bosses? I'm sure they'd love to hear about our little rogue project."

The rain started to come down harder now but Lassiter could sense Verris's self-righteousness; it radiated from him like heat, except it was cold, very cold. The man probably had a chunk of permafrost instead of a heart.

"I'll make it look like a Russian hit," Verris went on cheerfully. He stood up then and Lassiter followed suit. Apparently the meeting was coming to an end; she could hardly wait.

"You give Henry a state funeral. Flag on the coffin, twenty-one-gun salute, you give a nice speech, everyone cries, he'll be remembered as a hero, and life goes on."

"Not for Henry," Lassiter said. The rain was coming down really hard now, pounding the pavement and splashing her lower legs.

"Oh come on," Verris said. "Mutts like Henry were born to be collateral damage. Let's not pretend otherwise."

That's not how you felt back when you were begging him to work for you, Lassiter thought, sneaking a glance at him. He was gazing straight ahead, all puffed up with importance, loving his own genius. There was no way she could win this one.

"Do you have an asset in place?" she asked.

"I have the *perfect* asset," Verris replied.

Lassiter knew what that meant and her heart sank.

CHAPTER 7

Henry dropped anchor just off a secluded bit of Florida shoreline. They would be safe here for a while, he told Danny, and suggested she get a few hours of sleep to make up for what she'd missed. Danny laughed—after what they'd just been through together, she wasn't sure she would ever sleep again.

But even as she said it, she realized she had actually been running on fumes and was now so exhausted she was close to falling down on the spot. She stumbled down the few steps into the sleeping area in the Corsair's bow and was surprised to find it wasn't stuffy and hot; the owner had opted for air-conditioning.

As she lay down, she saw that the wide dark stripe running the length of the bow was actually dark-tinted Plexiglas, with three small hatches that could be opened for ventilation. She considered turning off the a/c and opening all three for fresh air, but before she could give that any further consideration, she dropped off into a deep, dreamless sleep.

* * *

The sun was a lot higher in the sky by the time she woke, groggy and heavy-headed, but more than anything, hungry. She gave herself a few minutes to become more alert, then had a look around the small galley. There were a few bottles of expensive imported beer in the mini-fridge but no food— no gourmet cheese, no caviar, no chocolate. It was so pristine she doubted there ever had been anything in it other than beer. Which she took as proof positive that the Corsair was owned by a man who never brought lady friends aboard.

Danny's stomach growled unhappily as she conducted a thorough search of the cabinets. If all she could find were smuggled drugs or diamonds, she was going to track down the owner and tear him limb from limb with her bare hands, just on general principle.

She was on the verge of despair when she finally discovered a box of saltines at the very back of the last cabinet. Just seeing the picture of the crackers was enough to make her mouth water. There had *better* be crackers in this box, she thought, because if it turned out to be a fortune in stolen gems or little plastic bags of cocaine, she was going to eat them anyway.

Nope, just plain old crackers, lightly salted and dry as a bone, which had to be some kind of miracle considering they'd been stored on a boat. The pictures on the box showed them floating in a bowl of soup or topped with cheese; nobody ever ate saltines plain. Unless there was nothing else in the pantry of your stolen Chris-Craft Corsair, of course. Danny told herself she was grateful, glad to have them, and she *wasn't* wishing they were Ritz crackers or cheese crackers, nope, not at all, not even slightly. These saltines were *divine*. The taste of edible *papier mâché* had been criminally underrated.

She emerged from below to find Henry had waded ashore and was now lounging on the beach, long legs stretched out and crossed at the ankles, and his ever-present Phillies cap pulled low to keep the sun out of his eyes. He looked up from his phone just long enough to give her a beckoning wave.

"Hungry?" she asked as she joined him, holding out the crackers.

He looked up from the phone again. "Very," he said. "But—" he tapped the end of the box. "Those expired three years ago."

"Really? They taste fine." She turned the box around and saw the *Best Before* date. Apparently Henry didn't know that *Best Before* wasn't the same as an expiration date. She considered explaining it to him, then decided it could wait for a later time when people weren't trying to kill them. Anyway, she was pretty sure the half-life for saltines was a lot longer than three years. Or maybe she was just so hungry she felt relieved that she didn't have to share them.

"How long have you worked with Lassiter?" she asked.

"You know my file," Henry said, not looking away from the phone screen.

"I do. Which was why I didn't believe the guy in the marina office," Danny said. "While he still had teeth, he said *you* were the rogue."

Henry glanced up at her briefly. "But you didn't believe him."

"I was ninety-nine percent sure he was lying."

"Yeah, there's always that damn one percent, eh?" He gave a small laugh.

Yeah, that damn one percent, Danny thought as she shifted from one foot to the other. Here in the light of day, out of state with a stolen boat and only some very old saltines for breakfast, she couldn't help wondering if she was doing the right thing. What if she had thrown her career away because she couldn't tell the difference between the good guys and the bad guys?

If so, what would happen when the *real* good guys finally showed up to bring her and Henry in? Was she going to spend the rest of her life in maximum security for being the stupidest DIA agent who had ever lived?

"Henry," she said, and he looked up from his phone again. "Has this ever happened to you before?"

"'This?'" He frowned. "Can you be more specific?"

"Your own government trying to kill you."

Henry gave a short laugh. "No. That's brand new."

"No, now really—you've been with the agency for a while," she said. "Can't *you* guess what this is all about?"

Henry gave her an arch look. "If I could, I wouldn't be taking this lovely vacation with you."

"When I'm head of the agency, we're going to handle retirement *very* differently," she promised him.

He was about to answer, then suddenly turned to look up at the clouds to the south and west. Danny heard the distant sound of an approaching aircraft. It gradually became louder until finally a twin-engine Aztec seaplane broke through the billows of white into the blue sky. It made a wide circle above them before it began to descend.

Henry's face lit up as he got to his feet.

The Aztec was similar to a lot of planes run by sightseeing businesses that catered to tourists along the Georgia and Florida coastline, although the logo on the side—Baron Air—was one Danny had never seen before. It was probably a one-man operation; many of them were. There was always more than enough business to go around in tourist season, and during the rest of the year there were courier jobs that the larger companies considered too small, too dubious, or too risky.

Danny watched the Aztec make a perfect, even graceful landing. It water-taxied over to them, maneuvering until it was right next to the Corsair. For a moment, she held her breath, hoping she was looking at the next step in solving all her problems and not one more bad choice. Then the pilot's side door opened and she saw a man with an impressive moustache smiling out at her. He was wearing a t-shirt, a vest with several pockets, cargo shorts, and motorcycle boots.

"Baron Tours here to pick up Brogan, party of two?" he said, eyes twinkling.

At a complete loss, Danny turned to Henry.

"Danny, meet the Baron," he said. "Middle-aged reprobate and the best pilot I know." Henry was grinning from ear to ear; she couldn't remember the last time she had ever seen anyone look so happy. "Baron, Danny."

"Hey, Toast," Baron said genially.

Danny grimaced, feeling her face grow warm again, now with mortification. In the DIA, once you got a nickname from a senior agent, you were usually stuck with it whether you liked it or not; complaining would only guarantee it would be permanent.

As Baron helped her board the plane, she spotted the tattoo on his right wrist, a green spade identical to Henry's, and felt herself relax a little. The two men had *that* kind of bond, which meant if she could trust Henry ninety-nine percent, she could trust this man just as much.

"Your burners, as requested." Baron handed Henry a plastic bag full of cell phones. "*But*," he added as Henry looked inside, "before you use them, maybe consider Cartagena as an option?"

Henry didn't say anything and Danny wondered if he was actually thinking it over.

"It's a nice life," Baron went on, addressing her, too, now. "You'd be anonymous, and *safe*."

Henry's eyes glinted and for a split second, Danny thought he was actually going to say yes. Then he shook his head apologetically. "Baron, we're in the shit here. I'm pretty sure Jack Willis is dead."

For the first time, Baron's smile vanished completely. "Jesus. Did anyone follow you?"

"No," Henry assured him.

"They will. Let's go. Hey, Toast, can I have one of those crackers?" he added, nodding at the box. "I skipped lunch. *And* breakfast."

Danny had actually forgotten she was still holding it and handed it to him.

"Brace yourselves," Baron said over his shoulder and revved the engine. "The ride tends to get pretty noisy."

Del Patterson was a man with a lot of problems.

Of course, his road never had been completely smooth. Something always went wrong, and if it had already gone wrong, it would develop further complications. From an early age, Patterson had had to learn how to think on his feet, make repairs on the fly, and never let his insurance lapse. This probably accounted for how he had ended up in the DIA, doing what he did. He was never more in his comfort zone than when he was outside of it.

Recently, however, the going was tough even for him. There was no time when he didn't have at least a dozen problems simmering on the verge of a rolling boil. A few were personal: he had lost his hair and gained a belly, he had the blood pressure of a man twenty years older and fifty pounds heavier, and the desire for a drink was starting to outweigh the desire *not* to have a drinking problem. As it happened, these were all due to ongoing troubles that either directly or indirectly posed a threat to the existence of the US or the world or both.

Not that he could share any of these burdens with anyone outside the agency. Patterson wasn't allowed to tell anyone where he worked. He couldn't even tell his family what he did for a living, which was why his wife was now his ex-wife and his kid was—well, he was a teenager and as far as Patterson knew, there was no cure for adolescence except growing up. And even that didn't always work.

Which was probably why Patterson had taken to fantasizing about spilling his guts to people with no security clearance, simply coming right out and saying, *I orchestrate strategic abductions and assassinations in foreign countries to ensure the safety of the free world,* if only for the shock value. Especially in situations like the one currently unfolding in the principal's office at his kid's school.

This wasn't the first time he'd been summoned here to sit through a detailed list of his son's high crimes and misdemeanors. Yeah, everybody knew that teaching was a difficult, frustrating, and thankless job, and being a principal was all that with a punchline on top. But sometimes Patterson had a powerful urge to interrupt the man's litany of complaints with something like, *Oh, gosh, I'm really sorry he's acting out again. I've been so busy on the other side of the world making sure the right people get assassinated for the sake of our national security—i.e. to prevent another attack on US soil—that I guess I missed all the warning signs.*

The man would probably swallow his tongue.

"Does he do this at home?" the principal demanded, jarring him out of his daydream.

"I don't think so." Patterson had no idea what he was referring to. "I don't know." He turned to his son, who was slumped in the chair beside him in the classic teenage position of defiant apathy. "*Do* you?"

His son shook his head and Patterson suddenly realized the kid was dying of embarrassment. Although he wasn't sure who the boy was embarrassed by, himself or the principal.

The principal's glower intensified. "Then can you tell me why, if it's inappropriate to do this sort of thing at home, you would think it appropriate to do it in your *science class?*"

"I dunno," the kid said querulously. "Probably because science is so wicked *boring.*"

Patterson was about to tell him what he thought of that statement when his phone rang. Sighing, he turned to the principal. "Excuse me, I have to take this," he said. "Try not to do anything incriminating until I get back," he added to his son as he got up.

The principal was unfazed by the interruption. He launched into a lecture, perhaps as a way to make sure the boy knew he was still being disciplined even while Patterson was out of the room. "Son, you're going a hundred miles an hour at a brick wall," he said. "*Slow down.* Every time you turn on that cell phone of yours, it gets you in trouble."

Words to live by, Patterson thought as he closed the door behind him. "Hello?" he said tensely.

"Well, I guess you *really* didn't want me to retire," said a familiar voice.

Patterson felt a sensation that he suspected was a lot like a sucking chest wound. "Henry! You're okay!" he babbled, barely aware of the bell ringing. Students flooded into the hall, brushing past him roughly. "Thank God!"

"Stop it." Henry's tone was flat and lethal. "Is Monroe dead?"

Patterson swallowed hard. "Yes."

"*Shit,*" Henry said, furious. "What about Jack Willis?"

"It wasn't *me*, Henry," Patterson told him desperately. "*None* of this was me. I *swear* it."

"Jesus, Del," Henry said. "I *trusted* you."

"You still can," Patterson told him urgently. "*I'm* the one fighting *for* you! Let me call you on another line."

There was a moment of silence that Patterson believed was a lot like the very last second of a hundred-foot fall, just before the impact.

"604-555-0131. You have thirty seconds," Henry said and broke the connection.

Patterson looked around desperately for someone he could borrow a phone from but the hallway that had been full of kids only a moment ago was deserted now. Where the hell had they all gone?

As if on cue, a couple of girls came out of a nearby ladies' room, whispering to each other and giggling.

Patterson hurried toward them, taking out his wallet. "I'll give you a hundred bucks for your phone for five minutes."

The girls looked at each other, then at him. They were dressed in what Patterson supposed was the height of teenage chic and made up to an extent that was practically kabuki, but he could see they were wary. They'd probably been warned about strange men offering them gifts or money. But they weren't on the street and he wasn't asking them to get into his car, he just wanted to borrow a phone. If neither of them said yes, he'd have to goddam *mug* them. Wouldn't the principal love *that*?

Finally, the taller one nodded. Patterson paid her, grabbed the phone, and moved away from the girls as he began dialing frantically.

"You can start with whose idea it was to send a team to Agent Zakarewski's apartment," Henry said as soon as he answered "Was that necessary?"

"Also not my call," Patterson assured him. "She's working for the inspector general, not me. Is she with you?"

"Yeah," Henry said. "Not voluntarily."

Patterson looked around. The girls stood a little ways up the hall whispering to each other. No doubt they could hear every word he said. Kids had ears like bats, especially when it came to things you didn't want them to hear.

"Listen," he said, unable to keep the desperation out of his voice. "This *isn't* something I want to say over a phone—I'm at my kid's goddam *school*."

"Del!" Henry snapped. "What the hell *is* all this?"

Patterson took a breath. "We have a... problem here." He lowered his voice and cupped his hand around the phone. "*Gemini*."

The silence on the other end was deafening.

"Your old friend," Patterson went on after a moment, "working with Janet Lassiter and her people. I can't stop them."

"What about Dormov?" Henry said. "Did he have something to do with Gemini? You remember *Dormov*? The guy I popped on the train because *you* told me he was a bio-fucking-terrorist. Was *he* working for Gemini?"

Patterson leaned against a row of lockers and closed his eyes. Now what was he supposed to say—that he'd been completely bamboozled by Janet Lassiter? It was true but Patterson knew how it was going to sound. Maybe if he apologized for not knowing he had been a sock puppet for Verris's sock puppet?

This wasn't how it was supposed to go, Patterson thought. Saving the world in the service of your country was supposed to be a *clean* job. The agency was supposed to be the *good* guy. He glanced up the hallway at the girls. They were smirking at him now. He felt like telling them they had a bright future as *Real Housewives*. Except they'd probably *like* that.

"So I was pulling a trigger for Clay Verris," Henry said.

Patterson let out a long breath. One of the main reasons he had quit drinking was his deep and abiding resolve to avoid the humiliation of hitting bottom. But somehow he had managed to do that very thing after getting sober.

"Henry, I regret my lack of candor, but listen—" Patterson said, babbling again.

"How many other times did you do this to me?" Henry demanded. "How many times did you spike a file and send me out to AMF someone who didn't deserve it?"

"*Never*," Patterson said promptly. "*Not ever*. This was a one-off, I swear on my son's life."

He could practically hear Henry thinking it over, trying to decide whether he was a liar or a fool.

"All right," Henry said after a bit. "Agent Zakarewski is not a part of this."

"Henry I can fix this, but I need *both* of you to come back," Patterson said.

Henry gave an incredulous laugh. "To *what*?" he said and broke the connection again.

Patterson stood in the hallway staring at the phone. It was pink—not just pink but *pink*, the *pinkest* pink he'd ever seen. He had no idea how he had failed to notice that.

"Hey, mister."

He turned to find the girl he'd borrowed the cell from standing behind him with her friend. "What do you want?" he asked, annoyed.

"If you're done, I want my phone back." Without waiting for him to answer, she plucked it out of his hand and walked off with her friend. Patterson could hear the beep-beep-beep of rapid texting.

He sighed. He had just made the most expensive phone call of his life and now he had to let the principal finish bitching at him. "Better put that in your spray-tan fund," Patterson called after the girl.

"Yeah, whatever," she said, still texting.

CHAPTER 8

Leaning against Baron's Jeep on the beach, Danny watched Henry take the SIM card out of the phone, break it in half, and grind the pieces into the sand with his foot. He looked pretty peeved and she didn't blame him. She felt the same after listening to the phone conversation he'd just had with his handler—correction: ex-handler. Henry had put it on speakerphone so she and Baron could listen.

Patterson's protests of innocence seemed sincere but in this business, everyone knew how to do sincere. And of *course* he was going to claim he'd had nothing to do with the assassins. What fool would *admit* trying to kill you? Hell, if you caught someone standing over you with a goddam butcher knife, they would still deny everything. *What do you mean, kill you? I'm not even mad at you! What knife? I didn't notice—how did that get there?*

But the crucial word in the conversation had been *Gemini*. She knew what Gemini was and she also knew that a lot of people at the DIA weren't overjoyed about its connection to the agency. But she'd never seen anyone react the way Henry and Baron had. They were actually spooked, and the name Clay Verris spooked them even more. Danny hadn't thought anything could shake Henry's composure, which spooked *her*. She had better find out as much as she could, she told herself, because if it scared Henry—well, she didn't even know how to finish that sentence.

She turned to him and said, "Okay. Gemini."

Henry's eyes were hooded as they swiveled to look at her. "How much do you know about them?"

"Privatized paramilitary, owned by Clay Verris." Danny watched his face carefully for a reaction to the name; there was none but Baron winced. "Agency does a ton of business with them. Is there more?"

The two men traded looks. "Baron and I served under Verris in the Marines—Panama, Kuwait, Somalia," Henry told her. "He started Gemini after he left the Service. Tried to hire us. We both said no."

"Except *I* was smart enough to move 1500 miles away," Baron added, chuckling.

"Yeah, that *was* pretty smart," Henry said, climbing into the Jeep's front passenger seat. "I blew that one."

Danny took a last look around at the beach and the gorgeous blue water where the Aztec was moored close to the shore. If the rest of Cartagena was this beautiful, she could understand how a person might decide to throw it all over for a place in the sun. She was far from ready to even think about that herself. But she wouldn't have minded turning her phone off for a week or two of vacation time here.

Assuming, of course, that things worked out so well that the agency not only let her keep her job but gave her a replacement for the phone she had tossed into Buttermilk Sound.

Now she was getting too far ahead of herself, she thought as she got into the Jeep's backseat. She had to take things one step at a time. Or in her case, one life-changing crisis at a time.

In spite of everything, Henry could feel himself un-tense as Baron drove them to his place. Baron had been trying to get him to visit for years—decades—and he had always managed to find reasons not to. Baron had accused Henry of dodging him and asked if it was because he was so completely out of the business. Henry had finally confessed that yes, he *had* been dodging him, but only because he didn't think he'd last even half a day in a place where he couldn't catch a Phillies game.

In truth, however, Henry had been afraid that Cartagena would seduce him the same way it had Baron and he would succumb to the pleasures of a life without stress or sniper rifles or targets, let alone the Phillies. He hadn't been ready to give any of that up yet, not permanently, and still wasn't. He had no idea when he *would* be ready; he only knew he wasn't there yet.

Baron drove them along a river lined with fishermen; a few of them were pulling in catches as they passed. Henry could hear Danny in the seat behind him moving from one side to the other, trying to see everything all at once. It was nice traveling with kids, he thought wryly; they weren't too jaded to appreciate the scenery. Ha ha.

Or was that less a joke than it was a message from his subconscious? He'd found himself thinking of Danny not as a daughter exactly, but someone similar, maybe a niece. Only he didn't have any brothers or sisters, so she would be kind of an adopted niece, like the daughter of a good friend. Except he couldn't imagine Baron or Jack Willis as her father. Not Patterson, either, not any more. And certainly not Lassiter—her species probably ate their young.

After several miles, Baron turned away from the river onto a road that he said led to the Old Town. "For some of us, Old Town is the *only* town," he said as they went through a fish market filled with people haggling or gossiping or whatever civilians did in the course of a typical day; Henry couldn't really imagine. He'd never gotten a handle on this kind of life. And yet when Patterson mentioned their having saved lives, these were among the ones he was referring to.

The fish market gave way to a church courtyard with a collection of impossibly beautiful statues of saints Henry was pretty sure he'd never heard of and wouldn't have believed in anyway. At one time, he'd have taken it for granted that Baron didn't, either, but now he wasn't so sure. Not that it mattered; saints or no saints, Baron was his brother. When Henry had called, Baron had dropped everything and come to help, no questions asked.

Baron slowed down and brought the Jeep to a stop in front of a large, two-story building painted bright canary yellow. Henry thought it was one of those boutique hotels that only the ultra-rich knew about. He turned to Baron, eyebrows raised.

"Here she is," Baron told him, obviously pleased at his reaction. "Casa Baron."

The house was even more impressive inside. Henry turned around and around in the entry hall, goggling at the staircase curving under a skylight, the polished tile floor, and the tropical plants in hanging baskets or in planters running along the walls. Baron pushed Henry gently toward the light and airy living room, still bright even though it was now late in the day. Danny made herself comfortable on the sofa opposite a floor-to-ceiling window overlooking the ocean. The water seemed to stretch out forever.

"Damn, Baron, you're the king of Cartagena," said Henry, taking in the high vaulted ceiling and wood beams.

"I get by." Baron chuckled with fake modesty as he went to the nearby drinks cart. "Plus, we got an awesome hardware store down the street. Henry loves hardware stores," he added to Danny, looking over his shoulder at her.

Danny shifted restlessly on the sofa. "Yeah, great. Let's make small talk. I want to know more about Clay Verris and Gemini."

Henry hesitated and looked at Baron but he was rattling glasses to show he was too busy with their drinks to answer.

"Verris tried to hire you," Danny prodded, "and you said no. So that's why you hate him, because he offered you jobs you didn't want? There's got to be more to it than that."

Henry shrugged.

"Come on, Henry," she said, slightly impatient now. "What *aren't* you telling me?"

The unadorned honesty of the question caught him off guard, although it shouldn't have. It was the only kind of question Danny had ever asked him, at least since he'd showed her the photocopy of her DIA badge. He sighed.

"Clay Verris gets billions every year to clear targets any way he sees fit," Henry said. "That's Gemini—off-book kidnappings, torture. They're who you call when you need twelve Saudi princes to quietly disappear. Or you want someone to train your death squads."

Danny's expression showed she knew that still wasn't everything and she wasn't going to settle for anything less than the whole story.

"When I was six weeks into sniper school," he went on after a moment, "Clay Verris put me on a boat, and took me five miles out. He tied weights to my ankles, then threw me overboard and told me to tread water until I couldn't any more."

Danny's jaw dropped. "He didn't know about your fear of—"

"*Of course* he knew." Henry couldn't help laughing a little. She may have had an exemplary record with the agency but she still had a lot to learn. "That was the point."

"So, what did you do?" Her eyes were wide and serious.

"I treaded water for as long as I could," Henry said. "Then I drowned. *Dead*."

Baron's bright, beautiful living room was gone and he was back in the ocean, sinking down into a cold, dark death, unable to feel his fingers and toes, his arms and legs too heavy to move, his muscles completely used up, drained and done. By then, his head was the only place he had any sensation. How icy the water had been as it covered his face. He could remember that so clearly, so vividly, the same way he could remember his father's enormous grin and the terrified little boy in those mirror shades. Dying in the ocean had seemed like the last bit of his father's malice, a booby-trap set to go off at a time and place where there was no loving mother to come to his rescue Henry's last breath had escaped him in a stream of bubbles as he died in the dark and the cold.

Abruptly he came back to himself and the late afternoon light in Baron's living room. Danny was sitting on the edge of the sofa cushion, waiting for the rest of the story, her eyes wide with dismay. They didn't do things like this where she came from, or so she thought. Baron had heard the story before—had one of his own that was just as bad—but even he looked a little spooked.

"He fished me out," Henry continued, speaking quickly now. "Put defibrillator paddles on my chest, shocked me back to life and told me I was now ready to serve under his command."

Danny's expression was horrified and revolted. Yeah, a *whole lot* to learn.

Baron came over with a bottle of Jose Cuervo Especial Silver and three shot glasses. He handed the glasses around and poured a generous measure into each.

"To the next war," Baron said, raising his glass. "Which is *no* war."

"*No* war," Henry echoed.

"*No* war," Danny agreed, which earned her a smile of approval from Baron. Henry expected her to cough a little and was surprised when she didn't. Then he remembered this was a woman who drank boilermakers.

"When I leave here," Henry said to her, "you're going to stay. The farther away I am from you, the better off you'll be."

"Sorry, that's not your call," Danny informed him in a final, almost prim-sounding tone.

"Yeah, yeah, I know," Henry said, exasperated. "You whipped the guy in the marina, you're a real badass. But this is different. You're not ready."

Danny's expression darkened. "Hey, *old guy*," she said, not at all prim now. "You want some teeth knocked out, too?"

Baron laughed like she'd found his ticklish spot. "I *like* her," he told Henry.

"I do, too," Henry admitted. "It's annoying as hell." He sat back on the sofa, suddenly feeling drained, as if he'd used the last of his energy to tell Danny the story about drowning. He ran a hand over his face. "Need some shut-eye, man."

"Sure," Baron said cheerfully. "You folks want one room or—"

"*Two*," Danny said, quickly and emphatically, as if it were crucial to make this clear. Then her face reddened with embarrassment. "Two," she repeated quietly.

"Hey, I can put him in the garage if you want," Baron offered.

"Separate rooms will be fine," Henry said. "I'm so tired I don't even care if there's a bed."

"There is one, use it or not—your call. Follow me." Baron chuckled. "Think you can manage the stairs, *old guy*?"

"Very funny," Henry said, then added, "Hope so."

CHAPTER 9

Henry had been awake for a few minutes, lying quietly to get his bearings, when he heard a flock of birds near the open window of his bedroom suddenly take flight. Something had startled them. The sound of startled birds was different from birds just doing their bird-thing and taking off; it was a very subtle difference but Henry had always been able to tell.

He rolled out of bed onto the floor, crept to the window, and peeked over the sill. Three houses away, a man in a black baseball cap moved from a higher roof to a lower one. There was a rifle bag over his shoulder. Henry could tell he was several grades above the guys that had come after him in Georgia. His cap was pulled low so Henry couldn't see his face but there was something familiar about his movements, like he was someone Henry knew or had at least seen before, although he was pretty sure they had never met personally. No one he came up against in the field lived to regret it.

The answer came to him unbidden: Gemini had sent him. The indoctrination and training gave their operatives a particular look—their moves, their posture, even how they carried their weapons (and used them). Verris was so particular about it, he trained all his guys personally to the point where they might as well have been clones.

Staying low, Henry dressed quickly, grabbed his burn bag, and slipped out of the room. He found Danny in a downstairs bedroom, sleeping as deeply as ever. She must have been right about that clear conscience thing, he thought. Hell, she had even been able to sleep on the goddam Corsair.

Henry crawled over to her bed, found the Glock in her burn bag, then put his hand over her mouth. Her eyes flew open and she looked terrified until she felt him putting the Glock in her hand. He uncovered her mouth.

"Two hundred yards away," he whispered. "Rooftop."

Danny nodded silently, all business now. Henry felt a sudden surge of affection for her. Even though she had a lot to learn, she was a quick study and she didn't whine.

"When he sees me leave, he'll follow," he said in a low voice. "Go with Baron, someplace safe. *Please*," he added as she opened her mouth to argue. She nodded again, reluctantly.

He found Baron on the couch in the living room. His friend had dozed off watching the flatscreen on the opposite wall. Henry's eyebrows went up; hadn't there been an art print hanging there yesterday when they had come in? Right now there was a Colombian game show on with a frantic host and even more frantic contestants, but fortunately the sound was off. The remote sitting in Baron's lap looked like something NASA would use to control satellites. If they could get the World Series in Cartagena, Henry thought he might have to seriously reconsider Baron's offer.

But not today.

He put his hand over Baron's mouth. Baron's eyes opened, found Henry. "Shooter, your three o'clock. Acknowledge," Henry told him.

Baron nodded, gestured for him to move back, and lifted the sofa cushion, revealing a respectable cache of weapons. Henry gave him a solemn look of admiration. Then he grabbed a case containing a disassembled sniper rifle, ammunition, and a few grenades for his burn bag, and tucked a Glock with a silencer into his waistband.

"You're a shitty houseguest, you know that?" Baron said in a half-whisper as he watched Henry tool up. "Most people bring flowers or a bottle of vino. How the hell did they find us?"

"Listen to me," Henry said. "Danny's good, she's *really* good. But she doesn't know how much she doesn't know. Take care of her, all right?"

Baron nodded.

"Thanks, brother," Henry said.

Henry got up and headed for the front door, keeping himself too low for a clean shot but not so low that he was completely out of sight. Bracing himself, he stepped outside, slinging the burn bag over one shoulder as he closed the door behind him. The bag was a bit heavier now but he didn't mind the extra weight. For a few seconds, he held very still, scanning his surroundings and listening.

Good morning, Cartagena.

He began walking briskly toward the center of Old Town, doing his best to look like he was off to spend the day sightseeing and shopping, and not at all like he was toting a bag full of weapons because someone was trying to kill him.

This guy was *good*.

Henry didn't catch a glimpse of him for at least ten minutes, and even then it was only by accident. Crossing a street, he happened to look down and saw his stalker's reflection in a puddle of water. Henry turned casually and, hiding the pistol in his hand behind his open shirt, fired at him. It wasn't his preferred method of taking a hostile down but it was a shot he'd made before.

Not today, however. The guy was gone and Henry knew he hadn't just rolled off the roof. Talk about reflexes, Henry thought, ignoring the hole he'd put in his shirt. His stalker must have moved as soon as he'd seen him start to turn, without even knowing Henry had a gun.

Better keep my head on a swivel, Henry thought uneasily.

Henry didn't pick him up again until he reached a parking lot almost ten minutes later. As he walked briskly along a row of cars, some impulse made him stop at a bright yellow VW bug and use its side mirror to check behind him. He caught a glint of metal and ducked a heartbeat before the mirror exploded into fragments of glass, plastic, and rubber.

Dropping to the ground, he crawled around the VW to the Jeep on the other side, dragging the burn bag with him. He waited a few moments and then used the barrel of the Glock to angle the Jeep's side mirror so he could see the rooftops behind him.

Nothing; his stalker had disappeared again. Being gone was a great idea; Henry decided to try it himself. He crawled under the Jeep to the other side and raised himself carefully, first to his knees and then to a half-crouch. The nearest street was about thirty yards away on his right. Henry hesitated, then made a break for it, forcing himself to stay low until he reached the street, where he straightened up and pushed himself into a sprint. Something whizzed past his head, close enough that he would have sworn he felt the breeze of it cutting through the air before it punched a hole in a brick wall on his right.

Henry veered into a narrow alley, sprinting faster than he had in a long time. The shooter was stalking him openly now, no longer caring that Henry could see him leaping from one rooftop to another. Like he wanted to show he could go just as fast as Henry on the ground, but without as much effort.

Time to turn and fight—gun time, not run time, Henry thought, hoping Danny and Baron were well out of harm's way. He ducked behind a telephone pole, worked the sniper rifle out of the bag and got it assembled.

Okay, Mr. I-go-so-fast-on-rooftops, let's see who you are, Henry said silently. He raised the rifle to his shoulder and looked through the scope.

Gone.

Fuck. Henry fumed as he scanned roofs through the scope. It took a few seconds before he finally saw a skewed line and a glint of metal and glass that didn't belong to the structure.

He adjusted his grip on the rifle. *Come on,* buddy, he said silently, *poke your head up so I can introduce myself properly. I'm Henry Brogan. And you are…?*

The guy's head rose slowly from behind the line of the roof and Henry froze.

The face he saw peering back at him through the scope was impossibly, unbelievably, and unmistakably his own.

CHAPTER 10

Henry had heard guys talk about this kind of shit, weird nightmares where they were tracking down a target, and when they looked through the scope, they saw their own faces looking back at them. It wasn't that unusual among snipers. According to common wisdom, if you had it more than twice a week, it meant you'd been on the job for too long and it was your subconscious telling you to quit. Some guys dreamed it the other way round, like what was happening to Henry now—they were being hunted by someone who turned out to be their doppelgänger. That one seemed to occur less often but it still wasn't unusual.

Henry had never had either dream. He only had one nightmare and it was all about drowning. It came and went in frequency and the details varied—his subconscious would swap out his father for Verris and vice versa and often he was simultaneously five and twenty-five as he drowned. He couldn't remember ever having the evil-twin dream. Therefore, as absurd as this was, he couldn't be dreaming. The man with his face was real—quite a bit younger, he saw now. But it was *his* face.

Except it *couldn't* be real.

Except it *was*.

Caught between real and unreal, Henry lowered his rifle.

The man on the roof responded to that with a burst of machine-gun fire.

Okay, that was *definitely* real, Henry thought, squeezing himself into the space behind the telephone pole while real splinters flew and real chunks of concrete burst from the real wall behind him. Apparently the guy was no longer worried about attracting attention. If he ever had been.

He fired another burst of real gunfire. Henry leaned out from behind the pole to answer with a burst of his own, just to make him duck, then scooped up his burn bag and ran like hell, although his legs were so shaky he stumbled and dipped from side to side like the ground under him was a rolling ocean. But those real bullets nipping at his heels straightened him out pretty quickly; again he pushed himself into a hard sprint, making for an abandoned building at the end of the alley.

Now he would see if all abandoned buildings really *were* alike, Henry thought, feeling surreal. Maybe the ones in Cartagena's Old Town were classier, dripping with history. The sign on the boarded-up entrance said something about how trespassers would be prosecuted. Next to it was a legal-looking notice he might have worried about if he hadn't been under fire. Henry raised his rifle and, still sprinting, shot out the boards, obliterating both signs. Tiny fragments of the road pelted him from behind as he made it to shelter.

This wouldn't fool the shooter, of course; the guy knew where he was. But at least he wasn't such an easy target. Or so he hoped, he thought as he scanned the place quickly.

It had been an apartment building, its three floors built around an open-air courtyard. Definitely nicer than the usual abandoned building—for all the good that would do him, Henry thought, going up the nearest staircase two steps at a time.

He found himself on a walkway with a broken railing on one side and several doors on the other—tenants could come out and see who was in the lobby. Through the street-facing window at the far end, Henry saw the shooter leaping from balcony to balcony of the neighboring apartment building as he parkoured his way down to street level.

The guy's head suddenly snapped up and around as if he'd actually *felt* Henry's gaze. He raised the rifle and fired even as he was rebounding from the railing of one balcony to the next one lower down.

Staying low, Henry moved toward the window, and returned fire, his bullets kicking up tiny puffs of powder at each spot where the shooter had been only half a second before. He got to the window just in time to see the guy hit the ground and run into the building.

Okay, how about a little game of Hide'n'Kill? Henry thought at him, crouching close to the wall. There was another set of stairs leading down to the lobby at this end, this one with a landing to break up the climb. Henry heard broken glass crunching under the shooter's feet as he approached it.

Henry leaned forward to peer between the broken staves of the railing. An object slightly smaller than his fist suddenly flew up and over in a curved trajectory that would end in his face. He batted it away reflexively while throwing himself backwards and covering his head with both arms. The grenade exploded in midair, making the walkway shake and taking a bite out of the railing. It also deafened Henry but he knew it had done the same to the shooter. He raised his head, brushed off the splinters and other debris, and crept forward to peer over the edge of the walkway.

The shooter was looking up at him from the lobby with a surprised expression on his face. On *Henry's* face.

Yeah, you're the junior *hitman here and it ain't gonna be* that *easy.* Henry felt a grim satisfaction although he could barely hear himself think over the ringing in his ears. The blast had been closer to the lobby so the kid probably wouldn't be doing any better. He hoped.

Doing his best to shake off the grenade's effects, Henry slung the sniper rifle over his left shoulder and grabbed the Glock from his bag. As he made sure the gun was loaded, he heard the sound of sliding metal, albeit faintly; his hearing was coming back. Well, his mother had always said strong eardrums ran in the family. *Thanks for the great genes, Ma. Now I'd just like to know how this bastard got my face—*

Abruptly, his gaze came to rest on a large mirror hanging over the staircase landing. It had been placed very high up on the wall and although it was fly-specked and filthy, it was still intact. Henry was mystified as to how it was there at all—something like that should have been carried off long ago.

Although now that he was really looking at it, he could see how high up it was—probably well out of reach for the casual scavenger, who preferred low-hanging fruit. Plus it was really *big*—as in *heavy*. Breaking a mirror like that might get you fourteen or even twenty-one years of bad luck.

He realized it had been placed there so people going up and down the stairs could see anyone coming the other way. Because passing someone on the stairs was also bad luck, wasn't it? He couldn't remember. Although he had a few little rituals—tapping his rifle stock before a hit, burning the target's photo afterwards—he wasn't superstitious so he'd never paid much attention to what was supposed to be good luck or bad luck. In Henry's experience, chance favored the prepared mind, especially in a situation like this. The way Junior was coming at him had nothing to do with luck. A guy who could travel by rooftops to stalk a target on the ground had to know the area *better* than the back of his hand, had to have burned it so deeply into his brain that he could do it with his eyes closed.

But even that wouldn't explain how he always seemed to know what Henry was going to do at the same moment he himself did, so well he could fire at him while he parkoured down the side of a building.

Or why he had Henry's face, which had to be completely impossible.

Maybe it was some kind of mind game, psychological warfare, one-on-one. But how—plastic surgery? A high-tech Halloween mask?

Henry shoved the questions aside; he could deal with impossible shit later. Right now, he had to press his advantage if he wanted to survive. *Think,* he ordered himself; there were more windows on the ground floor, which meant more light, making it easier for him to see what Junior Hitman was doing than vice versa.

Suddenly the already broken staves in the railing exploded into splinters as the guy opened fire on him. Henry fired back, belly-crawling to the stairs where he shifted quickly to feet first before moving down a couple of steps. Junior Hitman paced him; the reflection in the mirror confirmed to Henry again that what he had seen in the scope hadn't been a trick of the light. It *was* his own face, circa his early twenties. Henry remembered what that time had been like. He'd been all grown up but still a year or two away from being permanently set, like paint that hadn't quite dried or clay not yet fired—

barely not a kid, convinced he knew the good guys from the bad guys and the right things from the wrong ones, and utterly certain that when push came to shove, he could grab the world by the tail and swing it around over his head.

"Stop right there," Henry said sharply. "Who *are* you?"

Junior Hitman looked up at the mirror and didn't answer. Henry knew he could make out only a vague, man-shaped shadow among darker shadows. Despite having a better view of the kid, however, he didn't have a clear shot—not a non-lethal one, anyway. He didn't want to kill him before he got some answers.

"I don't *want* to shoot you," Henry called down to him.

"Fine," said the kid. "Then don't shoot me."

All the tiny hairs on the back of Henry's neck stood up. Over the years, he had heard his own voice often enough on wiretaps and bugs to recognize it. What the *fuck*—the kid had his face *and* his voice?

"Mind if *I* shoot *you*?" the kid asked, making Henry's voice sound offhand, like this was no big deal.

"Hey, I could have killed you on the roof," Henry said.

"Maybe you should have," said the kid.

Henry felt a surge of anger and exasperation. "Did they show you a picture of me?" he demanded.

"Yeah." Junior Hitman took another step up the stairs. "You're *old*."

You're gonna pay for that one, whether I shoot you or not, Henry promised him silently. "Kid, you take one step closer and you're going to leave me no choice."

The kid's reflection kept coming. Henry took a grenade from the burn bag and made a quick and dirty calculation by eye before pulling the pin and hurling it at the wall, intending to make the kid give ground in a hurry. The grenade bounced off a spot six inches away from the mirror and flew toward Junior Hitman. Eight ball in the side pocket—either he ran or it was game over.

What happened next went too fast even for Henry's eye to follow but he knew the move; he had done it himself once, in pure desperation:

Junior Hitman took aim at the grenade and fired, batting it back at the mirror. Before Henry could get both arms up to shield his head, it exploded in a burst of shrapnel, plaster, wood, and glass.

The shockwave slammed into him, flattened his lungs and midsection, punched his heart, drove his eyes against the back of their sockets, and made his brain ricochet around his skull. A split second later he registered the sting of countless fragments of mirror hitting his face and hands and larger debris pelting him like stones while clouds of dust billowed around him.

Henry turned his face away, pulled a fistful of his t-shirt up over his nose and mouth, and tried to take a breath, just to see if he could. For a long moment, his mashed-flat lungs refused to inflate. Then mercifully his chest expanded. He knew his heart was still beating—he could feel his pulse in his eyes.

As he raised his head, there was a sudden sharp pain in his cheek; something wet ran down his face. He felt around carefully with his fingertips, then removed a long shard of glass from a spot barely an inch below his eye. He reached for the burn bag and found it had disappeared along with a lot of the railing and part of the staircase. He was going to have to make do with the rifle, the Glock, and the two magazines of ammo he'd stuffed in his pockets. Once again, chance favored the prepared mind. He was just sorry he hadn't stashed ammo for the rifle as well as the Glock, so maybe this really was only pure dumb luck. If so, it might be the last lucky break he'd get for a long time since he and Junior Hitman had broken that goddam mirror.

Then he reminded himself he wasn't superstitious; the kid had to handle all the bad luck by himself. So maybe *that* was his last lucky break.

All he knew for certain right now was *pain*. *Everything* hurt, like he'd been tuned up for days by a team of experts. He could barely keep from crying out as he forced himself to get up and run down the closed hall just off the walkway. *You* can go *faster,* he told himself, keeping his eyes fixed on the staircase at the end of the hall. The stairs went up; he could do that. He could make himself climb the stairs because if he didn't move his ass, good ol' Junior Hitman was going to put him out of his misery.

The stairs led up to another dark hallway with a closed door at the end. Lines of light showed all around it; Henry ran with everything he had and hurled himself at it. The door broke into pieces when he hit and he stumbled forward onto yet another staircase, shorter than the others and made of iron. He didn't so much climb as he fell *up* the steps, then tumbled through an open doorway that spat him out onto the roof.

Sound was still so muffled that he wasn't sure whether he was hearing birds or traffic or the high-pitched tone that meant part of his hearing was dying off for good. He staggered across the roof to peer over the waist-high barrier that ran along all four sides. A graffito informed him that someone named Monte had been there.

Good for you, Monte.

It was about a thirty-foot drop to the ground, he estimated; a fall he could survive but not walk away from. Fortunately there was a fire escape that ran from the roof to the ground. It was pretty old but it didn't look like it was falling apart and Henry couldn't see any places where it had come loose. Still, there was a fair amount of rust; it was a gamble as to whether it would hold his weight.

Or he could just keep dithering until Junior Hitman caught up with him.

"Oh, hell no," Henry muttered. He stuck his sidearm into his waistband, slung the rifle, clambered over the barrier, and climbed down the first length of the fire-escape ladder. It felt solidly attached to the stone and so did the first platform but he didn't linger. The second platform, however, swayed as soon as he stepped onto it and he all but flung himself at the next section of ladder.

He reached the lowest platform to find that part of it *had* pulled out of the wall, along with the upper part of the last section of ladder, something he hadn't been able to see from his vantage point on the roof. He was still too high up to jump without breaking something. He'd just have to move so fast the goddam thing wouldn't have time to come apart under his weight.

The platform groaned but he made it to the ladder. Large flakes of rust on its rungs stuck to his palms, rubbed off on his shirt, fell into his hair. The ladder itself was a little shaky but it didn't start pulling away from the building until he was halfway down.

He froze, clinging to the rusty metal while he scanned the wall in the vain hope of finding some kind of protrusion he might grab onto and pull the ladder back toward the building.

And thankfully, he found it—a bolt slightly thicker than his thumb, sticking a few centimeters out of the stone at the level of his waist. As he reached for it, the rifle slid off his shoulder and down his arm to his wrist, but he managed to grab the bolt. It didn't give under his touch so he wedged his fingertips under the head and pulled.

The ladder tilted back against the building. Henry breathed a sigh of relief, then looked up, half-expecting to see Junior Hitman taking aim at him.

But he wasn't there—yet.

Still holding onto the bolt and attempting to keep his weight forward on the ladder, Henry tried going down a rung. Immediately, the ladder started to lean away from the wall; at the same time, the rifle slipped from his wrist onto his hand. Henry tried to counter the movement of the ladder by pushing forward with his body. The rifle slipped farther, from the back of his hand past his knuckles to the first joints of his fingers.

Henry groaned. He could let go of the bolt, flip the rifle strap toward his wrist and then grab the bolt again, although he would have to do it fast, before the ladder could tilt backwards. But the moment he let go, the rifle slid over his fingers and dropped to the ground while the ladder leaned even farther back than before. He braced himself, thinking the ladder would yank itself free and fall to the ground as well. Then there was a dull clang and the ladder stopped short; Henry had all of a second to see that it had caught on the platform above him before he lost his grip and fell the last several feet to the ground.

His breath went out of him in a painful whoosh. Damn, he kept getting the wind knocked out of him today. At least it wasn't another grenade. Nonetheless, it took every bit of effort in him to roll over and get to his feet. As he reached for the rifle, something zipped past his hand and kicked up some dirt. Henry didn't bother looking up before he dove behind a mango tree. Junior Hitman, right on cue—or maybe just ever so slightly late. Two seconds sooner and the round would have gone through his chest. After a few moments, he risked taking a peek around one side of the tree.

Gunfire shredded the foliage, took chunks out of the trunk. Junior Hitman was now coming down from the roof by way of the fire escape and shooting all the while. Henry decided not to stick around to see how he managed the last ladder. As soon as there was a break in the gunfire, he vaulted over the rough-hewn stone wall behind him and landed in a cluster of bushes on the other side.

Thorn bushes, of course—was there any other kind? Henry tore himself free and ran forward, into yet another square. Damn. Squares were definitely the big thing in Cartagena, squares and cafés, Henry thought. This one was paved with red clay tiles that were surprisingly clean and bright. Henry wondered who took care of them. Maybe all the café managers—Cartagena was a tourist destination, after all. Which was no kind of a damned thing to be thinking about right now. He looked around for something, *anything* that might help him—

Behind him a motorcycle engine suddenly roared into life. Henry felt his heart leap as he turned to see a small cluster of bikes parked under a mango tree between two buildings. A man was sitting astride one of them, strapping on a helmet while he chatted to a woman sitting in a car beside him. In spite of everything, Henry broke into a broad grin. The colors and design told him the bike was a Honda Enduro—just what he needed. It would go from road to off-road and back without missing a beat. Henry rushed at him, ignoring the pain in his legs and his ribs and every other part of his body.

The guy was saying goodbye to the woman and preparing to roll forward when Henry leaped, planting both feet in his back and sending him over the handlebars in a clumsy somersault. The woman gave a shocked screech and grabbed Henry's arm as the rider scrambled on the ground, shouting furiously in Spanish. He started to get to his feet, then suddenly cut off. For a moment, he goggled at Henry with an expression of fear and astonishment. Still trying to get out of the woman's surprisingly strong grip, Henry turned to see Junior coming over the stone wall without landing in the thorn bushes, rifle in hand, and that dumb baseball cap still on his head. Henry drew the Glock and squeezed off a shot. The woman gave him a hard yank; the shot ripped through the bushes and hit the wall, well wide of the kid.

Dammit, he just *couldn't* get a break, Henry thought. He twisted out of the woman's grip, gunned the engine, and sped away.

CHAPTER 11

As he flew down a narrow alley, Henry was as grateful for the Enduro's bark busters as he was for its maneuverability. The hand guards saved the skin on his knuckles as he swerved around cars and trucks driven by people who apparently took street parking literally—i.e. stopping wherever they were. They didn't seem to notice him zigging and zagging around them at high speed.

But now he really wished he'd paid better attention to the streets. Once he lost his lookalike assassin he wanted to get back to Baron's, if for no other reason than to put together another burn bag. With any luck, Baron and Danny would have left for parts unknown by then so he wouldn't be putting them in the line of fire. Although now Baron had to find somewhere else to live; Henry was going to feel bad about that for the rest of his life. Baron had made a beautiful home for himself, and he'd still have it if Henry hadn't dragged him into his problems.

Meanwhile, it was the start of the business day in Cartagena, which meant more traffic on the streets. Even as the thought crossed his mind, Henry spotted an incline leading up to a sea wall that seemed to be as wide as a lot of the alleys he'd been through, if not wider. He just hoped every other biker in Cartagena hadn't had the same idea. Also, that it was too early for tourists—he had a sudden mental image of people in straw hats and Bermuda shorts toppling over like bowling pins as he zoomed past them.

Nope, no tourists immediately ahead of him, and no other bikers, probably because riding on the wall was illegal. Well, they'd just have to add that to his rap sheet, Henry thought. Much farther on, where the wall made a kind of dogleg to the left, he saw a set of stone stairs coming up from the lower level. The Enduro could take them—it would be a rough ride but the bike could handle it. All he had to do was hang on.

He looked over his shoulder and then slowed to a stop so he could scan the traffic on the road in both directions. Had he finally lost the arrogant little son of a—

Nope, no such luck. Henry heard the sound of another motorcycle engine approaching quickly and he was pretty sure it wasn't the pissed-off Enduro owner coming after him on a borrowed ride. The engine was growing louder but he couldn't quite pin down the direction—

Abruptly, something flew at him on his left. Henry shot at it by reflex, not recognizing it as a motorcycle helmet until afterwards. If Cartagena had a helmet law, he'd just violated it twice over. As he stuck the Glock back in his waistband, he heard the engine rev again; in the next moment, he saw the kid bouncing *up* the stone steps on a stolen Honda Enduro of his own.

Henry didn't wait to see if the son of a bitch stayed in the saddle. He pulled the handlebars in a sharp turn and yanked the throttle to make the bike pivot on its rear wheel, and headed back the way he had come. A bullet whizzed past his left ear and he accelerated, crouching low over the handlebars, keeping one eye on the road and the other on Junior Hitman's reflection in the left-hand mirror.

He zoomed down the incline, pulled a hard left and shot across two lanes of traffic in an effort to put as many vehicles as possible between himself and the kid with his face. Just as he swerved around a brightly colored bus, he caught a glimpse of himself in one of his side mirrors. His face was covered with plaster dust, dirt, and streaks of blood, a lot of it from the gash on his cheek.

Good God, I look more like a homicidal maniac than the guy who's actually trying to kill me, Henry thought. No wonder the guy he'd stolen the bike from had seemed scared. He probably thought he'd been jacked by a psycho killer hurrying to his next mass murder.

Another bullet zipped past on his left side, so close Henry thought he smelled gunpowder. He worked the Glock out of his waistband, wrapped his arm around his body and returned fire. Junior Hitman gave a jerk as a round hit him in the ribs but it didn't send up a spray of blood or throw him off the bike, or even loosen his goddam baseball cap—the thing must have been superglued to his head. Although judging from his expression in the side mirror, it *had* pissed him off.

He was wearing Kevlar, of course, that was no surprise. But the impact of the round should have punched him right out of the saddle. Junior Hitman was one tough little bastard. Henry stuck the Glock back in his waistband and cut across two lanes of traffic with the kid still on his tail.

He made a sharp turn into another narrow alley, flying past an enormous colorful painting of a curvy lady that ran the length of a building. Henry turned again, zipped diagonally across a square, sending a flock of pigeons into startled flight, and into another street barely wide enough for the motorcycle to pass through before coming out on a main road.

Contemporary urban Cartagena was on his right now; after brightly colored Old Town, the ultra-modern skyline was jarring, a shock to the eye. Henry drew his sidearm again, tried another shot, and discovered he was out. Dammit, he thought, dumping the empty magazine. He put the pistol back in his waistband so he could get a fresh magazine out of his pocket and reload, while Junior went on taking potshots at him.

He stuck the magazine into his waistband and managed to get it into the Glock one-handed without dropping either of them or losing anything down his trousers. Baron had once bet him a hundred bucks he'd never be able to do that under fire. If he actually made it out of this with his head intact, Henry was going to enjoy telling him he was wrong. Although he should probably wait to collect on that bet until *after* he bought Baron a new house. Another shot flew past his shoulder; Henry checked his mirrors but Junior Hitman was gone.

Except he couldn't be—the goddam bullets were still coming and Henry could hear the roar of the bike behind him. He looked around frantically, checked the mirrors again. For a moment, he had an absurd mental image of Junior Hitman leaping the Enduro from one rooftop to another. From all-terrain to no terrain, he thought, swerving around a bus. Finally he caught a glimpse of the other bike's front tire in the right side mirror—but not on the road. Junior was speeding along the top of a wall barely wide enough to accommodate the bike's wheels.

Henry bared his teeth in a grim smile. It figured; the kid just couldn't resist showing off while making a kill. The problem was, the end of the wall was twenty feet ahead and it was at least ten feet off the ground—even an Enduro couldn't take a drop like that and keep rolling. Unless Junior Hitman could sprout wings, his *pièce de résistance* was going to end in pieces.

Now he heard police sirens and they sounded awfully close. Maybe Junior Hitman would try to impress them, too. As if the kid had caught something of Henry's thoughts, Junior suddenly laid the bike down on its side while gunning the throttle. The bike skidded off the wall without him and into the air, flying straight toward Henry.

Henry accelerated and passed a display of an old cannon half a second before Junior Hitman's stolen Enduro hit it and burst into flames. Yeah, the cops were going to be very impressed by *that* trick, Henry thought as the sirens screamed to a stop behind him. He hit the brakes hard and turned to watch.

Two motorcycle cops had just pulled up in front of the kid, who was standing on the wall and staring at Henry with obvious fury. This should be good, Henry thought, especially if the kid tried to sell them a story about having to lay it down to save it. But before the cops could draw their guns, Junior Hitman leaped down from the wall and banged their heads together, knocking them out. Then he grabbed up one of their bikes—another Honda Enduro. Apparently this was the bike of choice in Cartagena. Henry yanked hard on the throttle and got the hell out of there.

He headed away from the main road and back into the narrow streets of Old Town but the kid stuck with him all the way. If he couldn't lose him, Henry thought, he'd just have to knock him off the damned bike. One shot hadn't done it but five or six might.

Henry sped over a wood bridge well ahead of Junior Hitman, startling people walking on either side. He skidded to a stop, facing the way he had come, drew the Glock, and waited. A second later, the police bike appeared. Henry opened fire, sending everyone on the bridge into a shrieking panic as they ran or dropped to the ground, arms covering their heads.

Junior Hitman reared the bike up on its back wheel, practically dancing as he dodged the bullets—another miss. Henry took off again. The mirror on the left showed the kid trying to draw a bead on him, then giving up and gunning the bike forward as people ran for cover again.

Henry followed the road and found himself back on the highway with a stretch of sea wall on his left. This one was wider but Henry couldn't see any way to get up on it. He was looking around for something else when his right-hand mirror disintegrated in a burst of glass and cheap plastic. He ducked as low as he could and waited for something else to blow apart, hoping it wouldn't be his head.

Nothing happened. In the left side mirror, he saw Junior squeezing the trigger over and over, his face contorted with rage. Son of a bitch was finally empty. Henry had begun to think he had one of those magic movie pistols that never ran out of ammo. The roar of the engine behind him grew louder, rising in pitch as Junior closed the gap between them.

Another grim smile spread across Henry's face. The kid might be out of ammo but *he* wasn't—not yet, anyway— and he had no intention of wasting it on empty air. He swerved around the car in front of him and as Junior Hitman started to follow, he twisted around and shot the car's left front tire.

As soon as he did, however, he was sorry. Henry caught a fleeting glimpse of the driver's terrified face as the car spun out of control, tires screaming and sparks spraying up from the wheel rim grinding on the road. Junior Hitman veered into the next lane and kept going, not even glancing over his shoulder as the car collided with an SUV.

Great, Henry thought, pulling harder on the throttle; he'd just caused an accident and it hadn't even slowed the kid down. His moment of guilt was suddenly eclipsed by déjà vu. This stretch of road looked awfully familiar. Were he and Junior Hitman going in circles now?

No, that wasn't it, he realized, his heart sinking as he saw an even more familiar bright yellow house up ahead. *Please let Baron and Danny be inside, or better yet, far away from here,* Henry prayed. But of course they weren't—still no breaks today. Baron and Danny stood together as he blew past, their faces utterly astonished. Yeah, they'd recognized him all right, and they were going to recognize Junior Hitman, too.

Henry took another turn and headed for the heart of Old Town again. Maybe if he could get Junior into one of the narrower alleys—

The police sirens seemed to be getting closer. Henry wondered what was taking them so long as Junior Hitman drew even with him on his left. A cold chill swept through him; he could see the intent on the kid's face—*his own* face, *his own* expression, *his own* posture on the bike— and he was still trying to believe it was real when Junior Hitman jerked the handlebars and hit him.

Guys had tried this kind of Demolition Derby crap with him before; he had learned how to shift his weight along with the angle of the bike relative to the road. Henry felt a surge of intense gratification at the shocked expression on the kid's face. *I* told *you it wasn't going to be that easy,* Henry thought at him silently. *And if you thought* that *was a shock, get ready for this.* He swerved and knocked his bike into the kid, throwing in a hard left jab to his shoulder for good measure.

Junior Hitman went wobbly for a few seconds but he recovered his balance and kept the rubber side down, making it look as easy as flexing a muscle. Henry had been about his age when he had first learned the balance-counterbalance trick. It had taken a lot of hours of practice and he had sanded off a lot of leather and a few layers of skin in the process. Now he hoped having almost thirty years of experience on the kid meant he was thirty years better.

And if all else failed, Henry thought, he had the element of surprise. Junior Hitman hadn't thought he'd have such a hard time with a so-called old guy. Easing off the throttle, Henry dropped back and came up on the kid's left. *Okay, youngster, let's see how you do on your weak side. I've got twenty-plus more years of tricks, hacks and moves—what have you got?*

Reflexes, Henry discovered as Junior Hitman smacked him with his bike again, throwing a left jab at his head. Henry felt the kid's arm brush the top of his hair as he ducked, swerving away from the kid to stabilize himself. Except the kid came right with him like their bikes were tethered. He slowed, only to have the kid slow at the same moment, accelerated, and found the kid was right there with him like his reflection, or like they were doing some kind of synchronized dance at eighty miles an hour.

You little bastard, Henry thought at him, furious. But when he glanced over, Junior Hitman didn't look smug or pleased with himself at getting under the old guy's skin—he looked as if Henry was freaking *him* out.

Time to end this. Henry reached for the Glock in his waistband at the exact moment Junior surged forward and pulled over so he was directly in front of Henry.

Everything happened in only a few seconds, but later Henry's memory played it back in slow-motion:

The back wheel of Junior Hitman's Enduro suddenly rose up to eye level and wagged to the left. Henry sat back, trying to dodge it, and it smacked his shoulder.

The sensation of spinning rubber shredding his shirt was brief but vivid as Henry went down with the bike, just as vivid as the feeling of the road scraping away his jeans and the upper layers of his skin. At that particular moment, however, the only thought in his head was the hope that he wouldn't end up becoming an organ donor.

The outer side of his right leg felt like it had burst into flames but Henry shoved the sensation as far from his awareness as he could and concentrated on checking himself for broken bones. Nope, no fractures. He could file that with no wife, no son, no Paris, he thought, and rolled onto his belly, preparing to push himself to his hands and knees.

A crowd was gathering on the sidewalk, growing larger by the second. Apparently no one in Cartagena had ever seen a guy who'd just gotten his ass kicked and they were fascinated. Judging from their expressions, they were also squeamish. But not too squeamish to get him on video. Very few of them were actually looking at him directly; most were seeing him through their phone screens, although a couple of tourists had actual cameras. Monroe had been right; an hour from now, he'd probably be viral. *Motorcycle Maniac Lays It Down To Save It.* (Poor beagle.)

His grief for Monroe threatened to come bubbling up from where he'd buried it but Henry tamped it down again. There were other things to take care of first, the most urgent of them being to clear his head. He felt dazed and a little dizzy—no, a lot dizzy, he discovered as he struggled to his knees and then to his feet. Moving slowly, he straightened all the way up and immediately fell sideways, catching himself on a parked car. His inner ear didn't seem to know the ride was over—it couldn't decide whether he was still sliding along the road or spinning around in circles. The police sirens screaming in the distance like it was the end of the world didn't help.

Then he heard the familiar sound of an Enduro engine, coming fast, much faster than those screaming sirens. Henry took a deep breath; apparently he and the kid weren't done dancing. Dammit.

Henry limped away from the crowd into the middle of the street with the vague notion of drawing Junior Hitman away from the innocent bystanders; also the kid would have a harder time getting at him if he was standing in moving traffic.

Except the traffic wouldn't keep moving. Drivers slowed down to go around him, or pulled over and stopped altogether, because this was *not* his day. Should he put himself between Junior Hitman and the crowd, or face the crowds himself so they weren't in the kid's sights? Too late—the crowd had grown so large they were all around him and he couldn't think because the Enduro engine drowned out everything.

Henry's vision suddenly settled down and let him see the bike was coming right at him. Like a spear, like a lightning bolt, like a missile, and son of a bitch, he couldn't fucking move, not a step. He could only stand there, swaying a little while he waited for Junior Hitman to ride right over him. Maybe one of those distant sirens was an ambulance; with the way things were going, though, probably not.

He should close his eyes, Henry thought, but he couldn't do that, either. Nothing was working right today. Not his day...

Seconds before impact, Junior Hitman squeezed the front brake with just the right amount of pressure and the crowd gasped in perfect unison as the Enduro rose up on its front wheel *again*. It had taken Henry months to do an endo without sending himself over the high side, and even more time to do one that lasted longer than three seconds, and the kid had just done it twice.

Junior Hitman's eyes met his and all the tiny hairs on the back of Henry's neck stood up. He watched the kid shift the handlebars, making the bike actually *pirouette*. Henry kept watching, too transfixed to realize what was happening, until the still-spinning back wheel came around and whacked him. *Again.*

Henry felt his feet leave the ground as he flew through the air and crashed into the side of a parked car.

Bitch-slapped me with a motorcycle twice, Henry marveled, using the car door handle to drag himself to a standing position. He caught a glimpse of the driver hurriedly getting out on the passenger side and wondered if he should apologize. *Sorry, my insurance only covers collisions if I'm actually* in *a car.*

He turned just in time to see the kid had the bike down on two wheels and was skidding it sideways, intending to hit him with the back wheel a *third* time. Leaning hard against the car, Henry threw both legs into the air, feeling the heat from the muffler as the bike missed him by inches.

The tires screeched as Junior Hitman turned to face him. He took the bike up on its back wheel, revved the engine, and let it go at Henry riderless. Henry staggered out of the way; the front tire smashed the car's driver's side window and the impact threw Henry over the hood to land heavily on the street where he lay panting and gasping, unable to move.

Only he had to move, because Junior Hitman was *still* coming for him, like some kind of unstoppable robot killing machine. Henry struggled to get up but could only manage to crawl backwards while the kid advanced on him with a combat knife. And he wasn't even *breathing* hard, Henry saw. The muscles in his arms flexed smoothly and easily, his face was set in the stony mask of a professional determined to finish his mission. A pro didn't quit, didn't fail, didn't die; a pro accomplished the mission. Junior Hitman was about to accomplish his and Henry couldn't do a goddam thing about it. He had nothing left and the kid knew it. Nothing was going to stop him from finishing Henry off.

Every time Henry had gone out on a mission, it had been with the knowledge that he might not make it home. A body count as high as his pretty much guaranteed he was going to be a target himself someday; he knew better than to count on dying of old age. He had lived with that reality for a very long time without letting it get to him.

But of all the ways he had imagined his life would end, he had never envisioned this. It would never have occurred to him; it was patently impossible. Only it wasn't because here was the only other thing he hadn't seen coming: Junior Hitman.

Or maybe Junior Henry was more apt. Again, Henry recognized his own posture, the way he moved, even the way he held that goddam knife. More than that, he knew *exactly* what Junior Henry was about to do, how he'd counter Henry's self-defense moves, then how he'd counter Henry's counters, and so forth and so on, ad infinitum. It would be like they were fighting their reflections in a great big mirror.

Or it would have been except Henry barely had enough strength to crawl and he wouldn't be able to do that much longer. The kid would have no trouble finishing him off. He could just lean over and slash the femoral artery in his thigh. Henry would bleed out in a matter of minutes.

And to add insult to injury, he could tell that Junior Henry *still* didn't see the resemblance. Henry couldn't think of a more fucked up way to die.

At least the little bastard had finally lost his baseball cap. Like that mattered.

The screaming sirens were suddenly right on top of them. Henry heard two police cruisers pull up behind him as several more screeched to a halt in the street. The kid's eyes flickered from him to the uniformed officers now getting out of their cars, demanding to know what the hell was going on. Henry looked over his shoulder, saw their irate expressions. They weren't going to be too happy with Junior Henry, either, he thought, and turned to see if the kid was actually crazy enough to try fighting a mob of angry cops.

Except Junior Henry wasn't there, wasn't anywhere. All he could see now, besides what had to be most of the population of Old Town, were cops coming at him from all sides, more cops than he had thought were actually on Cartagena's police force. And every single one was furious with him.

Henry put his hands up as they closed in around him.

The cops hauled him to his feet and two of them pushed him up against the nearest cruiser so they could cuff his hands behind his back. Henry looked around, thinking the kid might be enjoying this portion of *The Kick Henry Brogan's Ass Show* from a nearby rooftop but there was no sign of him, not high up or at ground level. There were only a lot of innocent bystanders milling around, in no hurry to disperse despite the cops' efforts to shoo them away. Maybe they were hoping the kid would reappear and do some more tricks on another stolen police bike.

Henry looked around again and finally spotted Baron and Danny. They should have been far, far away but he couldn't help feeling relieved they were there. They were the only two people in all of Cartagena who didn't want to beat him like a big bass drum. Baron gazed at him with a pained expression and Danny was staring at the ground. Henry wondered if she was angry with him or just embarrassed. Then she stooped to pick something up.

Henry got only the briefest glimpse of what she was holding as the cops threw him in the back of the cruiser but it looked like a black baseball cap.

CHAPTER 12

Among the many historical sites in Cartagena, the most spectacular is the Castillo de San Felipe de Barajas, known as the most impressive fortress that Spain built in any of her colonies. It sits at the top of San Lázaro Hill overlooking quite a lot of Cartagena including the central police station across the street. Unlike the weathered seventeenth-century stone castle, the Policía Nacional building was bright, clean, with ultra-modern twenty-first century lines on the outside and, on the inside, dull tile floors and cement-block walls characteristic of institutions where people are not guests. Henry wondered if the cops here ever looked at the fortress and thought about how law enforcement had changed over the last three and a half centuries. Probably not. They seemed to be pretty busy, especially now.

In Henry's experience, getting arrested in a different language was a far wordier process than it was in English. In Cartagena, it was also more emotional, at least on this occasion. He had seldom seen local law enforcement anywhere so infuriated; the way they were acting, it was like he had broken every law on the books and then gone out of his way to personally insult all of their families. Of course, that may have been due at least in part to his American accent. Being an American had always been problematic in certain areas of the world and lately it seemed like there were more of these areas all the time.

But as Henry sat in the small, humid interrogation room sweating through his clothes while a continuing stream of cops, some in uniform, some in plainclothes, took turns ranting at him, he knew their outrage didn't stem from anti-American sentiment. From their perspective, he had come into their town and gone batshit crazy in the streets, and then, when they busted him for it, he claimed his evil twin was trying to kill him.

If he could have gotten a word in edgewise, perhaps he could have explained himself better. On the other hand, his Colombian Spanish was a bit rusty so he might have only made things worse. And it probably wouldn't have mitigated their anger at the accidents he and Junior Hitman had caused, not to mention the people they had endangered by shooting at each other. Cartagena was a tourist destination; batshit-crazy men running around with guns would kill their business and their economy. Worse, he fit the description of the *pendejo* who had knocked out two officers, stolen a police motorcycle, and then wrecked it doing tricks to show off.

He tried to point out that he couldn't have been that *pendejo*, he was the *other pendejo* on the *other* bike, whom the *pendejo* on the cop's bike had been trying to kill; they could tell the difference because that *pendejo* had been wearing a baseball cap—but it only made them angrier. Henry couldn't really blame them. If he'd been in their place, he'd have thought he was off his meds, too, and he'd have already called the appropriate institution to come and take him away. It made him wonder why he was still sweating in the interrogation room stone-cold sober and not floating on a Thorazine cloud in a straitjacket.

Probably because Cartagena had no institution for the criminally insane, he realized. The closest one would most likely be somewhere like Bogotá or Medellín, both of which were several hundred miles away; one hell of a drive. Maybe there was an ambulance on the way. Unless the authorities in Bogotá or Medellín were arguing with the Cartagena police about who was responsible for transporting him.

Henry began to think he was getting delirious from the heat.

He didn't know how many hours he'd been roasting alive in the interrogation room before he finally heard a new voice, female and very familiar. She was fluent and spoke calmly but firmly, laying it out for them without impatience or hostility but refusing to be argued with. Finally a uniformed officer came into the room, detached Henry from the table, and dragged him through the police station to the front entrance where Danny was waiting.

The grey-green suit coat, white blouse, and blue jeans she was wearing gave her an air of untouchable authority, underscored by the badge on the lanyard around her neck: *Homeland Security*. Danny gave him an authoritative look as they stepped outside. Nope, he wouldn't argue with her, either, Henry thought as he stood blinking in the late afternoon sunlight.

The officer said something to her that might have been either an apology or a proposal of marriage. She responded in a professional tone that had a slight hint of kindness, perhaps telling him to go now and sin no more. Then Baron pulled up at the curb and she hustled Henry into the car.

"Sorry, Baron, but your place is burned," Henry said. "Get me somewhere I can see him coming."

"You got it," Baron said.

The view from San Felipe Castle was spectacular. As he sat on a low wall with Baron and Danny, Henry could see Old Town as well as the skyline of twenty-first-century Cartagena, all against a backdrop of Caribbean blue, a shade unique to this part of the world.

Baron had brought them up here by way of what he claimed was a shortcut, which turned out to involve a lot of stairs. Baron had managed them easily and Danny had simply trotted up one set of steps after another with little apparent effort. Henry had been panting before they were even halfway to the top. The Enduro could have handled all those stairs but it was probably illegal to ride a motorcycle in a national monument.

There had been a time when he'd have climbed up to the top of the castle without even thinking about it, no matter how hard his day had been.

Yeah, and there had also been a time when he wouldn't have missed the shot in Liège, which was why he'd decided to retire in the first place.

Damn. No matter what he did, he *could not* get a *goddam break*.

The sun was starting to set now; this close to the equator, night would come quickly. He had to make some decisions about what to do next, the sooner the better.

"I wanted to go in there guns blazing," Baron said, grinning. "She thought the diplomatic approach made more sense."

"Gunfire would have been kinder," Henry said. "She shredded those poor guys."

Baron chuckled. "So, now what?" Both he and Danny were looking at him expectantly.

"I need to get to Budapest," Henry replied.

"What's in Budapest?" Danny and Baron asked in perfect unison.

"Jack's informant—Yuri." Henry stood up and stretched. A plan was coming together in his mind. The adrenaline that had kept him alive while Junior Hitman had been trying to kill him was gone and he had been holding off fatigue by sheer willpower but he knew he wasn't going to last much longer. He had to find some way to keep his mind engaged and focused, or he was going to start feeling instead of thinking. If he did that, he might lose it and losing it was *not* an option, not now.

"These guys aren't after me because I'm retiring," Henry went on. "They're after me because they think Jack told me something classified. Yuri ought to know something about that."

Baron laughed a little, shaking his head. "Sorry, partner. My Aztec doesn't have that kind of range."

"Yeah, I was hoping we might *borrow* something that does. Maybe a G."

Baron's expression was solemn. "Wow. Taking someone's Gulfstream. You'd really have to *hate* a guy to do that." His face suddenly lit up with a broad smile. "And I know just the fella. Gimme a minute." He took out his phone and moved away a few yards.

"I'm so fired," Baron sang to the tune of 'I Got A Woman.' *"Yeah, I'm so fired! I'm so fired and I don't caaaaaaaaare!"* On the last note, the jet lifted into the air, then banked gently as Baron put the last faint glow of sunset behind them.

In spite of everything, Danny smiled as she continued tending to Henry's various cuts and abrasions. The Gulfstream's medikit was quite extensive, which was a good thing since Henry's injuries were, too. Danny had had to pick more than a few chunks of dirt and grit out of the long, deep scrape on his outer thigh. It was an awful process but Henry barely flinched. And he'd seemed all but unaware of all the cuts on his arms and just below his collarbone.

But the worst injury besides his leg was the one she was working on now, a gash where something sharp had been driven into his face scarily close to his eye. She used a cotton ball soaked in witch hazel to clean away the dried blood and dirt caked around it so she could see exactly how bad it was. It wasn't long but it was deep. She saturated another cotton ball with hydrogen peroxide and warned him it was going to sting before applying it to the wound.

He winced a bit but that was all. She supposed a little sting was nothing compared to getting bike-fu'ed by a homicidal maniac—but not just any homicidal maniac. She knew Henry had seen his face. And vice versa, although Henry had been so covered with dirt and blood, the other guy may not have spotted the resemblance. Hell, she might not have recognized Henry herself if they hadn't already met.

"Henry?" she said tentatively. No answer; he didn't want to discuss it but Danny decided to plunge ahead anyway. What the hell, she was wiping up his blood; she was entitled to some answers. "Did you ever have a kid? A son, maybe?"

He gazed at her through hooded eyes. "No, why?"

"The guy on the motorcycle—did you notice anything *funny* about him?"

"Yeah," Henry said. "I noticed he was very good."

"I meant his *face*," she said, applying the first butterfly bandage to his cheek. Stitches would have been better but she wasn't skilled enough at facial sutures so butterflies would have to do. "The *similarity*?"

Henry gave a resigned sigh. "Yeah, I noticed that, too."

"So you never had a long-term relationship?" she asked, putting on the next bandage.

"Not unless we count you."

Danny couldn't help laughing at that one. "Is it possible you had a kid without knowing it?"

"*No*," he said firmly. "Zero chance."

"Then…?"

"*Danny*." He hadn't raised his voice but she got the hint. Instead of pushing him, she tucked two bloody cotton balls into a small plastic bag and pushed it under her seat with the other item she was hanging onto.

"Thank you, by the way," she said.

Henry's eyebrows went up. "For what?"

"Leaving Baron's apartment so he and I wouldn't be targets," she replied. "Also for coming to get me in Georgia when you could have just run for your life."

Henry chuckled. "Just wanted to put you on a private plane and give you a free trip to Hungary."

"Where I'm going to find…?"

"Hungarians," Henry said. "When I saw him it was like I was seeing a ghost."

"A ghost with a gun?" Danny said.

"It was like it was every trigger I ever pulled," he said, surprising the hell out of her.

She was still trying to figure out what to say to that when he lay back and closed his eyes. The conversation, like the first aid, was over.

CHAPTER 13

The mansion Clay Verris called home was one of many stately old houses that Savannah was famous for, although it wasn't actually in the city itself but several miles away in the countryside, well off the beaten path followed by historic tours. It sat on several well-kept and heavily-surveilled acres of land and had its own lake just a few steps from the front door. The clear placid water reflected the place perfectly, so that from a certain distance, the house seemed to be sitting directly above its upside-down double. It was the kind of image many photographers found irresistible but the very few people allowed within Verris's established perimeter knew better than to bring a camera.

In the twenty-three years Clay Verris had been in residence with his son, there had been very few intrusions. The security details stationed well away from the house had occasionally redirected hikers with broken compasses and, on one occasion, escorted someone claiming to be a herbalist off the property. But no one had ever come close to breaking into the house.

Nonetheless, Verris had put in an alarm system, just in case. The Gemini personnel he had tasked with the installation told him that it was a bit tricky to install something so high-tech without compromising the house's historic character. Verris had told them this meant either the tech wasn't high-tech enough or they didn't know what they were doing; which was it?

The alarm system had gone in without a problem, and so had all the updates. Verris tested it from time to time and was satisfied that there was no way anyone could get into his home without being invited.

So when he woke just before dawn, he knew something was wrong. He was a man who slept soundly and well; *thoroughly* was the word he liked to use. His training and conditioning were also thorough, and as a result, he had an extremely heightened awareness, which was how he knew he had awakened because there was someone else in the house.

He lay very still, waiting for noises that might give some indication of how many hostiles he might have to deal with and where each of them was. Later he would determine how they had breached the perimeter and broken in without setting off the in-house alarm. The overnight security team would regret their negligence for the rest of their miserable lives, if not longer.

It seemed like an hour before he finally heard another sound, this time from his son's bedroom. Verris tensed; was this some kind of drunken prank? There had been an incident before, but that had been in his office in the compound. At times, personnel got rowdy there but they wouldn't *dare* break into his house, he was sure of that. If this was an outsider, though, a lot of heads were going to roll.

Without making a sound, Verris got up, put on his dressing gown and crept down the stairs. The light in Junior's room was on and shouldn't have been. His son was still out of the country; after his mission to take out Brogan had gone pear-shaped, Verris had told him to sit tight in a Colombian safe house and await new orders. He had issued that command personally and his son was nothing if not reliable and obedient.

Verris drew the pistol in the pocket of his dressing gown and, hugging the wall outside his son's room, peeked around the open doorway.

The man sitting on the bed was the spitting image of Henry Brogan as he had been at the age of twenty-five, and he was alternating between tweezers and a pair of angled metal tongs to pick shrapnel out of his side, dropping the fragments on a monogrammed towel.

It was a tedious, awkward process, complicated by the attendant bleeding. Every time he removed one of the larger pieces, a little more blood would dribble down his side— not so much that he was in danger of losing consciousness, just enough to make a messy job that much messier.

Verris was rarely taken by surprise but he really hadn't seen this coming. The only thing more surprising would have been finding Henry Brogan himself sitting on the bed with him. Now *that* would have been a sight and Verris almost wished he could see it. But it would never happen. The physical resemblance was only skin deep; past that, Junior was Verris's son clear through to the bone.

He slipped the gun back into his pocket and stepped into the open doorway. The man on the bed looked up at him, then went back to what he was doing.

"I told you to stay in Colombia and await orders," Verris said.

Junior looked up at him again. "I wanted to talk to you."

His son's voice was just a little too loud to be acceptable. The kid knew it, too, Verris thought, gazing at him sternly. Junior stared back, tongs in hand, refusing to admit he was in the wrong. All sons did this from time to time, even the best and most dutiful of them. It was how they tested the structure they'd been given. They needed to see if it held. A good father made sure his son knew that it would, that it was one of the few things in life he could count on never to fail him.

Junior could push pretty hard sometimes. It took almost half a minute before he finally dropped his gaze.

"Sorry," he said.

When Verris didn't respond, Junior looked up at him again, his expression turning wary.

Verris was staring through him now and Junior knew that meant he'd crossed a little too far over the line. He tried to go back to picking shrapnel out of his side but he couldn't get a good hold on anything. The bleeding had increased.

Verris turned on his heel and went to his study. The retina scanner was a bit slow to unlock the door but he was in no hurry. He got his first-aid kit out of a cabinet behind his desk and gave it a full ten-count before going back to his son's bedroom.

Junior's expression was relieved if still a bit apprehensive when he reappeared. Verris shoved everything Junior had been using off the bed and had him lie down on his uninjured side while he finished removing the shrapnel for him. *Boys will be boys,* Verris thought as he soaked up the excess blood with cotton batting. No matter how old they got, they had to learn some lessons more than once. With any luck, this one would sink in hard enough to leave a mark as a permanent reminder. Verris loved his son but there were moments when Junior came uncomfortably close to genuine rebellion. That wasn't supposed to happen... yet.

Verris adjusted the long-necked high-intensity reading lamp on the nightstand, then offered Junior a syringe of lidocaine. Junior shook his head. He was facing away so

Verris allowed himself a fleeting smile of approval. At least Junior had never had to relearn the lesson about overcoming pain. In truth, Verris had never known anyone else who was as adept at conquering their own physical discomfort.

But that didn't mean Verris wanted to prolong it. Enduring pain put unwanted stress on even the healthiest person, not just physically but mentally as well. He worked as quickly and as gently as he could, dropping each fragment in an empty compartment of the first-aid kit so Junior could hear it and know it was out.

It wasn't the first time Verris had pulled shrapnel out of a soldier, and he'd done so under much worse conditions—but there were more fragments than he'd realized, many of them tiny. He couldn't risk leaving any behind—sepsis was no joke. He'd seen guys keel over with crazy-high fevers, bodies shutting down because some ham-handed medic had done a half-assed patch job. The men and women under Verris's command died in combat like the warriors they were, not flat on their backs in delirium from massive organ failure.

He disinfected Junior's wounds again before he started suturing. Just as he finished closing the first laceration and was about to go onto the next, Junior suddenly said, "He's... very good."

Verris didn't have to ask who *he* was. "The best," he replied. "That's why I sent *you*."

"He knew every move of mine before I made it," Junior went on. "I'd *have* him, right *there*—then when I pulled the trigger, he was gone. Like a ghost."

"Did you happen to get a look at his face?" Verris asked, finishing with another laceration.

"Not really," Junior said. "I saw him up the stairs in the abandoned building, through a dirty mirror."

"Thought you were on the roof," Verris said sharply.

Junior sighed. "I was but he got a line on me. Had to jump down."

"What do we always drill?" Verris asked him, his voice brisk. "Hold the high ground, put his back to the wall and—"

"Don't let him off," Junior finished in unison with him. "The whole thing was weird. *Wiggy.*"

"How?" Verris asked as he started on the last wound in need of suturing.

"Like I was watching it all, but—" his son hesitated. "But I wasn't actually there. Who is he?"

Junior being a little spooked wasn't the only thing Verris found worrisome. He had trained his son to stay squarely in the moment, to focus on the immediate situation, but the way Junior was talking, it sounded like he was distancing himself instead. This was no good; Verris knew he had to nip that in the bud before Junior developed any seriously bad habits, like over-thinking, or wondering about the nature of his existence.

"Junior, the thing you're struggling with—that *strangeness*—it's fear." Verris tied off the last suture and sat him up so he could look directly into his eyes. "Don't hate it. Lean into it. *Embrace* it. *Learn* from it. Then overcome it."

Junior nodded, looking sheepish.

"You're right on the threshold of perfection, son." Verris held up his thumb and forefinger with the thinnest sliver of a gap between them. "This close." Pause. "You hungry?"

"Yes, sir." Junior nodded again, this time with enthusiasm.

"Bowl of cereal sound good?" Verris asked.

"Yes, sir," said Junior.

Verris saw his gaze move to the framed photo on the nightstand. It was the two of them, taken on one of their hunting trips when Junior had been eight or nine and they'd shared a less complicated existence.

He smiled at his son and took him into the kitchen.

* * *

The blown-up bus lay on its side, burn marks obscuring most of the large curved script that ran the length of it below the shattered windows. From where he stood in the roped-off observation area, Junior didn't have to see the words clearly to know they said *City Transportation Company*. He'd been fluent in Arabic, both Modern Standard and Egyptian, for over half his life.

The scene in front of him was equally familiar: civilian 'casualties' lay motionless on the ground around the bus, dropped by 'insurgents' who had taken up positions behind it and picked them off as they crawled out of the wreckage. There were no live rounds, of course—they were all armed with tasers. Some of the civilians had been desperate enough to try for one of the low buildings that served as a village or neighborhood or installation or whatever the war games scenario called for. A few of them had made it but without weapons; they were pretty much sitting ducks. Eventually the insurgents would come out from behind the bus and advance on the village, 'killing' anyone they found.

In any case, the insurgents were in for a fight. As an observer, Junior had access to all the feeds for the exercise; his phone screen showed today's designated good guys, an elite team of fighters coming in on the other side of the village, as yet undetected by the insurgents. Their uniforms were Libyan Army but there was an extra patch on their sleeves that identified them as Gemini support troops.

He watched as the Gemini team secured the other half of the village before preparing to attack the insurgents. They'd save civilians if possible but the insurgents were the priority, not rescuing non-combatants, and judging by the size of the Gemini squad, the mission was no prisoners. So they probably wouldn't be taking civilians with them, either.

Junior knew that in a combat situation, it wasn't always possible to rescue every innocent soul caught in the crossfire, but he also knew deep down he would never be able to abandon someone he *could* help, even if he was ordered to. That seemed to go against every principle his father had raised him to live by.

Then again, so did disobeying a direct order, yet he had done exactly that when he had left Colombia to come home, and his father had let him get away with it. But he hadn't been in a combat situation with a team. The only team combat he had ever seen was in exercises like this one.

He had certainly been in a lot of those, more than anyone else in Gemini. He had taken his lumps and dished some out as both a designated good guy and an insurgent, although never as a civilian. When he had asked Verris why, his father had told him it was because unlike everyone else, he had never been a civilian and never would be. Verris had made it sound like one more extraordinary achievement that proved Junior was elite even among the hand-picked elite that comprised Gemini personnel.

Why his father would be proud of him for that, however, was beyond Junior's understanding. If he'd never been a civilian, it wasn't by choice. It wasn't that he *wanted* to be a civilian—he didn't. *Never* to have been one, though— that was different from being career military. Junior thought it sounded more like he was missing a big chunk of the human experience and that didn't make him elite. It made him a freak.

Which he probably was to all the other Gemini soldiers. For them, the Gemini compound was a specialized training ground. For him, the training ground was home.

But if the exercise he was watching had been an actual mission and he had been part of the squad fighting real insurgents, they wouldn't have spared even a second to think what a freak he was.

Still, he had a feeling his never having been a civilian showed in ways that he wasn't aware of, that there was something about him other people felt was wiggy or off, even if they didn't know what it was.

He turned his attention back to the exercise, where the elite team members were now engaging the insurgents and showing them what they thought of fighters who killed unarmed civilians. The uniformed team was going full-on, like it really was fighting insurgents and this wasn't a training exercise where both sides were armed only with tasers.

Training had to be tough and a good part of that was so soldiers gained a level of conditioning to be able to withstand punishment—a punch, a beating, a cattle prod, even a stab wound or a gunshot—and not be too traumatized to get up again. But Junior thought these guys had bypassed tough and gone to unadorned brutality. There had to be a limit to how many times you could tase even the hardest hard-ass before doing serious damage. At the very least, it wasted juice.

The guys playing the insurgents gave as good as they got, all for the sake of keeping everyone's training at peak. But this didn't look like training. The so-called good guys seemed to be enjoying themselves too much. So were the guys playing the insurgents—some of them had apparently discovered their inner bad guys and were gleefully letting them out to play. One rather protracted fight gave Junior the definite impression a score was being settled and that was nothing short of unprofessional. Conduct unbecoming, for sure.

Junior looked around at the other personnel who weren't part of the exercise. Generally, anyone not tapped for an exercise gave the field of action a wide berth. But more than a few soldiers had paused in the observation area to check things out, although they hadn't stayed long, and if they'd thought the exercise was getting out of hand, they hadn't said anything to him about it. But they probably wouldn't have anyway. Everyone was polite to him but even those who were friendly kept their distance, never going out of their way to get to know him, like they didn't know what to make of him. Like he was a freak.

In any case, Junior knew what his father would say if he shared his misgivings about what was going on in the current exercise. Verris would tell him to remember these guys were still learning. None of them came from his privileged background—they hadn't grown up learning how to conduct themselves, how to channel their thoughts and emotions, how to conquer fear by first embracing it, how to focus their minds properly, how to achieve complete dedication to a mission without letting it become personal. And of course, none of them could manage physical pain as well as he could.

His father had told him many times he was especially proud of him for that. Physical pain was the biggest problem for a soldier. Compartmentalizing was a skill and most people could learn how to do it if they were dedicated enough. But physical pain was something else altogether. Even the strongest soldiers could be worn down and defeated by pain.

That includes you, Junior, his father had said. *You have a remarkable ability to keep pain from taking over your state of mind and affecting your judgment. But even you can't do that indefinitely. Pain weakens the body, interferes with the mind, and eventually soldiers succumb.*

They can't help it. They're captured or killed, because they either make mistakes, or they simply don't have the physical strength to defend themselves.

Can't the lab just make better painkillers? he'd asked Verris. *Stuff that won't get you stoned, then wear off after four measly hours and make you an addict?*

Easier said than done, his father had replied. *I've spent a good part of my career trying to find ways to pain-proof the men and women under my command. Drugs don't work the same for everyone and a lot of them create more problems than they solve, like addiction. I've come to the conclusion that the only real solution is endogenous—something within the soldier's body, part of the physical organism.*

Junior hadn't been sure what that was supposed to mean but it had sounded weird and creepy and possibly dangerous. Maybe it was just because his father had referred to the human body as an organism. His father always talked like that but sometimes he sounded scary even to him.

Behind him, he heard the sound of soldiers suddenly snapping to attention; his father had arrived. Only people with Gemini training could salute audibly. Those who managed not to be completely intimidated spoke to him: *Hello, sir. Good afternoon, sir. Good to see you, sir.* His father let the pleasantries bounce off his impenetrable shell as he joined Junior in the observation area.

"Some new faces out there," Junior said, nodding at the soldiers.

"Yep. They'll be the first boots on the ground in Yemen." His father spoke with undisguised pride.

If that was true, Junior pitied the Yemeni. He wondered what uniforms they would be wearing— certainly not Libyan. Unless his father had done another of those convoluted deals he was so famous for. In which case, Junior pitied everyone involved. Except his father, of course.

"Do these guys know the rules of engagement?" he asked Verris. "Or are they more 'if it moves, shoot it?'"

"They're *elite*," his father replied, even prouder. "*Disciplined*. And if they have a clean shot at their target—say, through an apartment window—they'll *take* it. Why don't you think about that on your way to Budapest?"

Junior turned to look at him in surprise.

"Henry's just landed," his father added. "Pack your bags, you've got a flight to catch."

CHAPTER 14

Danny had been to Europe a number of times for the DIA. She had noticed that in winter, you could tell when you'd passed from Western Europe to Eastern Europe when the fur coats appeared. People wore a lot more fur in Eastern Europe, particularly in the northern regions where, if someone said they were freezing, it wasn't hyperbole.

Until now, however, she had never been to Hungary and she was feeling slightly awestruck, almost as if she were a kid seeing the Old World for the first time. Of all the cities she had been to, she had never felt the presence of history as much as she did in Budapest, where it seemed to be in the very air she breathed.

In Rome and Moscow, the present and the ever-oncoming future had an immediacy that overrode the past even when you were looking at a relic as enormous as the Coliseum or standing in a cathedral commissioned by Ivan the Terrible.

But in Budapest, the past seemed to have grown stronger with time, holding its own no matter how demanding or urgent the concerns of the day might be, giving the city no choice but to co-exist with it as best it could. And nowhere was this more evident than at the Budapest University of Technology and Economics. The old friend Danny had phoned told her it was Hungary's answer to MIT, which made it MTI—Magyar Technologia Intezet.

Clever, Danny had said, but how was their biology department? Specifically, human biology.

Her friend, an old submarine crewmate who now worked as an interpreter at the UN, had assured her the whole place was full of whip-smart students who were already shaping the future of their various chosen fields. The name she had given Danny was of a doctoral candidate who was so bright she'd been invited to participate in some highly advanced gene-sequencing projects while she was still an undergrad. Danny hoped she lived up to the hype.

The library where Anikó suggested they meet looked more like a cathedral to Danny. It was also enormous but she had no trouble finding her. Among all the students sitting at the long polished tables, some with notebook computers, some with pads of paper, and some with both, she was the only one reading a comic book.

"Anikó?" Danny asked her in a hushed tone.

She looked up and smiled. It was hard to believe she was working on her doctorate. With her shiny black curls, pink cheeks, and large dark eyes, she looked about twelve. Or that might have been because of the comic book.

Sitting down across from her, Danny put two plastic bags on the table. One held a few bloody cotton balls; the other contained a dirty black baseball cap. "Thank you for your time. Here are your samples."

Anikó took one in either hand, studied them for a moment, then nodded. "This I can do for you in… two days."

Danny was already pulling crumpled bills out of her various pockets and piling them on the table between them. She always kept several different currencies in her burn bag, mostly Euros; she had changed some of it into forints but the exchange rate the teller had given her was terrible. Anikó would probably get a better deal. She certainly didn't look unhappy to see all those Euros.

"No, this you can do for me in two *hours*," Danny said. Anikó's wide dark eyes went from the small crumpled fortune on the table to her. Danny shifted position in the chair, getting more comfortable. "I'll wait."

A little over two hours later, Danny was sitting on a bench in the garden outside the library, waiting for Henry and Baron while she tried to get her mind around the new reality contained in the envelope Anikó had given her. She actually found herself hoping Henry and Baron would be late. Then she could worry about them. Worry was a normal thing, part of the normal world. Only the normal world didn't exist any more. Thanks to the thing in the envelope that Anikó had given her, nothing would ever be normal again.

But of course they weren't late.

"Hey," Henry said, quickening his pace as he came toward her with Baron. "We got a time with Yuri. Meeting him at the—" The look on her face finally registered and he broke off. "You okay?"

Danny held up the envelope Anikó had given her with the lab results. How could something as normal as an envelope contain something so unbelievable? "I think I know why this guy is as good as you, Henry."

Henry's eyes widened; Baron looked like he was waiting for a punchline.

She took a deep breath and plunged on. "He *is* you."

Henry and Baron looked from her to each other and back again.

"Huh?" Henry said finally.

"There's a lab in there," she continued, tilting her head at the building behind her. "I gave them samples, yours and the baseball cap he was wearing."

The expression on Henry's face told her he didn't like that one bit. If it had been her, she wouldn't have, either, but she'd have wanted to know.

"He looked so much like you, I thought he had to be your son," she went on. "So I—well, they did the test three times. Your DNA and his. All three came back 'Identical'. Not 'Close'. *Identical*. As in 'same person'... He's your clone."

He's your clone.

He's your clone.

Your clone.

Your clone.

Clone.

Henry plumped down on the bench beside Danny. She looked pretty freaked out. So did Baron. Which was almost funny—if they thought this was crazy-town, they should have seen the view from *his* side of the looking glass.

"They thought *I'd* made the mistake," Danny was saying. "That maybe I'd given them samples from just one person. But I didn't. He's *you*."

"It's impossible," Henry said after a bit. He turned to Baron to see if he thought so, too.

Baron looked as stunned as Henry felt. "You know what Verris always used to say about you—'I wish I had a whole corps of Henrys.' I thought he was just blowing smoke."

"My clo—" Henry looked pained. "Hell, I can't even say the goddam word." He shook his head. "The way he was coming at me, it was like he was... *bred* for it." Suddenly he was back on that street in Cartagena, the guy swatting him with the back wheel of a motorcycle, trying to smash him with the front wheel. And when all of that failed, pulling his combat knife. If the police hadn't shown up then, Henry knew the guy would have gutted him, and the last thing he would have seen as the knife went in was his own face.

Talk about being your own worst enemy—*literally*. Henry winced; that should have been funny but it wasn't. The whole world was out of kilter, and so was he. And there was no going back.

"I don't—" Danny started and then had to take a steadying breath. "Henry, who the *hell* have we been *working* for?"

And *that* was why he had to keep it together, Henry thought, sitting up straighter. His reaction would have to wait. His whole life had been about serving his country, protecting the good people from bad guys, foreign or domestic. Good people like Danny and Baron, not to mention all the people who were just doing the best they could to get by, unaware of what bad guys like Clay Verris were up to in secret laboratories. Henry couldn't quit on them even if he quit the agency. When he had joined the Marines, he had taken an oath to bear true faith; that oath didn't come off with the uniform, it was for life. And if he was ever in danger of forgetting it, the green spade on his wrist would remind him.

Semper fi.

"There were always rumors about the agency lab and their experiments," Henry said as the three of them walked through a Budapest park together, on their way to meet Yuri. In the aftermath of the bomb Danny had dropped on him, he had all but forgotten why they'd actually come to Budapest in the first place.

"How is it even *possible*?" Baron said.

"It's complicated," Danny told him, "but doable. They take the nucleus of a somatic cell from a donor—in this case, Henry. Then they take an egg cell, pull the genetic material out of it, transplant the donor cell into it. That's the science."

Baron looked openly impressed. "You get that from your lab friend?"

Danny shook her head. "Google."

Henry blinked at her, incredulous. The world had spun so wildly out of control that anyone could find instructions on cloning on the goddam *Web*. "I always thought if they could do that they'd make more doctors or scientists, not more of *me*," he said. "They could have cloned *Nelson Mandela*."

"Nelson Mandela couldn't kill a man on a moving train from two kilometers," Danny pointed out.

Henry grimaced. If she was trying to cheer him up, she was doing a lousy job.

"Hey, I'm not happy about this, either. I risked my *life* for them," Danny said. "So they could do *this*?"

"You risked your life for your *country*," Henry corrected her. "Like your father did."

"My country." She gave a harsh, bitter laugh. "I don't think I like the way that's working out."

"The DIA is an agency—it's *not* your country," Henry said. "Be glad you didn't have to wait, say, twenty-five years to find that out."

Baron patted her shoulder. "Listen, if you ever want to junk it all and come be VP of Baron Air, I'll make a position available."

Danny gave him a sad smile. "If my father were here, he'd find out who was responsible for all this and beat the crap out of them." She sighed. "But he's *not* here."

"Then I guess it's up to us," Henry told her.

* * *

The Széchenyi Baths were not a single building but a whole complex of magnificent old structures built around thermal springs. Yuri had waxed rhapsodic to Henry about the beautiful architecture and how relaxing and therapeutic the baths were, and yes, the buildings *were* gorgeous, great architecture, yeah, yeah, yeah. But standing with Danny and Baron on a balcony overlooking the multitude of happy bathers enjoying themselves in the sunshine, Henry had a hard time appreciating Yuri's choice of meeting place.

When Yuri had said baths, Henry had imagined Turkish baths with steam rooms, popular among spies and mobsters because you couldn't wear a wire or hide a weapon when you were dressed only in a towel. He had been fully prepared to strip down and sit in a steam room for the sake of getting some answers.

Instead, he was meeting Yuri at what was essentially a gigantic municipal swimming pool.

Although in hindsight, Henry supposed he should have known—the mention of *thermal springs* should have given him a clue that there was more to the place than steam and whirlpool baths. He could see the pools weren't very deep; the average adult didn't have to tread water to not drown. There weren't any children, either—apparently thermal springs weren't advisable for little kids—so there wasn't a lot of laughing and splashing.

No, Henry realized, he was wrong—there wasn't *any*. The people here were practically sedate. He spotted a couple of older guys who had set up a chess board on a marble surface near a set of stone stairs; Henry watched them in astonishment. He'd seen people playing chess in parks— retirees making a game last all day, or young show-offs playing speed chess with ten people simultaneously and beating all of them for ten bucks per checkmate. But who the hell would go to a *swimming pool* to play chess?

Well, these guys, obviously—and now that he was looking, he saw they weren't the only ones. But even seeing it with his own eyes, he was having trouble getting his mind around the idea that anyone woke up in the morning and decided to go to a swimming pool for a game of chess.

Of course, when *he'd* woken up this morning, he hadn't thought clones were possible, let alone that someone would clone *him*. He couldn't get his mind around that, either, and he wasn't sure he ever would. God only knew what he'd find out when he woke up tomorrow.

If he woke up tomorrow—the younger version of himself was trying very hard to keep that from happening.

Where the hell was Yuri, he wondered, listening to happy Hungarian conversation over the musical sound of rippling, bubbling water. "Everything okay with you?" he asked Baron, who was now keeping watch by the stairs to his left.

"All good, no worries," Baron replied.

"Copy that." Henry glanced at his watch, feeling on edge, and not just because Yuri had made him come to a giant swimming pool and was now about to be late. As of today, he would probably feel on edge for the rest of his life. The world had become a very unfamiliar place in the brief period of time since Monroe and Jack had died and Verris had sent a hit squad to kill him and the exemplary agent standing next to him, an agent who had never gotten a single demerit. *Congratulations, here's your reward: a bullet in the head.*

"Henry," Baron said.

Henry turned to see a man standing in the doorway behind him. He was dressed in the standard outfit for anyone not actually in the water—a bathrobe and flip-flops—but unlike the other baths patrons, he didn't look at all innocuous. He was shorter than Henry but built like a brick wall.

"Mr. Brogan!" The man smiled brightly and beckoned for Henry to join him.

Henry shook hands with him and then turned to Danny and Baron. It was obvious that Yuri's warm greeting didn't extend to them. They both nodded to indicate they didn't mind waiting for him on the balcony. In a situation like this, only one on one was acceptable; two plus one was asking for trouble and three to one would result in casualties all round.

In any case, Henry was sure that Yuri wasn't going to try anything tricky in a place like this, not in a bathrobe and flip-flops. But he did insist that Henry trade his street clothes for the same outfit—Yuri had even brought bathing trunks for him, which he said Henry was welcome to keep. He had to insist, he added when Henry hesitated, looking dubious. They needed to blend in. People didn't come to the baths to hang around fully dressed. Henry's friends should do the same, Yuri said with an appreciative look at Danny, but it wasn't as important. They could remain on the balcony and the locals would assume they were American tourists with body image issues.

Henry put on the bathing trunks and bathrobe, leaving his clothes in a changing room, and was greatly relieved when Yuri led him to a nearby bench and invited him to sit. He had been prepared to bite the bullet and go into one of the pools if Yuri had insisted, but apparently the bathrobes were camouflage enough.

Henry could see why Jack Willis had liked the guy. Aside from the fact that his slightly florid complexion indicated a fondness for vodka, Yuri exuded an air of cheerful corruption and casual treachery, qualities that were absolutely necessary for survival under a corrupt, treacherous regime. He was a spy's spy—he probably had dirt on Putin and Putin probably knew it. Putin probably also knew that as long as he left Yuri untouched and happy, the dirt would stay under the rug.

"Before we begin," Yuri said with that same delighted smile, "I must confess—I have admired your work for many years!"

Henry blinked at him, surprised. "So you know who I am?"

Yuri laughed. "'Long-time listener, first-time caller,' as they say in your country. I would congratulate you on your retirement but your last job has some loose ends, yes?"

"Well…" Henry tried not to squirm. "My government lied to me and tried to kill me, if that's what you mean."

Yuri laughed again. "In Russia, we call this 'Tuesday.' But you Americans—it hurts your feelings. So…?" He raised his eyebrows.

"So why was Dormov going back to Russia?" Henry asked.

"Yes, down to business! Very American—you are a very busy man!" Yuri's delighted smile faded and his expression became thoughtful as he looked up and down the hallway. It was empty except for the two of them. "We were both friends with Jack Willis," he went on after a moment. "He was a good man, and like you, I mourn his death. The reason you are here and I have not killed you—yet—" there was a brief hint of a smile on Yuri's face, "—is, we share a common enemy."

"Clay Verris?" Henry guessed.

Yuri nodded, his face solemn. "He lured Dormov to the West. Funded his lab. And now you've met the fruits of their labor. Dolly the sheep was cloned in 1996. And in '97…"

"*I* was the sheep," Henry said. It still seemed unbelievable but now he was starting to feel less astonished and more like he'd had something stolen from him, something both enormously significant and priceless that he would never get back.

"Perhaps you should take it as a compliment. Verris took your DNA and raised the boy as his own son, trained him to be the perfect assassin."

"So why did Dormov leave?" Henry asked, even though he was pretty sure he knew the answer, at least in part.

"We tried for years to lure him back home," Yuri said. "Nothing worked. Then last year, Dormov and Verris had a falling-out. Dormov became frightened; he reached out to me. We had indications that Dormov had made a breakthrough with modified human DNA that could lead to mass production. But Dormov wanted soldiers who were both stronger and smarter. Verris wanted—" Yuri paused, looking troubled. "Something else," he said finally.

"Something else," Henry echoed. He had no idea what that meant but he was sure it was nothing good.

Yuri looked into his face and now the cheerfully corrupt, pragmatically treacherous spy was gone, replaced by a man who had encountered something he could not bring himself to justify or accept. If it was true that everyone had a price, it was also true that everyone had a line they wouldn't cross for any price.

"Mr. Brogan, you are the best at what you do," Yuri said earnestly. "But you're still a man. You get tired, you have doubts, fears—you feel pain, even remorse because you have a conscience. This makes you sub-optimal as a soldier. You're less than perfect and so less profitable." Yuri leaned toward him and lowered his voice. "Clayton Verris is playing God with DNA. He must be stopped."

Henry sat in silence. A few days ago, he had understood the basic structure of the world. It was a messy, unhappy, dangerous place and he had chosen to spend his life working to alleviate those things, or at the very least, to keep them from worsening.

But then he had come home from Liège and retired and suddenly the world was upside down and inside out, and everything he knew was wrong. He'd killed a good man and his younger self was trying to kill him to cover it up—sent by the bastard who'd tricked him into killing a good guy in the first place. Henry wondered what Verris had told his clone. Dormov's spiked file had said he was a bioterrorist. Verris had probably told the clone Henry ate young children alive. Hell, in his early twenties, he might have bought that himself.

Henry was quiet for a long moment, letting the other man's words sink in. "If this is as dangerous as you say, why not just send a missile? Take out the whole lab?"

Yuri gave a single, humorless laugh. "That is what we are doing—except *you* are the missile! I wish you luck!"

The Russian stood up, stretched, and tightened the belt on his bathrobe. "And now, you'll have to excuse me, I must go kill a Ukrainian oligarch." He looked up and down the empty hallway. "Just kidding!" he added loudly, then winked at Henry as he drew his finger across his own throat, mouthing, *No joke.*

Yuri turned to leave, then stopped. "One last thing I meant to tell you. Your escape from your home two days ago? *Amazing* work! I was on the edge of my seat the whole time!"

Henry's jaw dropped. "How do you even *know* about that?"

Yuri shrugged good-naturedly. "What can I say? I'm a super-fan." He ambled up the hallway, his flip-flops smacking against the soles of his feet.

Damn, Henry thought, staring after him; the Ukrainians just couldn't get a break, either.

* * *

Danny and Baron were waiting for him on the balcony. They listened intently as he told them what he'd found out from Yuri.

"Do you believe him?" Danny asked when he'd finished.

Henry nodded. "I'd trust him more than anyone at the agency right now."

"Well that's sobering," Baron said. "You guys up for defecting?"

Danny elbowed him in the ribs. "We just have to find that kid." Her eyes were large and serious. "You aren't going to be safe until we do, Henry. None of us are."

Who are you calling a kid? Henry barely managed not to say it aloud. "Okay, we find him. Then what?"

"You *talk* to him," Danny replied, as if this should have been obvious. "He doesn't know what he is; he doesn't know who you are to him. Maybe you'll get through."

"Seriously?" Henry gave a short, hard laugh. "If a fifty-year-old version of you suddenly shows up saying you're her clone, that would calm you down?"

"Fifty-one," Baron put in.

Henry turned to give him a death-ray glare.

"Just sayin'." Baron shrugged.

Danny touched Henry's arm gently. "Maybe he's the mirror you don't want to look into, Henry. But he's our best shot at getting to Verris."

Henry couldn't decide whether he wanted to hug her or shake her till her eyeballs rattled. Then he grinned as a better idea occurred to him.

"Let's go get a cup of coffee," he said.

"Where?" Baron asked.

Henry looked down at himself. He was still in the bathrobe and trunks. "Anywhere we don't have to take off our clothes."

CHAPTER 15

"Janet Lassiter?"

Lassiter was sitting at her usual table in the Copper Ground coffee shop, staring out at Savannah's early morning traffic while she waited for her usual order, which seemed to be taking more than the usual amount of time today. She turned to find a tall, dark-skinned man who looked vaguely familiar standing over her. He wore a narrow blue bike helmet, a tight, colorful shirt, dark shorts, and had a worn canvas bag slung across the front of his body.

Of course he looked familiar, Lassiter realized; he was a bike messenger, most likely the one who almost ran her down every other day.

"Who wants to know?" she asked, knowing full well she wasn't going to like the answer. No one she had any use for would trust anything important to a bike messenger.

He pulled a cell phone out of his bag. "I've got a message for you, ma'am, from a man who transferred a thousand dollars into my Feathercoin account just to make sure you got it."

"Does this person have a name?" Lassiter asked archly.

"His name is, 'Thousand dollars into my Feathercoin account.'"

Lassiter considered asking what he called the guy for short but she didn't feel like giving the smartass another straight line. Instead, she fixed him with a cold stare. Maybe she should shoot the messenger, she thought. A slug in the knee from the .38 in her purse wouldn't kill him but it would hurt like hell, force him to find a less obnoxious line of work, and teach him not to get mouthy with short, older women. Then she motioned for him to go ahead.

The messenger cleared his throat and began reading from the cell phone screen. "'Hello, Janet. Before you try to kill me again, consider this…'"

In her peripheral vision, Lassiter could see people turning to look at her with unabashed curiosity about the killer drinking coffee among them. It took an enormous amount of effort not to show any reaction herself. You couldn't let the enemy see they'd had any effect on you or you'd be at their mercy. They were always trying to knock you off-balance, make you look crazy or stupid or even scary.

"'Your home address is 1362 Carrol Grove. The security alarm code is 1776,'" the messenger continued. More people were staring, craning their necks, even standing up to get a look. Dammit, now she was going to have to move, Lassiter fumed. And she would have to change the security code while she packed.

"'You awaken at 6:12 every morning and stop for your decaf soy latte with an extra shot by 6:42,'" declaimed the messenger, obviously enjoying himself. "'Every night, you stand in front of your huge living room window sipping a Jose Cuervo margarita with *Forensic Files* on the TV.'"

Lassiter thought he had paused for breath but he tapped the screen and put the phone back in his bag. Apparently that was the message in its entirety. Lassiter felt let down in spite of herself; anticlimax wasn't like Henry.

The people around her, however, seemed to think the show wasn't over. Lassiter imagined kneecapping the messenger and maybe the wide-eyed couple at the table on her left, but then her own cell rang. She touched the Bluetooth clipped to her ear.

"This is Lassiter," she said briskly.

"There are shooters at your ten and two," Henry Brogan said. "Get up out of that chair and you *will* be AMF'ed." He almost sounded polite, as if he were trying to be helpful.

Lassiter's head snapped towards the window, scanning the buildings at ten o'clock and two o'clock. They were mostly high-rises with plenty of glass that reflected the bright morning sunlight, making it impossible for her to see anything. There might have been no one out there—or there might have been a whole platoon keeping her covered from multiple floors. She thought the former was more likely but she had known Henry Brogan for too long to risk calling his bluff. If she died today, it wasn't going to be in a goddam coffee shop with a smartass bike messenger and a bunch of goddam over-caffeinated hipsters watching as she breathed her last.

"If I thought the world needed another me, I would have had a kid," Henry said.

Lassiter wet her lips. "That program pre-dates my arrival at the agency. You must know that," she said in a stiff, professional tone. If she sounded boring, her audience would lose interest.

Henry laughed. "Oh, that's a *perfect* DIA answer. Always cover your ass, deny everything, and if something goes wrong, *duck*!"

He said the last word so loudly, Lassiter did exactly that, putting her hands over her face to protect it from flying glass. Except there was no glass, no gunshots from ten o'clock or two o'clock, just the bike messenger staring at her like she'd gone crazy and a café full of people who probably thought they were watching a reality show.

"Now tip the nice bike guy," Henry ordered her in a condescending tone.

Lassiter sat up, smoothing her hair and squaring her shoulders. She pointed an index finger at the bike messenger. "You—" She lowered the finger ninety degrees and aimed it at the front door. "Can go."

The messenger gave her a parting sneer and Lassiter did likewise, listening to the *tik-tik-tik* sound of his bike shoes on the floor. If he had really thought he was going to get a tip after *that* shit-show, maybe she *should* have kneecapped him, just as a life lesson.

But the good news was, the rest of the coffee shop rabble took the messenger's departure to mean the show really was over now and turned their attention back to their own phones or tablets or laptops. Except for the wide-eyed couple at the table on her left; they seemed to be hoping for a better finale.

Lassiter turned in her chair, pointedly giving her back to them and everyone else, mostly so she could search the buildings and the street for sniper rifles. She still didn't see anything at ten and two, either up high or at ground level. Brogan had to be bluffing, she was almost certain of it, but in this business, you didn't stay alive by being *almost* certain.

"I have an agent of yours here with me," Henry said. "Danielle Zakarewski. She wants to come in."

"Fine." Lassiter decided to kneecap Zakarewski just on general principle.

"Like me, she's a patriot," Henry went on. "But *un*like me, she wants to spend the next couple decades scoring touchdowns for you assholes. Her safety is non-negotiable. Remember I've got you covered. Ten and two, Janet."

Lassiter was vaguely aware of a barista calling out something about a decaf soy latte with an extra shot for Janet but it was just background noise.

"You *cannot*—" she started.

"The *only* person I'll hand her off to is the person you sent after me in Cartagena," Henry said, talking over her. "So don't bother sending anyone else."

"Oh, a family reunion?" Lassiter gave a short humorless laugh. "How sweet."

"Keep it up, Janet," Henry said, "and you'll be the first person I ever killed for free. How soon can you get him to Budapest?"

Lassiter gave another short laugh. "How about five minutes? Does that work for you?"

There was a long moment of silence. Lassiter smiled with grim satisfaction. The smug bastard hadn't seen *that* one coming.

"Good," Henry said. She could practically *hear* him pretending she hadn't just blindsided him. "She'll be at the courtyard of the Vajdahunyad Castle at midnight tonight. Enjoy your latte." He hung up on her.

Oh, she was going to enjoy her latte, all right—she'd enjoy it a hell of a lot more than Henry would enjoy what happened next, Lassiter fumed, putting her phone away. In fact, she should have been enjoying her goddam latte right now—where the hell *was* it? She looked over at the pick-up counter, frowning like a thunderstorm. If that barista had forgotten her order, Lassiter was going to rain so much hell down on her she'd be scarred for life.

Henry sat back in his chair. Danny half-expected to see steam coming out of his ears. Baron signaled their waiter for another round of espressos but she wasn't sure

Henry really needed more caffeine. On the other hand, he *had* set the meet for midnight and they needed to stay awake even though they were all still jet-lagged. Well, she was, anyway; Baron was such an easy-going, roll-with-the-punches kind of guy, she wasn't sure he even got headaches. As for Henry, she was starting to think he was Superman's secret identity.

Baron nudged her elbow. "In case you're wondering, AMF stands for—"

"Adios, motherfucker," Danny finished for him. "Yeah, I know."

Both he and Henry stared at her, startled.

"Oh, come *on*," she said, rolling her eyes. "What am I, a five-year-old?"

Henry shook his head. "A better question is, how the *hell* did *he* know I was here?"

CHAPTER 16

Vajdahunyad Castle was in the middle of the City Park of Budapest, which according to Danny's phone was the oldest urban green space in Europe. Or was it the world? Henry had forgotten already. He did remember Danny telling him that Vajdahunyad Castle wasn't just one big fortress like San Felipe Castle back in Cartagena but actually a complex comprising several buildings. Henry had chosen it as a meeting place because both park and castle were located in the middle of Budapest. He thought Danny would be much safer there. If Junior tried to abduct her, the city's narrow streets would slow him down. Unless, of course, he went vaulting over the rooftops instead, although Henry didn't think he'd try that with Danny. If he did, Henry was sure Junior was more likely to end up splattered on the sidewalk than she was.

But now as he sat in the car with Danny a few hundred yards from the entrance to the Vajdahunyad Castle complex, Henry was beginning to think this wasn't such a good idea after all. It was all he could do not to keep himself from calling the whole thing off and taking her as far away from Junior as possible.

There was no question that she was a tough professional; he'd seen her in action and he knew she was anything but helpless. Or a coward, although Henry thought that a good part of her courage was down to youth and inexperience— she didn't know how bad the bad guys could be. Of course, if she stuck with the DIA she was going to find out; she'd encounter things that most civilians never had to deal with, never even imagined. Right now, he wished more than anything that Danny Zakarewski was a civilian.

He could see how nervous she was; it made her look even younger than her years, which in turn made it harder for him to justify sending her to meet a trained killer without so much as a nail file for defense. His instincts were telling him to get her out of there, to protect her, not expose her to danger.

If Danny had known what he was thinking she would have accused him of sexism and ageism and who knew how many other -isms—capitalism, anarchism, antidisestablishmentarianism—all while going upside his head. So much had changed since he'd started out in the DIA as a young, strong, capable agent whose career was on the rise. The world was so different these days that sometimes he wasn't sure what planet he was on. And now Danny was the young, strong, capable agent whose career was on the rise, while he was getting older.

Or trying to.

Danny took hold of the car door handle, then paused. "This *is* going to work, right?"

"Yep," Henry assured her, hoping he wasn't lying.

"How do you know?" she asked.

"He's not *exactly* me but I know his taste," he replied.

Danny turned to get out of the car, then turned back to him again. "Wait a second. You're *attracted* to me?"

I talk too goddam much, Henry thought unhappily. "Me, personally, right now? *Hell* no," he said. "But a younger, less mature version of me? Probably."

She laughed and he laughed with her, as if they weren't both scared shitless. He couldn't let her do this, he thought, and opened his mouth to tell her it was off.

"Henry?" she said.

His name hung in the air between them and he could hear all the unspoken questions she wanted to ask:

Do I have a hope in hell of getting out of this alive? Do you? If we don't, is this something worth dying for? Is anything worth dying for? Is this really what our lives have been leading up to and is it right, is it good? Are we good? Will it even make a difference? Will anyone care what happens to us?

Even after twenty-five years, he still knew all those questions by heart. With any luck, she would get more answers than he had.

All of this ran through his mind in less time than it took for him to smooth an errant strand of dark hair back from her face. "When I came to get you in Georgia," he said quietly, "I didn't have to *think* about it. It was instinct, wanting to keep you safe. He's got that, too—he's not going to hurt you."

He could sense her seizing on that and holding it close, willing it to be true.

"And hurting *you* doesn't help him," he added. "What he wants is *me*. In his sights."

Danny took a deep steadying breath, got out of the car, and walked toward the entrance to Vajdahunyad Castle without looking back.

Henry stared after her, all his instincts still screaming for him to call it off.

* * *

Danny walked across the footbridge at an even pace, not slow, not fast, toward the Gatehouse Tower of Vajdahunyad Castle. The outside of the castle was surrounded by very bright, yellow-gold lights; although the illumination spilled over a bit on the inside, the place was still very dark and shadowy. The gate was up, its sharp points hanging over the entrance. She was pretty sure it was normally lowered after hours but Henry's clone was clever enough to fix it so she wouldn't have to scale the tower to get in. And the open gate absolutely did not in any way remind her of an animal's gaping jaws, not even a little.

On the other side of the bridge, the paving went from smooth to brick. Danny still didn't hurry, except as she passed under the raised gate; she did a quick little trot, so as not to be under those pointed metal bars for more than a second.

Which was silly—why would the clone agree to meet here only to impale her with a metal gate? Henry's words came back to her: *Hurting* you *doesn't help him. What he wants is* me. *In his sights.* She really hoped Henry was right, at least about the first part. And anyway, clone-Henry would have orders from Janet Lassiter to take her back to the States safe and sound. If he were going to disobey those orders and kill her, he could have done it when she was on the footbridge. Or he could shoot her right now.

Danny felt a rush of shame for being so scared. She wasn't doing this alone. Henry and Baron had her back and she had theirs. The three of them were a team.

Her steps began to slow until she came to a stop, with a church on her left and on her right a statue sitting on a bench, mostly in shadow despite the spillover from the lights outside. Count Sándor Károlyi, according to the information she'd downloaded to her phone, but for the life of her she couldn't remember the name of the church opposite. Then she discovered that she couldn't get her feet to move, either.

"Forward *march*," she whispered between clenched teeth. "Yo left, right, left."

Nothing; her feet might as well have been super-glued to the bricks.

"Yo left, right, left," she whispered again—still nothing. Maybe she should try counting cadence. *I had a dog, his name was Blue, Blue wanna be a seal too…*

No, she was damned if she was going to make a fool of herself while clone-Henry watched. And he *was* watching her, she saw, from behind an iron gate off to the side of the church's front door. Danny felt an intense surge of hostility and indignation. How long had he been there? Could he tell how spooked she was? Goddammit, it was after midnight in a castle that had been Bram Stoker's inspiration for Dracula's crib. Anyone *not* creeped out would have to be made of stone.

Well, apparently *he* was. He didn't look even mildly nervous as he opened the gate and beckoned to her. He was a clone made of stone. A stone clone. Danny had to bite her lips to keep from laughing. If she did she might not be able to stop, and hysteria was hardly the most constructive course of action.

She gave him a hard glare as she walked past him into a small courtyard. He was still watching her closely. Was he wondering how long she could keep it together without losing her shit? Let him, she thought; she would show him she wasn't some poor little victim he could bully.

The moon was high in the sky. It was on the wane but still bright enough that, along with the flow-over from the lights outside the castle, Danny could see his face quite clearly, in more detail than the few glimpses she'd had back in Cartagena. This wasn't simply a strong resemblance—it really was *Henry's* face, his and none other, minus a few years and maybe some mileage. The way clone-Henry was staring at her so coldly, with no sign of recognition, was even more unsettling than Dracula's castle at midnight. It was like she had taken a wrong turn and walked into a parallel universe where she and Henry had never met on the dock, and instead of teaming up with Baron they had become enemies.

"Lovely courtyard," Danny said. It was a silly thing to say—the courtyard was lovely but only if you wanted to make a horror movie where everybody died horribly in the end. She had just wanted to see if she could speak without her voice shaking and was surprised at how calm and undaunted she sounded.

"I'm sorry, ma'am," Henry's clone said with Henry's voice, "but before we go any further, I have to ask you to strip."

Danny gaped at him. Her attention had snagged on the word *ma'am*. "I beg your pardon?"

"So I can check you for a wire," he added, as if that made it reasonable.

"Wait a second," she said. "Did you just call me '*ma'am*?'"

"*I* was raised to respect my elders," he told her in a slightly reproachful tone that suggested he thought her upbringing left a lot to be desired. "Your clothes, please."

That *ma'am* was going to cost him dearly, Danny vowed as she took off her top. His death would be slow and merciless; it would last for *weeks*. No, *months*. She toed off her boots, pushed her jeans down and stepped out of them. Now she was standing in the middle of a horror movie set at midnight in her underwear. And her socks. She stepped back into her boots but she was pretty sure that wasn't an improvement. At least she had put *nice* underwear in her burn bag—not that she had ever imagined *this* scenario. Although it was a good bet that someone somewhere did, frequently.

She tried to block the idea but it was too late. What had been thunk could not be unthunk, as her grandfather used to say. Meanwhile, Henry's clone stood in front of her in his fatigues and his Kevlar vest and his combat boots. Was he enjoying this? Did he feel powerful because she was half-naked and vulnerable? That was the whole idea, of course, to make her feel weak and powerless. But why was he just standing there? What was he waiting for—another opportunity to call her *ma'am*?

Or wasn't she naked enough?

A cold rage bloomed inside her. She didn't know what she would do if he went there. But if she just stood in front of him waiting for it she might begin to tremble, and she was goddamned if she would let him see that.

Danny put one thumb under her bra strap and pulled it away from her shoulder slightly, her expression both questioning and hostile. No, she was wrong—she *did* know what she'd do. Screw the plan.

Clone-Henry shook his head awkwardly, averting his gaze for a moment before he looked at her again and then away, over and over. It was as if he was trying to look at her without looking at her.

The memory of Henry in her bedroom turning his back while she got dressed popped into her mind and suddenly she understood. This *wasn't* a power trip for clone-Henry—he was embarrassed. No, it was more than that—he was *ashamed*.

Good, she thought at him. *Suffer, you bastard.* And that was only the truth—clones *were* bastards. They didn't exactly have mothers, either, which made them *double* bastards. Maybe she could find some way to work that into the conversation before the night was over.

"Turn around, please," he said.

Danny made a snappy about-face and allowed herself a fleeting smile of spiteful triumph. Then he came up close behind her and she wished she hadn't just snapped to and obeyed him like that. She had already yielded to his authority over her by undressing; obeying his next order so promptly told him she accepted him as being in charge. Lesson learned: the next time somebody ordered her to strip at gunpoint and told her to turn around, she was going to flat out refuse. What were they going to do, kill her? If they planned to do that anyway, she didn't have to make it easy for them.

And the other lesson learned: she was a cockeyed optimist to posit *next* time when she didn't even know if she'd survive *this* time.

Her optimism dwindled considerably when the clone's Kevlar vest touched her bare back. She forced herself not to flinch as he ran his hands quickly over her body from neck to thighs. But even as he did it, she could sense he was trying to be impersonal, detached, to touch her without touching her the same way he had tried to look at her without looking. He almost managed it... *almost*. Being impersonal and detached was impossible when you were ashamed of what you were doing in the first place.

It was only when he ran his fingers through her hair that she actually jumped. "I see you like to be thorough," she said.

"Caution has kept me alive, ma'am," he said, and she added another week of suffering to his miserable future. "You can get dressed now."

As soon as she was decent again, he handed her a phone. "Call him."

Danny hesitated, then decided there was nothing to be gained by giving him a hard time now. She punched in the number; he took the phone back from her and put it on speaker.

It rang once. "Yes?" said Henry.

"In twelve minutes, I'm going to put two bullets into the back of Agent Zakarewski's head," clone-Henry said.

Danny all but heard Henry's blood pressure jump a hundred points. "*Your orders* were to deliver her safely—"

"*My orders* were to kill *you*," the clone said, and Danny felt a cold chill run down her spine. Their voices were as identical as their faces; it was like listening to Henry argue with himself in the throes of a dissociative breakdown. "Do you know the Quartz Chamber in the catacombs?"

"Oh, *hell* no," Henry replied angrily. "We're doing this someplace *visible*. Where I can *see* you."

"And now we're at eleven minutes," the clone said and hung up on him. For all the tough talk, he looked unsettled. Danny wondered if he'd also heard the similarity of their voices. Then he noticed her watching him and motioned at the gate. "We're going for a ride."

She added another week to his slow, painful death, just on general principle.

The taxi had an official-looking strip of black and yellow checks under the windows on either side and a light on the roof that said taxi. But Henry's clone told her it was a *hyena*, which was some kind of widespread scam aimed mostly at tourists.

"The scam also works on anyone too drunk to see straight," he said as he motioned at the driver with the Glock. "Yeah, that's right, buddy, take the rest of the night off. And tomorrow, find a new line of work," he called after the fleeing man. "Any cab without a company logo showing on the doors or the hood is a hyena," he went on to Danny. "That's how you can tell the honest taxis from the scammers. Now get in, you're driving." She did so and he climbed into the back seat directly behind her.

"Okay, buddy, where to?" she said with a nervous laugh.

"You're not a *real* cab driver," he said sourly.

"According to you, neither was the guy you chased off," Danny said evenly. "Either way, you still have to tell me where we're going if you actually want to get there."

"Jaki Chapel," the clone said in a low voice that was practically a growl.

"Jaki Chapel, huh? Sounds nice. You'll have to direct me," she told him.

"I can't do that unless we're moving."

Danny started the car and put it in drive. Hungarian taxis weren't much different from most other cars, although when she shifted gears, it felt like she was using a crowbar to move thick, heavy chunks of metal. Steering was even more of an effort. Fortunately the Budapest streets were deserted at this hour so she was unlikely to hurt anyone except herself and clone-Henry. Most likely herself; she had a feeling this model hadn't come with airbags.

"Taking this cab was a smart move," she said after a bit, adjusting the rearview mirror so she could see him. "Where are you from anyway?" His eyes met hers. "Your formality—it sounds Southern to me."

Clone-Henry looked annoyed. "No disrespect but I'd prefer not to chat just now."

"There it was again," she said, stubbornly cheerful. "Georgia? Texas?"

"It's better if we just don't talk."

Danny didn't ask him if that was because a butcher never made friends with cattle; there was no need to rile him unnecessarily. But she had no intention of making things easy for him, either. She wasn't cattle.

"Look, if you're going to use me as bait and possibly murder me, the *least* you can do is indulge me with some conversation." She gave his reflection a brief, pointed stare.

The clone let out a heavy, resigned breath. "I was born just outside Atlanta."

"I knew it!" Danny hit the steering wheel with one hand in triumph. "You and Henry have a *lot* in common."

"I doubt *that*," the clone replied.

"You'd be surprised," she assured him. "You know, *I* started out surveilling him, too. Then I got to know him. He's got a big heart." Pause. "Like you."

She practically heard his hackles go up. "What would *you* know about *my* heart?"

"I know you *have* one," she replied. "And I know it's telling you that something about this job you've been given isn't *right*."

There was an almost imperceptible moment of hesitation before he said, "A job's a job."

"This is nice, actually," Danny said as she parked the taxi in front of a church. "Usually when I travel I don't get to do much sightseeing." Clone-Henry yanked her out of the driver's seat without bothering to close the car door. "And I *love* old churches," she went on inanely as they went in through the front entrance. "So this is Jaki Chapel. It's Romanesque. Beautiful. *Ow*," she added as he poked her in the back with the Glock to make her walk faster down the main aisle.

When they got to the communion rail in front of the altar, the clone yanked her into an alcove on the right and pushed her toward a set of stone steps going down.

"Basement?" she said, forcing a light tone. "You must really know your way around Budapest churches."

"I watch a lot of Nat Geo." He motioned at the stairs. "*Down.*"

The steps were narrow and uneven and she was afraid of losing her balance and falling because he kept prodding her with the Glock. That would be another *two* weeks added to his agonizing death, she thought poisonously.

When they reached the bottom he gave her a nudge into a passageway lined with shelves and lit by bare bulbs strung overhead, spaced about fifteen feet apart. Were they five watts? Less? She could barely see, and if clone-boy poked her with that Glock one more time, she was going to shove it up his nose sideways—

Her toe hit something and she stumbled, nearly falling on her face before she caught hold of a steel rod sunk solidly into the floor. Which, she saw now, wasn't hard-packed dirt as she had originally thought but concrete covered with ages of dust and grime. She looked up and suddenly found herself staring into the dark, empty eye sockets of a very, very old skull. It was one of many on the shelf in front of her. No, actually one of thousands on a multitude of shelves on either side of the passageway, all stacked one on top of another, from the gritty cement floor up past the string of bare light bulbs and disappearing into the shadows above.

"Wow," Danny breathed, staring upward. The clone gave her another push. "I wonder how many people are buried down here." He didn't answer and she resisted asking him if he had missed Catacombs Week on Nat Geo.

There was a rusted iron gate ahead; as they got closer, Danny saw part of a broken padlock hanging from the hasp. Signs in four different languages, including English, declared, *This Area Strictly Off Limits.*

The clone gave her another poke with the Glock, motioning her forward. Whoever had raised him to respect his elders had obviously failed to mention it was rude to poke them with a handgun. Instead of giving in to the urge to stick the Glock up his nose, however, she pushed the gate open. "But it says off limits."

"That's very funny," he said, his voice flat.

The passageway ahead was even narrower and more dimly lit. He caught her arm. "Stand over there," he said, pushing her up against another steel support rod. "Don't move."

Danny watched as he wedged a grenade into the mouth of a skull on a shelf one up from floor level, then attached a tripwire, which he connected to another skull on the shelf opposite. It was about six inches off the ground and, in this light, invisible.

Messing with the dead like this had to be some kind of serious desecration, Danny thought, the kind of thing even a hard-headed non-believer would want to avoid. But clone-Henry wasn't fazed in the least. Maybe he really was a stone clone. Or maybe he'd just never seen a horror movie.

He reached up with the Glock and shattered the bulb above them. As they continued along the passageway, he broke the rest of them so that the only illumination came from his flashlight.

"If you knock out all the lights," Danny said, "how are you going to see your own tripwire on your way out? A grenade is no joke. I mean, I get what you're doing—darkness neutralizes his biggest strength. And close-quarters favors you, right? He can't throw a grenade without killing me, too. But what if he uses tear gas? Or a sleep agent?"

He shoved her through another doorway into a large round area with a few dim naked bulbs dangling well out of reach. *This must be the Quartz Chamber,* Danny thought. It, too, was lined with shelves of skulls and bones bolstered every few feet by metal support rods. As far as she could tell, there was no other way in or out. The clone dropped his backpack on the cement floor and pulled out what seemed to be a compact gas mask equipped with night vision. He put it on but left it sitting up on top of his head.

"Okay, I see you're way ahead of me," she said. "Gas mask *and* night vision together, very smart. But can I ask you something?"

"Would you actually stop talking long enough for me to answer?" clone-Henry said with a fed-up edge in his voice.

Danny smiled inwardly. She was getting to him. "How much *do* you know about Henry?" she demanded. "What have you been told?" He dragged her over to one of the steel support rods. "Did anybody tell you *why* they want him dead? Did you even *ask?*"

The clone gave a heavy, put-upon sigh. "The guy cracked," he said, pulling some zip-ties out of his backpack. He bound her wrists with the rod between her forearms, positioning them so she couldn't try chewing herself free and so tightly she couldn't slide her arms up or down. That was a real problem; pretty soon she was going to lose feeling in her hands, and if she complained he'd make them tighter. "He killed eight ops in a single night. *And* his spotter."

"*That's* what they told you?" Danny said incredulously.

"*That's* what he *did*," the clone corrected her.

"Not exactly!" Danny fumed, forgetting she was trying to make *him* lose it. All at once, she was close to tears and didn't care if it showed. "I was *with* him the night all those operatives got hit. They'd been sent to kill him. And *me*—by *Gemini*. Think about that: Henry saved my life even though I was *surveilling* him!" She was shouting at him now, full of rage at the way everything she said just bounced off him while he rummaged around in his backpack.

"And *not* that it matters," she went on at high volume, "but his spotter was shot in *Virginia*, the rest of those men went down in *Savannah*. Henry can shoot long distance but not *that* long. I—"

Clone-Henry suddenly stood up again. "You know what?" Without waiting for an answer, he mashed a thick piece of duct tape over her mouth, pressing hard for a couple of seconds. "That's better," he said.

"Fuh *yuh*," she replied, enunciating as clearly as she could.

He screwed a silencer onto the end of the Glock and started shooting out the light bulbs in the chamber, spraying glass and fragments of bone into the air. Danny wanted to kick him for violating a place where the dead from ages past had been laid to rest with the idea that they would rest undisturbed for all eternity, but she couldn't reach him.

He was about to shoot out the last light when the grenade went off.

CHAPTER 17

Yanking the mask down over his face, Junior ran into the passageway, his heart pounding with a mix of anticipation, excitement, and confidence. The explosion that had blown his target to pieces had also blown the world back into its proper orbit. Everything was now in order again. As soon as he finished mopping up, his next mission would be waiting—

He stopped short. The goggles were very high resolution, letting him see, in various shades of luminous green, the iron gate now hanging crookedly from one hinge, and the crater that had been blown out of the cement, with countless bone fragments and shards spread all over the blast zone. But there were no splatters of blood and tissue, no body parts, no dead or dying old guy. Had the son of a bitch somehow set off the mine from a safe distance? No, impossible. Even with night-vision goggles, Brogan couldn't have spotted the wire unless he'd known where to look for it and there was no way he could have known that. He couldn't even have *guessed*.

Light exploded in his face, so blinding it hurt his eyes, and he staggered backwards, tearing off the mask, blinking rapidly to try to clear his vision. He reached out, blindly sweeping his arm around until his hand hit a steel rod; he grabbed it and held tight. At the same moment, he sensed something moving in front of him.

As he raised the Glock, a shot knocked it out of his hand, stinging his palm. His vision began to clear and he caught a glimpse of a red flare sizzling on the cement a second before something slammed into his head. The force of the blow sent him flying and he landed hard, the back of his skull rapping sharply on the cement.

Furious, he made to get up but someone put a heavy boot on his chest, grinding the heel into his solar plexus so that he could barely breathe. Junior tried to feel around in the bone fragments, which made the boot on his chest press harder. Nearby, another hissing flare threw shifting red light over everything. He raised his head and felt the muzzle of a rifle between his eyes.

His vision cleared some more and he saw it was the old guy he had failed to kill in Cartagena. He couldn't believe it. Brogan had to be at least *fifty*. How could anybody so *old* fight off someone as young and well-trained as he was without help?

Brogan flicked on his rifle's Tac Light, shining it directly into his eyes, then proceeded to pat him down, relieving him of both the pistol in his ankle holster and the commando knife in his forearm sheath. How hard had he hit his head just now, he wondered as he watched Brogan's movements, because it was like he was watching himself. Only he knew *he* was sitting on this goddam concrete, refusing to give the pain in his head any place in his thoughts. So he *couldn't* be watching himself.

Except he was.

No. Junior squeezed his eyes shut for a moment. He couldn't see properly. It was a trick of the very dim light.

Brogan stepped back, picked up one of the sizzling flares, and motioned at him with the rifle.

"Up."

Junior got to his feet. All at once, they were eye to eye, and there was no denying the face staring back at him was his own. There were more lines around Brogan's eyes, his skin wasn't as tight or as smooth, and his lips were rougher. It was like looking into a mirror that showed him how he was going to look in nearly thirty years. And it wasn't just their faces that were identical, it was their expressions, too. He had no idea how long he and Brogan stood staring at each other before Henry poked him with the gun and marched him back to the Quartz Chamber.

The first thing Brogan did was pull the tape off Zakarewski's big mouth and cut her free from the pipe. Apparently her constant talking didn't get on *his* nerves. Maybe that was some kind of old person thing.

"Thank you," Zakarewski said.

"Thank *you* for the tip about the grenade," said Brogan.

Junior's mouth fell open, which the two of them thought was hilarious. Zakarewski scraped something off the back of a front tooth with one finger, then held it out to him. The light in the chamber was bad but he knew the small black object on her fingertip was a mic.

He looked from it to her and then to Brogan. "She was talking to you the whole time," he said, trying not to sound impressed and failing.

Brogan shrugged. "Hey, you either search somebody thoroughly or you don't. Being thorough will keep you alive." He took another flare out of his pocket and handed it to Zakarewski. "Know how to light one of these?"

"Jesus, Henry." She rolled her eyes as she lit the flare. Brogan was now walking a slow circle around him, like a drill instructor conducting an inspection, and it was a real effort not to squirm. Dammit, Brogan stood like him, moved like him, even gestured like him.

"For the record," Brogan said after a bit, "I don't *want* to kill you. But I will if I have to."

He tried to make himself stare through the old guy, the way his father did when he was mad at him, but he couldn't. Maybe his father would have had a much harder time with someone who looked exactly like him.

"What did Clay Verris tell you about me?" Brogan asked.

Junior kept his lips pressed together, refusing to answer.

"Okay, then, let *me* tell you about *him*," the old guy went on. "I happen to know Mr. Verris *very* well. How did he start you out—hunting? Birds and rabbit, right? Then when you were about twelve, he moved you up to deer."

Junior refused to look at Brogan, concentrated on keeping his face a stony mask. But he couldn't help thinking the man saw something about him—his eyes, maybe his posture or even his breathing—that told him he was right.

"I'm guessing you were nineteen or twenty the first time he ordered you to shoot a person. Any of this ringing true? He also told you to *lean into* your fear because 'you're a warrior blessed with great gifts to defend the weak.' Right?"

Junior forced himself to stand motionless and silent despite the anger building inside of him.

"But he just couldn't stop the noise, could he?" Brogan said. "That secret part of you that always felt a little different than everybody else. The part that made you feel like a weirdo."

"You don't know *shit*!" Junior blurted, unable to help himself.

Brogan laughed. "Kid, I know you inside out and backwards. You're allergic to bees, you hate cilantro, and you always sneeze four times."

"Everybody hates cilantro," Junior said, wondering if Brogan really didn't know that.

The old guy kept talking. "You're meticulous, thorough, disciplined, relentless. You love puzzles. You're a chess player, right? Good, too, I bet. But you suffer from insomnia. Your mind never lets you sleep and even when it does, it attacks you with nightmares. I'm talking about those three-o'clock-in-the-morning, someone-please-save-me nightmares."

Junior began hoping the ceiling would cave in; anything to shut the old guy up.

"And then there's the doubts," Brogan was saying. "Those are the worst. You hate them, and you hate yourself for having them because they make you feel weak. A *real* soldier doesn't doubt, right? The only time you truly feel happy is when you're flat on your belly about to squeeze a trigger. And in that moment, the world makes perfect sense. How do you think I know all of that?"

"I don't give a shit how you know anything," Junior told him contemptuously.

"Look at me, dummy!" Brogan shouted. "Look at *us*! Twenty-five years ago, your so-called father took *my* blood and *cloned* me. He made *you* from *me*. Our DNA is identical."

"He's telling you the truth," Danny put in, her voice quiet and matter-of-fact.

"Shut up!" Junior shouted. Were the two of them high or merely batshit? Everybody knew Clay Verris had adopted him, it wasn't any kind of big state secret. But what Henry had said about his DNA had to be a steaming pile of horseshit. It *had* to be.

Except it explained how Brogan had his face.

No, it was crazy. Even though they looked alike, it *had* to be crazy. Cloning wasn't a real thing, not with humans.

"He chose me 'cause there's never been anyone like me," Brogan went on, "and he knew one day I was going to get old and then you'd step in. But he's been lying to you the whole time. He told you that you were an orphan. And of all the people to send after me, why would he send you?"

"'Cause I'm the *best*," Junior informed him.

"Oh yeah?" Brogan shocked him by putting the barrel of his gun right up to his ear. "You're obviously *not* the best. For one thing, you've got a hard-ass head. But I guess this was supposed to be your birthday or something. I had to die and you had to do it. As long as I was alive, Clay's little experiment was somehow incomplete. *That's* the maniac you're pulling the trigger for."

"Shut your mouth about him," Junior said, his anger and frustration turning to rage. "You're just trying to rattle me."

"I'm trying to *save* you," Brogan replied. "What are you, twenty-three? And still a virgin, right? Dying to be in a relationship and connect, but terrified to let anyone near you because what if someone saw who you actually are. If they did, how could they ever love you? So everybody else are only targets, and you're just a real good *weapon*."

The bullshit psychoanalysis finally pushed him over the edge. Junior grabbed the end of Brogan's rifle and yanked it toward himself, hard. Brogan came with it and Junior kneed him in the groin, making him let go of the weapon as he fell. Junior reached for it but Brogan surprised him by kicking it straight to Zakarewski, then gave him an elbow to the head. Junior sprawled on the dirty stone floor, rolled over quickly to see Brogan had drawn his commando knife; he flipped himself to a standing position and kicked it out of Brogan's hand.

That blow hurt, he could see it in his face. *This will hurt worse,* Junior promised him silently as he lowered his head and charged him like a linebacker, driving both of them into the wall of bones.

The impact sent clouds of dust billowing into the air as the shelves collapsed and bones that had lain undisturbed for hundreds of years broke into pieces and flew in all directions. This was the perfect place for Brogan, Junior thought—buried under a mountain of old, forgotten bones. He pulled away from the old guy and his hand fell on a broken thigh bone with a viciously jagged end. Junior tried to jab it into Brogan's throat and discovered Brogan had also found a jagged femur and was trying to do the same thing to him.

More bones cracked and scattered as he struggled to get on top of Brogan, trying to get the upper hand. He almost had him a couple of times but before he could drive the jagged bone into the old guy's throat, Brogan would somehow find the strength to heave him off or go upside his head, or trap his leg and twist it, forcing him to let go before the old guy broke his knee. Junior just couldn't get the better of him. But at least Brogan wasn't getting the better of him, either—

"Drop it!" Zakarewski yelled suddenly, aiming the rifle at him. Junior looked at Brogan's face covered with dirt and bone dust. Brogan's face; *his* face. He couldn't deny it, now or ever.

"*Drop it!*" Zakarewski yelled again, louder now. "I *will* shoot you!"

"*Don't shoot him!*" Brogan yelled.

Junior saw her freeze. *Thanks, old man,* he thought with a grin. She really *wouldn't* shoot him, not if Brogan told her not to. He twisted his left hand out of the old guy's grasp and punched him. At this angle he didn't have the leverage for a knockout blow, but the feel of Brogan's jaw slewing sideways gave him a moment of satisfaction before the old guy surprised him with a hard jab to his throat.

He fell away from Brogan, rolled over, and got to his feet, rubbing his neck and coughing. Zakarewski had a clean shot now; she could drop him easily.

Only she still couldn't—he saw it in her face. No matter how much she wanted to, she just couldn't put a bullet in someone who looked so much like her hero. Good to know, he thought just as Brogan used the linebacker charge on him.

It crossed his mind as they crashed into another section of wall that Brogan's old-man shoulder didn't have as much muscle on it as his but it seemed to be just as strong, and damn, this wall was so thick with bones, they were tunneling through it with their bodies.

Some kind of barrier broke apart behind him and then all the bones and shelves were gone, everything was gone, even the dust. Suddenly they were hurtling out and down through dark empty air and before he could even wonder what was waiting below them, they plunged into water, momentum still driving them downward.

Son of a bitch—they were in the goddam *cistern*.

Now the old guy was flailing with all his might, his movements desperate and panicky. Right—that would be Brogan's special problem with water; it scared the shit out of him. Junior grinned triumphantly. This was such a lucky break—it was like Fate itself wanted Henry Brogan dead.

Crashing through a wall of bones into thin air took Henry completely by surprise. He had barely had any time to look up information about the catacombs and most of what had come up on his phone had been in Hungarian.

He had no idea how long the fall would last or what might be waiting for them at the bottom but he did his best to keep Junior Hitman under him. Landing on him would give him a better chance of surviving the impact—better than Junior Hitman's, at least.

Unless there was no impact and they fell forever.

The thought was fleeting, there and gone in a tiny fraction of a second, and it should have been ridiculous, utter nonsense. On the other hand, he had just crashed through a wall of bones in the middle of the night going mano-a-mano with his clone. The bar for strange and farfetched was higher than it had ever been. But the possibility of landing in water had never occurred to him.

All thought ceased as he thrashed madly with his arms and legs, trying to get to the surface. But this time, the weights on his legs weren't just impossibly heavy, they were alive and actively fighting him, trying to drag him down into the dark. This wasn't how the dream went—the weights were always inanimate objects.

Which meant this was no dream. It wasn't Hell, either— otherwise his father would have been there laughing at him and telling him to *concentrate*, dammit, this was *easy*. No, he was awake and alive, and if he wanted to stay that way he had to *get the hell out of the goddam water* NOW.

Henry finally kicked free of the hands pulling at him and propelled himself upward. When he finally broke the surface, he caught a glimpse of Danny high overhead, holding a flare as she peered down at them from the hole he and Junior had punched in the Quartz Chamber. He was about to call out to her when the kid surged up out of the water and threw himself on top of him, trying to push him under.

Instead of resisting, he let the clone push him down with a force that actually pushed him away. Henry slipped around him and broke the surface again, looking for some way to get out of the water. Off to his left, he spotted a jagged ledge, the remains of a floor or platform. As he started to swim for it, Junior Hitman's hands clutched his shoulders hard from behind.

Henry jerked his head back sharply, hitting the clone in the face, grinning when the kid yelped in surprised pain. Treading water, he turned to see the clone coming at him with his nose bleeding profusely and a broken femur in one hand.

How the *hell* had he managed to hold onto that, he wondered as the clone jabbed it at him. Henry put his hands up as if he were going to try to push him away, then let the clone get just close enough for another, harder head-butt before he swam for the ledge.

No yelp this time but Henry knew that one must have hurt him a lot more. His clothes dragged heavily on him as he pulled himself out of the water onto the ledge and rolled over onto his back, out of breath. Something on his neck was stinging. Henry touched the spot and his fingers came away bloody. Then all at once the kid was there with him, leaping up out of the water and onto the ledge seemingly with no effort at all.

Henry threw one arm across his face. The clone knocked it away easily and pounced on him. His nose was still bleeding copiously but he seemed oblivious to it as he put both hands around Henry's neck and squeezed.

Henry tried to pull his hands away, fighting to breathe, but his air was already cut off. Dark patches appeared in his vision and the light from Danny's flare above him began to fade out. Henry tugged on the clone's wrists and forearms but it was like pulling at steel bars. Dammit, instead of drowning, he was going to suffocate *out* of water like a goddam fish. Henry was vaguely aware of a splash as something else fell into the water but he was too busy losing consciousness to wonder about it.

"Get your hands off him!" Danny yelled from somewhere off to Henry's right. He felt Junior's hands loosen but only for a moment before he started to squeeze again.

And then impossibly, there was a gunshot. Even more impossibly, Junior fell back from Henry.

Air rushed into Henry's lungs in a noisy, torturous wheeze. He could hear the clone panting with shock and pain, as if he had never been shot before. Henry managed to prop himself up on one elbow and saw Danny treading water and aiming a Glock at the clone.

The woman could tread water *and* shoot a Glock, Henry marveled. If this was the DIA agent of the future, he was retiring just in time.

The clone was staring at her, too, astonished and indignant. Henry half-expected him to yell something like, *No fair, that's cheating!* And then fling himself at her. Except he couldn't. His nose wasn't bleeding as much any more but now Henry saw a lot more blood on the front of his shirt.

Danny had maneuvered herself so that she was right beside Henry. With her free hand, she used the ledge to steady herself and took aim at the kid again. It was a tremendous physical effort but Henry reached over and somehow found the strength to push her gun hand down.

Danny stared at him wide-eyed and he knew she was wondering why he was stopping her after she had finally managed to shoot him.

Junior Hitman seemed even more astonished. "I'm not *you!*" he shouted suddenly, his face contorting with rage and pain. "You hear me, old man? *I'm not you!*" He rolled off the ledge into the water.

Danny quickly boosted herself up out of the water next to Henry while he peered through the gloom, listening for the sound of the kid coming up for air. For a long time, he heard nothing and he wondered if the gunshot had weakened Junior so much that he had drowned. There was something terribly perverse about that.

Finally he heard the small splash of someone breaking the surface somewhere far away. He looked at Danny, who nodded; she'd heard it, too. This pool, or whatever it was, was a hell of a lot larger than he'd thought. And it wasn't stagnant, which meant it had to let out somewhere.

"You think he's gone?" Henry said after a bit. His chest was tight and every muscle in his neck felt sore; it hurt even just to swallow.

"I think so," Danny replied.

"Where did you hit him?"

"In the shoulder." Danny's voice was calm and even.

"Then he'll recover," Henry said, staring at the water. He half-expected some new menace to suddenly surge up out of it. *Just when you thought you were safe from your clone in the catacombs.* Damn, he really was loopy from lack of oxygen.

Danny moved his hand to his neck. "Keep pressure on that and wait here," she said as she got to her feet. "I'm going to see if we can get out of the cistern without having to climb back up to the catacombs."

"This is a *cistern*?" Henry said, horrified.

"Well, it ain't an indoor swimming pool," Danny said with a grim little chuckle. "Once I find a way out, I can call Baron to come get us."

Henry was flabbergasted. "You've got a waterproof phone?"

"No. I've got a regular phone in a waterproof case," she said over her shoulder as she disappeared into the shadows, leaving Henry to wonder how the hell she'd slipped *that* past Junior.

* * *

Baron had been waiting almost twenty minutes in a back alley outside a disused service entrance to the catacombs before Henry and Danny appeared. Henry had one arm slung across her shoulders, leaning on her like a wounded soldier. That was curious enough but what made it genuinely strange was the fact that they were both *wet*. He couldn't wait to hear *that* story.

"It's not often you see a guy get his ass kicked on *two* continents back to back. Hop in!" He opened the passenger-side doors. Henry sprawled across the back seat while Danny took shotgun. Baron closed the door for Henry, then hurried around the front of the car to hop into the driver's seat. "Where to?"

For some reason, Danny found that funny; Henry didn't. "Georgia," he said wearily. "It's where Verris is."

This time, they were flying away from the oncoming day, chasing the night into the west while the clock ran backwards. Baron wasn't singing, which Danny actually missed, while Henry resisted her attempts at first aid.

He didn't have a whole lot of new injuries but she was concerned about the laceration on his neck. It wasn't especially deep but it had been made with the jagged end of a very old, very dirty bone in a cistern and there was a high risk of infection. Henry had finally let her sterilize the wound and put a bandage on it. But every time she tried to check for inflammation, he waved her off.

"Advil?" she offered, showing him the bottle.

He shrugged. She gave him two; he held up four fingers so she gave him two more. The rule of thumb in the field was, doubling the dose of an over-the-counter medication made it prescription-strength. But another rule of thumb said this was only a stopgap and you were supposed to get out of the field ASAP. Danny didn't know whose thumbs the rules were based on but she was pretty sure they weren't Henry's. He tossed back the four pills and chased them with whiskey. Well, at least alcohol was a disinfectant, she thought, and maybe its depressant properties would put him to sleep.

"Try to get some rest," Danny said.

Henry didn't answer. She hesitated, then decided to take her own advice in the seat behind him.

CHAPTER 18

Clay Verris was in his office watching feeds from several different pre-dawn exercises when the guard on the ground floor called to inform him Junior was on his way up with blood in his eye. She also advised the commander that his son had sustained a GSW in his left shoulder, although it didn't seem to be serious.

Verris thanked the guard and made a mental note to leave a plus sign on the performance sheet in her file. He didn't like being disturbed while he was monitoring exercises unless it was important. A less perceptive guard would have figured there was no point in interrupting him to tell him he was going to be interrupted; fortunately, this one knew Junior *always* took priority.

Junior had been very much on his mind since this second debacle with Henry Brogan. Verris had known full well that Brogan wouldn't be easy to eliminate. But he'd been surprised when the kid had called him from Cartagena to report the target had gotten away.

Then again, it *had* been a rushed assignment. Brogan had to be neutralized as soon as possible and there hadn't been much time for the kid to study up on him, watch footage, get acquainted with his moves. Not that Verris had really wanted Junior to get a close enough look at Henry to recognize him at that point—not until he was ready to know the truth about who he was.

Originally, Verris had planned to lay it all out for him on his twenty-first birthday. But when it had arrived, he was still so damned *young*. It wasn't education and training that he lacked, Verris realized, it was seasoning.

Education had been important in Verris's family. His father had always said that training without education produced a waste of good man flesh (women included). During Verris's time in the Marine Corps, he'd seen how true that was. The problem, however, was not so much with the man flesh involved as it was with those in command. Most of them regarded soldiers as something to be supplied and replenished, one more military consumable: cannon fodder. Talk about a waste of good man flesh! They should have been producing *warriors*, not fresh meat for slaughterhouses like Vietnam or Iraq.

Long ago, Verris had come to the conclusion that just as war and other conflicts had many facets, so, too, were there different kinds of warriors. Junior was the warrior Henry Brogan could have been if he'd had the right education and guidance, while the guys he'd been watching tonight were another kind altogether. When they hit the ground in Yemen, the whole world was going to sit up and take notice, especially the US. They were going to see that Gemini warriors were the new and improved future of military man flesh, women included; women especially.

He would never have been able to accomplish this in the Corps, no matter how high he rose in rank. If he had stayed in the Marines, they only would have held him back. So he had quit and started Gemini. He had thought for sure that Henry would want to be part of it—the private sector had so much more to offer, starting with better pay. But Henry had chosen to stick with government work and let the DIA recruit him. He'd always had a thing about serving his country. He was committed to it and Verris hadn't realized how strong that commitment was; Henry had never acted like a flag-waving robot.

It didn't make any sense until Verris considered that this was what happened when kids grew up without a father. They had to put something in that empty space and for Henry, it was his country. Admirable? Maybe, but it meant that Henry would never be able to achieve his full potential. All things considered, he'd done pretty well, overcoming his deprived background and making something of himself.

Still, Verris couldn't help thinking how much more Henry could have accomplished if he'd had the care and guidance of a father. Verris had promised himself that if he ever became a father himself, he would be right there in his kid's life, 24/7.

As time passed, Verris had seen he wasn't going to have a conventional nuclear family. If he wanted to be a father, he would have to adopt. That was all right with him but there seemed to be a shortage of newborns and adoption agencies tended to favor two-parent families, not single ex-military men who couldn't talk about what they did for a living because it was classified.

Then he had gotten wind of Dormov's work and right away he'd known this was how he could make his fondest dream a reality—he could give Henry Brogan a do-over. He could raise him right, make him into the warrior he should have been. He could train him to grow into his strengths unhindered by the psychological damage of a childhood and adolescence living in poverty without a father.

Henry Brogan 2.0—all of the shine, none of the whine.

The road hadn't been completely smooth. But Junior was fast becoming the warrior Henry would never be; the kid was going to achieve the perfection that Henry had never had a chance at.

Verris had wanted so much to tell Junior that but the kid simply wasn't ready yet. Junior was educated, he was trained, he was a warrior. The problem was, there was still too much of the adolescent in him.

Gemini's psychologists told him he had to be patient. Every person matured at a different rate, and in general the male of the species usually lagged behind the female. Verris was just going to have to watch and wait, they said, play it by ear.

So he'd done that but Junior still wasn't ready at twenty-three and Verris was damned if he knew what was wrong. There shouldn't have been anything holding him back. Finally Verris realized the solution had been right in front of him all along: Henry Brogan.

Junior would never come into his own as long as Henry Brogan was alive.

It was so obvious, he should have seen it right away, Verris thought. But it wasn't just that Henry had to die— *Junior* had to be the one to kill him. Then Junior would be able to take his rightful place in the world as who and what he was.

Then he would be perfect.

Henry Brogan was broken and flawed. Junior was the new, improved version, and best of all, he was Verris's son. Verris would continue to make sure Junior knew he had a father every moment of every day. That would make sure he *stayed* perfect.

* * *

Another soldier would have stopped at the infirmary to have his gunshot wound checked out and clean up a little before he reported in, but not Junior. Junior would know Verris had already been informed of his failure to accomplish his mission for the second time. He wouldn't wait to account for himself.

He didn't knock, either, to Verris's annoyance. Verris blanked and muted the feeds. He'd been watching the exercises long enough that he had a pretty good idea of how they were all going to go. If anything blew up that wasn't supposed to, he'd hear it.

But Jesus, the guard in the lobby had been right— Junior was very much the worse for wear. He looked as if he'd gone swimming with all his clothes on, then slept in them while they dried.

Verris waited for Junior to say something but his son just stood in front of his desk giving him a hard stare. Finally, he leaned back in his chair. "Tell me something," he said, looking directly into those glaring eyes. "Why is it so hard for you to kill this ma—"

"Do you know how much I *hate* Big Hammock park, Pop?" Junior demanded.

Alarm bells went off in Verris's mind. It was never a good sign when Junior started a conversation with something he hated. The bizarre juxtaposition of his birthday with his second failure to accomplish his mission meant he had let himself be distracted by irrelevant shit. Verris was tempted to give him a sharp, hard slap in the face, like hitting a radio with a loose connection. But a good father *never* struck his son in the head, not off the training field.

Maybe this was a childish attempt to divert attention from his failure, or even to deny his own responsibility: *I failed to kill Henry Brogan because you've been forcing me to go to Big Hammock park on my birthday.*

Junior should have been a little too old for that one but you could never tell with young people. Whatever was going on with him, Verris knew he would have to take it step by step and see where it led.

"Come again?" Clay said, careful to keep his tone neutral.

"Every year since I was twelve, we shoot turkeys there on my birthday. I always hated it—I mean, I was an *orphan*, right? How did we even *know* when my birthday was? But you never seemed to notice so we just kept going there."

At least he hadn't gone soft about turkeys, Verris thought. He had raised Junior with the idea that those who couldn't kill what they ate were too weak to fight for their own lives or anyone else's. But the kid still wasn't making sense and if he didn't start soon, he'd have to call in PsyOps.

Aloud, Verris said, "Fine. Next year we'll try Chuck E. Cheese."

"Yeah?" Junior tilted his head to one side. "Who's 'we'—you, me, and the lab guys who made me?"

Verris kept all expression off his face although he felt like he'd been punched between the eyes. "Oh."

He had known that despite all his efforts to shield Junior from the truth, there was a possibility he might find out that very thing he wasn't ready to know. But Verris had always thought that if such a thing happened, it would be here at the Gemini compound, where he would be able to manage his son's reaction to some degree (and also know whose big mouth to staple shut).

Over the years, Verris had supervised Junior's life as well as he could, restricting his contact with other personnel. That had worked pretty well throughout Junior's childhood and his teen years, when even the best kids could become rebellious and uncooperative. It wasn't so easy to do that with an adult, however, even one conditioned to follow orders and not ask too many irrelevant questions.

The other soldiers tended to keep their distance from the CO's son, which helped to minimize the amount of rumor, gossip, and general scuttlebutt that came Junior's way.

This wasn't always easy on the kid. Sometimes Verris caught him looking longingly at a group of soldiers going off for a drink together after an exercise. Whenever that happened, he would draw Junior's attention away with something more suited to his intellectual and physical skills and abilities, and pretty soon the kid seemed to forget all about trivial shit like drinking buddies. Protecting him until he was ready to know the truth was more important than anything else.

From time to time, though, Verris had wondered if he should have told Junior everything as soon as he was old enough to grasp the basic biology. Maybe if he had grown up with the knowledge, it would have normalized everything and there would have been that much less to agonize about later.

Or maybe Junior would simply have found another reason for an existential crisis. Kids were good at that.

And it was all moot because his son was still standing in front of his desk, glaring at him, waiting for him to explain himself.

"I, uh, I always believed you'd be happier not knowing," Verris said finally.

"*Happy?!*" Junior gave a short harsh laugh. "The only time I'm happy is when I'm flat on my belly about to squeeze a trigger."

The alarm bells in Verris's mind were louder this time. He had heard those words before but not from Junior and he was damned sure it wasn't a coincidence. This was worse than he'd realized. Not only had Junior failed to kill Henry Brogan again, but somehow Henry had found out about Dormov's program and used the information to get into Junior's head. Verris wasn't sure what was more disturbing—Henry's finding out about the program or his having cornered Junior long enough to tell him about it. And how the hell he could have found out in the first place—

Budapest. That Russian rat Yuri, friend to Jack Willis.

Dammit, Verris thought; if he had called in an airstrike on Willis's yacht while he and Brogan had still been hugging it out like teenage girls, this whole thing could have been avoided. He would never have had to tell Junior he was a clone and this rite of passage wouldn't be necessary.

No.

That would have been easier but there was something else to consider: the symmetry of Junior supplanting Henry by punching his ticket. That was so beautiful, so elegant, so perfect. And Brogan deserved nothing less. The arrogance of that self-righteous prick, putting on that hitman-with-a-heart-of-gold act, refusing to come work with him at Gemini, as if he was actually better than his old CO. As if he was too good for Gemini.

Brogan must have been livid when he found out who Junior was. He had said no to Verris and Verris had gotten him anyway. Not only that, he'd *raised* Junior to work there, actually *bred* him for it. If anyone was too good for something it was Junior. He was too good for the DIA or any other crappy government agency.

"I mean, this wasn't some *mistake*." Junior planted both fists on his desk and leaned forward. "It's not like you got somebody pregnant and then had to man up and raise me. No, you made a *decision*. You had a scientist make a *person* out of another *person*."

"No, that's *not* what—"

"That's *exactly* what happened." He straightened up and looked down at himself, putting his hands on his chest and midsection with the fingers splayed, as if he were trying to feel how substantial he really was. "And why, of all the shooters in the world, did you have to send *me* after him?"

"Because he's your darkness," Verris replied. "You had to walk through it on your own."

Junior gave him a hard look. "Maybe *you're* my darkness."

Christ, Verris thought as a knot started to form in his stomach.

"That lie you always told me, about my 'parents' leaving me at a fire station. I *believed* it. Do you know how that made me feel?"

"That was a necessary lie," Verris said.

"*None* of this was necessary! You *chose* to do all of this to me!" Junior paused, looking lost and sad. "Can't you see how *not okay* I am?"

Verris had had enough. "Bullshit."

Junior gaped at him. The kid hadn't seen *that* coming.

"Don't forget who you're talking to, Junior," Verris went on while the kid was still off-balance. "I've been in battle! I've seen soldiers go over the edge because more was asked of them than they had to give. And I promised myself that I would *never* let that happen to my kid, that I would *never* let *anything* in life squeeze the strength and spirit out of my son and toss him aside. And nothing will! That's not you, that will *never* be you—I made sure of it. Because you have what Henry Brogan never had—a loving, dedicated, *present* father who tells you every goddam day that you're loved, you matter! Jesus, kid, the whole point was to give you all of Henry's advantages without any of his disadvantages—all of his gifts without his pain! And that's what I did!"

The knot in Verris's stomach loosened as Junior's expression went from abject and accusing to thoughtful. He had always been able to talk the kid down and smooth him out, and thank God he still could. He got up and went around the desk.

"Come here," he said. Junior went to him and he took his son in his arms. He was the good, loving, present father, always ready to give advice, wisdom, and comfort.

"I love you, son," he told Junior, hugging him tighter. "Don't let yourself down."

At the edge of a remote airfield a few miles away from the Gemini compound, Henry and Danny waited while Baron bid a fond farewell to the Gulfstream. Saying goodbye was one of Baron's rituals. He had told Henry once that he always tried to part on good terms with any plane he had flown. *Because if we should meet again,* Baron had said, *and it happens to be a life-or-death situation, I want to make sure I'll be welcome in the cockpit.*

Henry had smiled and nodded politely. Pilots were a superstitious bunch. They all had their own personal rituals. Even Chuck Yeager had had a good-luck routine where he asked one of his ground staff for a stick of gum. Anything that made Baron happy and confident was fine with Henry. (And just to be on the safe side, he hadn't mentioned breaking the mirror in the abandoned apartment building.)

"Like so many of my encounters, it was short but sweet." Baron blew a kiss at the nose of the Gulfstream. "Thanks, darlin'. No matter what happens after this, we'll *always* have Budapest."

Danny laughed a little but Henry felt a sudden odd chill, brief but intense enough to raise goosebumps on his arms. *Goose walked over my grave,* his mother would say when it happened to her. It rattled him. Maybe he *was* getting superstitious in his old age. Or he was entering his second childhood and tomorrow he'd be stepping over cracks in the sidewalk.

"So, what's next?" Baron said as he joined him and Danny.

"Well, we can't stay in the open," Henry said, "and we need some ground transportation."

"I'm pretty sure there's a truck around here somewhere," Baron said. "I never saw an airfield without one."

"When we were coming in to land, I saw an open-air barn over there, just past the tree line." Henry pointed at the other side of the runway. "We can hole up there for a bit while we figure out our next move."

He should have been beyond tired, Henry thought as the three of them crossed the airfield together, but somehow he wasn't. It was as if he was running on a reserve of energy that he'd never known he had until now. Or maybe it was adrenaline afterburn. Whatever was keeping him upright, he was glad to have it. Otherwise he would have been dead on his feet.

And then just as they reached the barn, he was.

As a Marine, Henry had learned how to override his circadian rhythms and function whenever he had to, day or night. By personal preference, however, he was a night owl. Like most kids he had loved staying up late, but Henry had a special affinity for the nighttime. Nighttime was always the right time—cool stuff happened at night that never happened during the day, and a lot of daytime things vanished after the sun went down, e.g. there was no school, no chores, and best of all, no bees trying to kill him.

Unfortunately, there were other ways to get stung.

As soon as Henry felt the dart hit his neck he yanked it out, but it was already too late. He knew what it was and who had done it to him. His own fault—he'd opened his big mouth back in Budapest and told the kid how to kill him.

Well, he was going to regret that for the rest of his life, which would last for maybe two more minutes before his throat swelled shut. Unless his blood pressure fell too rapidly—then he'd skip suffocation altogether and go straight to cardiac arrest.

He was barely aware of hitting the ground. Baron and Danny were talking frantically, Baron saying something about an EpiPen and Danny telling him this wasn't his original burn bag. Their hands ran over him in a quick search in case he had an EpiPen on him but the feel of them was far away, muted and muffled, and their voices seemed to slide away from him.

Henry's head rolled to one side. His younger self was marching forward out of the shadows, pistol raised. On his left, he saw Danny kneel to pick something up: the dart.

"Don't move!" Junior Hitman said loudly.

Danny held the dart up. "What was in this?" she demanded just as loudly.

"Bee venom," said the clone.

Even in his semi-conscious state, Henry couldn't help thinking how smart it was. A dart was like a stealth bee—he couldn't snap one of those clean out of the air with a cap. Not even with a Phillies cap.

"You can't! He's allergic!" Danny took a step forward and the clone fired—two quick shots, one at her feet, one at Baron's. Near misses, warning them to stay put.

Henry's vision started to brown out as it became more difficult for him to breathe. Apparently he was going to suffocate after all. Not as showy as being killed with a motorcycle but more effective. Once it started, there was no fighting it off, shooting it, or outrunning it. Unless someone interrupted it with an EpiPen, it would continue to its inevitable conclusion. The end. Game over.

The dark patches in his vision were spreading as Junior stood over him. Damn, the kid looked *exactly* like him at twenty-three—not just his face but his posture, the way he held his weapon. Henry even recognized the mix of emotions on Junior's face as he watched the target dying. Clay Verris had literally turned him into his own worst enemy. That was all kinds of wrong.

His thoughts faded as a new feeling took hold of him, a sensation of loosening, becoming untethered, like a boat that had been untied from a piling and was starting to drift, except the movement was upward.

This really was it, Henry thought. He was wheels up on his last flight, the one you took without a plane. Junior could finally go home and tell Daddy he'd taken out his old self.

In the distance, Danny was saying, *Please,* please *don't do this!* And Baron was yelling, *Breathe, Henry, breathe!* His old friend didn't know he was already catching an updraft.

Then somebody stabbed him in the arm.

The pain pulled him back from the edge of unconsciousness. The floating sensation was gone; he felt the hard ground under him again. He could breathe more easily now. It was a tremendous effort to open his eyes but when he finally forced his lids apart, he saw a face above him, so close it filled his vision. His own face but younger.

"Epinephrine," his younger face said with his voice. "And an antihistamine." Henry felt another sharp pain. "You're going to be fine."

Henry's breathing was almost back to normal now. On his left, Danny started to cry with relief. He wanted to tell her not to do that, there was no crying in assassination, not even when someone was trying to kill you. You were supposed to suck it up, tough it out, walk it off. But when he rolled his head around to the other side, he saw Baron's face was wet, too.

"Hey," he croaked at Baron.

Baron nodded at Danny. "What she said."

Danny laughed through her tears as she and Baron helped him sit up. A few feet away, Junior sat on the ground in front of him, long legs folded. Henry had a moment of envy; his own flexibility wasn't what it had once been. But he was still alive, thanks to his clone's sudden attack of conscience. The kid looked like a man who had awakened from a troubling dream to find himself in unfamiliar surroundings—unsure, bewildered, and lost. Henry could relate.

"I'm sorry," Junior Hitman said after a bit, and Henry knew he wasn't only apologizing for trying to kill him. He was sorry about being a clone and not knowing it, sorry the world had gotten one over on him, sorry for things he didn't even know how to articulate yet. Henry had seen the expression before in the mirror.

"It's all good," Henry told him. "All this shit's been pretty hard to accept."

The kid looked up at him, wary.

"So, you came here to kill me with bee venom," Henry went on. "But you also brought the antidote with you?"

The clone gave an awkward shrug. "You said you were allergic; I figured maybe I was, too, and I ought to start carrying an EpiPen, just in case."

"You decided that when—tonight?"

Another awkward shrug.

"Guys, I hate to break up the kumbaya of it all," Baron said. "But how the hell did you always know where we *were*?"

His younger self hesitated. "Do you trust me?" he asked Henry.

The question jerked an incredulous laugh out of Henry. "Damn, you've got nerve."

"Yeah, I wonder where he got that," Danny said, amused.

The clone produced a combat knife from an ankle sheath and held it up in a silent question.

Henry nodded. He *did* trust the kid. Strangely, he felt like he'd always trusted him.

Junior Hitman got up on his knees, took hold of Henry's left bicep and pushed the point of the blade into a spot a couple of inches below the curve of his shoulder.

"Jesus!" Danny said, flinching; even Baron caught his breath. Henry held still. It didn't tickle but it wasn't the most painful bit of impromptu field surgery he had ever endured. It wasn't even the worst thing that had happened to him tonight. Danny was rummaging around in her burn bag and Henry knew she was looking for something to use as a bandage. Ms. First Aid to the rescue.

After almost half a minute, Junior sat back and showed Henry a small black square on the tip of his knife. "They chipped you," he said. "Remember that surgery on your torn bicep, three years ago?"

Danny was already painting the incision with something cool that stung slightly. "I feel stupid," she said as she wound a strip of cloth around his arm and tied it. "I should have guessed. It's so obvious."

"Everything's obvious if you know," Henry said darkly. He plucked the chip off the end of the knife and flicked it into the darkness.

"Verris—" Baron started.

"*You* know him, too?" The kid looked at Baron in genuine astonishment.

"We served in the Marine Corps with him—Panama, Kuwait, Somalia," replied Baron. "Can you take us to his lab?"

The kid nodded. "Sure, but why?"

"We need to shut him down," Henry said. "You and me, together."

Junior Hitman nodded. "I'm parked on the other side of the runway."

Junior's heart beat faster as he drove toward the Gemini compound. He glanced at Henry beside him. Henry was so sure of himself, so steady and focused, a man who always knew what he was doing. Clay Verris had raised *him* to be like that but he could never quite get there, no matter what he did.

Like now—he knew he was doing the right thing, throwing in with Henry and the other two. He had been lied to and used and it had left him feeling wobbly and precarious. He wasn't sure what was going to happen when they got to the Gemini lab. What was he going to do? Or maybe the real question was, what would he be able to do?

Everything had always been so clear when he had trusted his father and believed in him. Any time he was confused, his father would straighten everything out. Not any more. He'd never be able to turn to his father again for answers or clarity or reassurance or anything else. But Henry seemed to have faith in him. He could tell even though Henry had never said so.

He wanted to ask what Henry expected of him, what they were going to do not just when they got to the lab but afterwards, for the rest of their lives. But what he heard himself say was, "You grew up in Philly, right?"

Henry raised his eyebrows, a bit surprised by the question. "Hunting Park," he said. "A place called The Bottom."

"'The Bottom?'" Junior frowned, unsure of what to make of that. Henry's life was completely beyond his experience. He was quiet for few seconds, then decided he had to know. "Who was my—our—mother?"

"Helen Jackson Brogan," said Henry with pride in his voice. "She was the strongest, most capable woman I've ever known. Worked two jobs for forty years." Pause. "And she spanked the *hell* out of me."

"Did you deserve it?" Junior asked, honestly curious.

Henry chuckled. "Usually. Does being angry and stupid and never trying at anything mean you deserve it? I don't know." His voice turned thoughtful. "My—our—father wasn't around much. He left when I was five." Pause. "I could never shake the feeling that when she looked at me, she saw *him*. So I went off and joined the Marines, grew up, made some friends—*real* friends, not Badlands punks whose biggest accomplishment when they grew up would be making parole. I found something I was good at and I even got medals for it. By the time I got out with all my shiny medals on my chest, she was gone. And I became… *this*."

Junior didn't take his eyes off the dark road ahead but he could feel Henry's gaze on him.

"You should walk away while you still can," Henry told him.

"It's all I know," Junior said.

"No, it's just all he *taught* you," said Henry. "Stop now and you can still be something else."

Junior gave a short, sarcastic laugh. "Like what? Doctor? Lawyer?"

"*Husband*," Henry corrected him. "*Father*. All the things this job gives you an excuse *not* to be. I threw all that away, man. You can do better than that."

Junior was seized with a sudden intense desire for that to be true, even though he'd never once wondered about having any other kind of life. He had never seen himself doing anything else, never thought he would want to. That was a failure of imagination, he thought; his father had worked very hard to stifle it.

"And while I'm at it," Henry said, "what the hell is your name?"

"Always been Junior. For Clay, Junior," he added in response to Henry's incredulous expression. "Only I'm not so sure about that any more."

"That's another reason to quit," said Henry.

Junior let out a long breath as he took the turnoff for Glennville. He *was* going to quit, not just because Henry had told him to, but because after this, he would have no choice. And that would be the easy part.

The lights were on in the Winn-Dixie—the manager always came in extra early to get ready for the day. The public library on the next corner was still dark, as was the high school farther up. But the traffic lights were already in regular service; the one at the first intersection went red as soon as he was in sight of it. He never could beat the lights in Glennville.

"This is home," he said.

Henry looked around. "Nice town." The other two in the backseat made murmurs of agreement.

Junior blew out a short breath that wasn't quite a laugh. Glennville had been shabby and in decline for as long as he could remember. It was a sad, rundown place that offered no future, only the remnants of an undistinguished past. The town might have already faded out of existence if Gemini hadn't been around as life support. Gemini kept Glennville alive because it suited Clay Verris to do so. The town made great camouflage.

"It won't be easy getting in," Junior said.

"You're our ticket, man," Henry said. "With you, we can walk right in through the front door."

Junior gave a short, soundless laugh. "Yeah? Then what?"

"We talk to him, together," Henry replied. "You and

me. If he has any humanity left in him, he'll listen."

Junior frowned. "What if he doesn't?"

Henry shrugged. "Then we both kick his ass. Together. You and me."

They were still sitting at the light when the phone in Junior's shirt pocket rang. He took it out and showed Henry the screen: DAD.

"Guess who," Henry said, amused.

In the backseat, Baron sat forward eagerly. "Ooh, can I answer? *Please* let me answer. I want to be the one to tell him we're all BFFs now."

For a moment, Junior was tempted; then he put the phone to his ear.

"Hello?"

"Are you with Brogan?" Verris asked, his voice urgent.

"Why would I be with *him*?" Junior said, trying to sound innocently offhand and not at all like the man he was supposed to have killed was sitting next to him. "You sent me to AMF him, didn't you?"

"Doesn't matter," Verris said. "Just *run*!"

"Huh?"

"*Run!*" Verris yelled. "Get away from him. *Now!* Please, Junior! I just want you safe!"

Junior laughed, slightly bewildered. "Why? Because I'm your favorite experiment?" The traffic light changed from red to green and he put the Jeep in gear.

"No, because I'm your father and I love you, son. Run!" At the same moment, Junior saw a bright white flash ahead of him and knew immediately he was in trouble. They all were.

Releasing his seatbelt, he opened the door. "Everybody out!" he yelled and jumped.

* * *

As soon as Henry saw the flash, he knew even before he heard Junior yell that they were on the wrong end of an RPG.

"*Bail!*" Henry shouted. He tumbled out of the Jeep, rolling over and over on the asphalt, coming to rest not far from Danny, who already had her weapon in hand. Before he could look for Baron, the RPG hit.

The sound of the blast was merciless. Henry covered his ears, felt the ground shake as the shockwave slammed into him; he had a glimpse of Danny sliding backwards on her stomach as the explosion shoved her off the road. He put up an arm to shield himself from chunks of asphalt and dirt flying at him. The blast blew a crater into the street and flipped the Jeep into the air end over end like a flimsy toy; it was completely engulfed in flames. Squinting against the brightness and the heat, Henry saw both doors on the passenger side flapping open but only one on the driver's side. Then, over the stink of hot metal and burning tires, that smell hit him in the face, forced itself up his nose.

"*Baron!*" Henry jumped to his feet and ran toward the burning Jeep but the heat was too much for him, the heat and the smell, awful, sickening, and all too familiar from his time in the Corps, the smell that told him Baron hadn't made it out with the rest of them.

And now Danny was pulling on his arm, telling him he had to back off, she knew, she knew, but he had to stay back.

"Are you hit?" he asked her.

She shook her head and kept on trying to pull him away from the burning wreckage. Henry looked around, his eyes stinging from the smoke, until he finally found Junior standing on the other side of the street.

In the light from the flames, Henry could see the storm of emotions on his face—horror, fear, guilt, disbelief, betrayal. It hadn't been Henry's chip they had zeroed in on—Junior had removed it. Henry felt his heart break all over again, for Junior, for Danny, for himself, and for Baron.

Junior's eyes met his and for a long moment, something like a powerful current of energy ran between them, holding them there in the terrible light from the burning Jeep. Henry couldn't move, couldn't speak; he could only stare.

You should have run, Henry thought at Junior, and it was almost as if Junior really *were* his younger self and it was possible to tell the twenty-three-year-old Henry Brogan that it wasn't too late to take a different direction. *You should run for your life—your real life, not whatever this is. You should run and never look back.*

And then, as if Junior had heard what Henry was thinking, he turned and ran into the darkness.

CHAPTER 19

Danny was sobbing as she yanked at Henry's arm, trying to get him farther away from the Jeep still burning in the middle of Main Street. "Henry, I'm sorry! I'm so sorry but please, *please*! We have to *go*!"

Henry pushed her hands away, twisted out of her grip. "It's my fault, I brought him into this." He wiped his eyes, stinging from the smoke. The stench of burning tires mixed with *that* smell turned his stomach. "I told you to go home, man—" He broke off as he heard the sound of another vehicle approaching.

"*Henry!*" Danny bellowed, practically in his ear. "We have to go *now*!"

The headlights of a Gemini vehicle cut through the fire and smoke. As it got closer, Henry could see there were several Gemini soldiers hanging off it ready for action; mounted in the center was an M134 Minigun.

But it was the sound of gunfire and glass breaking behind him that stirred him into action. Danny had shot out the front window of a liquor store and she was dragging him toward it. She managed to pull him inside just as the vehicle came to a stop. The soldiers jumped off and fanned out on the street, taking aim.

He and Danny dropped as everyone opened fire.

Bottles exploded, spraying glass and booze in all directions, shelves broke and collapsed, the doors of refrigerated cases cracked and shattered, their contents disintegrating.

Keeping their heads low, the two of them belly-crawled toward the back of the place so that they were practically wiping the floor with their faces. Machine-gun fire shredded the walls, punching out chunks of drywall and wood to mix with the booze and broken glass on the floor. If they kept this up, Henry thought, the Gemini team were actually going to cut the building in half sideways. He and Danny had to get out of here before the entire structure collapsed in on itself.

He looked at Danny, brushed a scrap of wet paper from her cheek. Maybe the alcohol would disinfect any cuts they got from broken bottles. Maybe he could think up some other absurdities to help him avoid wondering how he was going to live with himself after what had happened to Baron.

Henry wrapped his grief for Baron into a tight little package and stowed it away next to Jack Willis and Monroe. He had to concentrate on doing everything he could to make sure the same thing didn't happen to Danny Zakarewski, the exemplary agent who'd never gotten a demerit, recently undercover as a grad student in marine biology. She had signed up to serve her country and instead it was serving her up as toast. She hadn't asked for any of this. Maybe she even wished she really was a grad student in marine biology; he certainly did.

She turned to look at him then and flashed him a grin as they continued to inch forward. He promised her silently that he absolutely would not let her buy it on the floor of a shot-up liquor store; he would get both of them out of there alive. Danny would go home and live a long and fulfilling life, while he was going to live long enough to shoot Clay fucking Verris in the fucking face.

They finally made it to the storeroom. The back door was heavy-duty metal. Yeah, this was a small town, all right—security door in the back, no shutters up front. Henry wondered if the owner was insured for damage due to domestic terrorism—probably not. Most insurance carriers wouldn't cover war or so-called acts of God. No doubt Gemini would take care of all the damage and fix the new giant pothole in the road as well. It probably wouldn't be the first time.

Henry heard more shelves collapsing out on the sales floor as well as the creak and groan of load-bearing walls that hadn't been made to withstand heavy artillery and wouldn't be able to bear their load much longer. He reached up for the door lever and a burst of machine-gun fire nearly took his hand off. He sneaked a quick look behind and saw it was only the Jeep out front now. The soldiers would have circled around to cover the back door. The bastards knew exactly where they were and wanted to keep them pinned down. If the building didn't collapse and bury them alive, the soldiers would either ambush them when they came out or come in and finish them off.

Henry conveyed this to Danny in a combination of whispers and sign language, then reached for the lever a second time. Again he had to yank his hand back while bullets punched into the metal.

When he tried a third time, however, nothing happened. Henry couldn't help grinning. Four thousand rounds per minute was lethal but it ate ammo fast. While the guys out front were reloading, he got the door open and he and Danny slipped out into the alley behind the store, still keeping low.

* * *

From where he stood on the gravel roof of the Masonic Hall in the very center of downtown Glennville, Clay Verris listened to status reports on his comm unit while he kept an eye on the action at street level. Using binoculars, he saw the soldiers had moved around to the back alley behind the liquor store, ready to greet Henry and Zakarewski if they managed to get out. He didn't think they would, not without getting at least winged by the M134.

The back door of the liquor store swung open but Verris couldn't see much else—Brogan and Zakarewski were crawling on their bellies. If they stood up, the soldiers would say hello. It would be a kind of Butch and Sundance moment, only not as cinematic—

His anticipated triumph cut off; underneath the four thousand rpm music of the M134, he heard the sound of police sirens. Glennville's small-town police force was riding to the rescue. They took their police vehicles home with them; it was the sort of thing they did in small towns. After Glennville's station house closed at nine, emergency calls were forwarded to Chief Mitchell's home phone. It must have been ringing off the hook with panicky citizens reporting that World War III had broken out on Main Street.

Verris had intended to call the chief as soon as Henry Brogan's plane had landed but Junior's belated adolescent crisis had distracted him. It was crucial to keep Mitchell and the rest of his Barney Fifes from cluttering up his battlefield. If any of them got hurt, the county authorities would open an investigation and who knew where *that* would end. At the very least, it would be inconvenient.

Verris tapped a button on the comm set he was wearing. "Chief Mitchell? Clay Verris. I need your units to stand down. We're engaging with a terror cell that has a weaponized biological capability."

"*Shit*," Mitchell said, in direct violation of FCC regulations governing acceptable language on police frequencies. Not that Verris was going to file a complaint.

"Federal authorities have been notified and are en route," he told the chief.

"Affirmative. Keep me posted, Clay," the chief said.

"Yes, sir," Verris said in his best just-doing-my-job voice. "Will report back to you shortly. Thank you."

He clicked off before Mitchell could enlarge on how grateful he was that Gemini was on the scene to save Glennville from evil terrorists, or to tell him to call if he and his men could help in any way, although the latter was highly unlikely. If you wanted to keep civilians out of your face, all you had to do was say *weaponized biological capability* and they vanished as if by magic. They wouldn't even ask if they could observe. Nobody in their right mind wanted to be within sight of people infected with Ebola—what if they sneezed while you were downwind? Mitchell was probably hiding under his bed with a ten-gallon bottle of hand sanitizer and a twenty-gallon barrel of Savannah Bourbon.

Now, where the hell was Junior?

Henry and Danny lay on the ground amid some overturned trashcans while the Gemini soldiers fired on them, keeping them pinned down. Maybe Verris planned to come and finish them off personally since Junior wasn't going to do the job. In any case, it allowed Henry to figure out the position of each shooter just by listening. When he had pinpointed each one's location, he conveyed this to Danny in sign language and was gratified to see she knew what he wanted to do.

He and Danny mouthed the countdown together silently: *Three, two, one.*

Go.

They rose up back to back, and took out their targets. Three, two, one.

And that's why a machine gun is no substitute for someone who can actually shoot, Henry told the Gemini soldiers silently as he and Danny ran down the alley to the next building. This one was a lot larger than the liquor store and more substantial, not as easy to destroy with an M134. Henry shot out the lock but just as he opened the door there was a second shot. Danny cried out in pain and fell to her knees with a ragged, bloody hole in one thigh.

Henry looked back toward the liquor store and saw one of the soldiers had dragged himself up on the side of a garbage can and was taking aim, about to fire again.

Henry let out a wordless yell of rage and put a round through the guy's forehead before dragging Danny through the door.

Junior's shoulder hurt like hell. Rolling out of the Jeep had partially reopened the gunshot wound. He could thank the ham-handed medic on the plane for that.

He'd told her to just get the goddam bullet out and close up the hole but she'd tried to insist he get undressed and put on scrubs. He'd had no intention of letting his father see him in *scrubs.* The medic had kept arguing with him about hygiene this and sterile that and he'd finally gotten so frustrated he'd removed the goddam bullet himself with his combat knife. Then he'd told her if she didn't want to close the incision he could handle that, too, with a sewing needle and some dental floss.

For a moment, he thought she might go off on him; instead, she gave a resigned sigh and told him to take his shirt off—just his shirt, he could put it back on later—and lie down. Even though she used glue instead of stitches, she had injected his shoulder with lidocaine before he could tell her not to. She gave him a couple of other injections she claimed were antibiotics but Junior knew there was something extra in them; he could feel analgesics at work.

The medic had probably thought she was doing him a favor. In fact, the drugs had screwed up his sensory control. The painkillers were starting to wear off and his usual techniques for managing pain weren't working as well as usual. And of course she hadn't given him any extra pills for later, expecting him to march over to the infirmary and see the doctor right after they landed as if he were some delicate flower of a civilian who needed to be hospitalized for a mere flesh wound!

Still, he probably shouldn't have parkoured his way up to the roof of the Masonic Hall with his shoulder in that condition. But he knew his father would be up there watching everything and it was the only way to get to him without some bodyguard tipping him off in advance.

It wasn't really that the pain was too much—he had managed to get the better of it so it was now background noise rather than a blaring siren. But it had put him in a foul mood, too foul to tolerate his so-called father's son-I-love-you horseshit. Especially not after that RPG.

Just the sight of Verris standing there looking down on Glennville like he was a heroic general overseeing a battle to decide the fate of the world made Junior want to kick his ass.

Fuck it, he thought and drew his sidearm. "Stand your men down, Pop," he said. "*Now.*"

Verris turned, saw the gun in Junior's hand, and looked positively delighted. "You did the right thing," Verris told him happily. "Getting away from Brogan—"

"I did the *cowardly* thing!" Junior shouted at him. "And it makes me *sick*!"

His so-called father shook his head. "I was asking too much of you," he said in a soothing, reasonable tone. His father was *handling* him again; it made Junior want to punch him. "I see that now. But that doesn't mean you—"

"He deserved better than a missile fired at his car, Pop!" Junior said angrily. "They all did!"

"It doesn't matter what he deserves. He has to die," said Verris, his voice still relentlessly reasonable but with an undertone that suggested Junior was starting to try his patience.

"*Are you gonna call these clowns off?*" Junior demanded. His shoulder was throbbing like a second heart, pumping angry pain all through him.

"No," his father said. "But *you* can. All you have to do is fire that sidearm and take command." He spread his arms; there was a radio in his left hand.

What. The. Fuck? Junior looked from Verris to the radio and back again. Was his father telling him to shoot *him*—kill *him*? Junior had thought he might have to fight Verris and subdue him. But *kill* him? Was this *really* what his father wanted? It didn't make any sense.

Over the years, Verris had been harsh, rigid, immovable, domineering, tyrannical, and sometimes unforgiving, but everything had always made sense— granted, a very twisted kind of sense, like Verris wanting him to kill Henry. That was pretty demented—the whole clone thing was batshit—but he had always been able to follow his father's thinking. Not now, though; he didn't get this at all.

Verris spread his arms a little wider: *I'm the target, shoot me.* "Well?" he said.

Junior had never done anything that didn't make sense to him and he wasn't going to start now. He holstered his weapon.

Verris's hopeful expression turned to disappointment. Junior decided he could live with that. If this was his idea of being a good father, God only knew what the man thought a bad one would do.

But he could show Verris that a good soldier could do the right thing without shooting his own CO. Junior approached him slowly and reached for the radio he was still holding out to one side.

Verris seemed to move impossibly fast as he reached around Junior, put his free hand inside the back of his shirt and yanked hard, pulling him down onto the gravel surface of the roof.

"I don't think so," he said, stepping back from him easily, lightly, almost as if he were dancing.

Junior pushed himself to his feet, trying to ignore his screaming shoulder and the feel of blood oozing from the wound, which had opened a little more.

"A loving, dedicated, *present* father," Junior said, making it an accusation.

Verris darted forward and gave him a hard right that rattled his teeth. Junior staggered back a few steps but managed to stay on his feet. Before he could get his fists up, however, Verris pounced again and got both hands around his throat. Junior returned the favor.

It was like grabbing a handful of writhing snakes made of cartilage and muscle, all fighting to get away from him. The old man was in exceptional condition and crazy-strong—his fingers felt like steel bands. If he couldn't break away, his dedicated, loving, *present* father was going to crush his throat, and then maybe pitch his body off the roof.

His vision started to dim. If he fell over, Verris would land on top and that would be the end. Fortunately, his sense of balance was still functioning—he let his hands fall away, then stamped hard on Verris's instep while simultaneously punching both the man's forearms upward, breaking his hold. His father staggered back and they locked eyes.

Felt that, didn't you, Junior thought at him. *Come at me again, you'll feel worse.*

But Verris didn't come at him. He gave a short laugh and pointedly turned his back to look down at the street again, letting him know he was too busy to waste any more time teaching him a lesson he should have already learned.

Junior lowered his head and charged. The two of them went down hard, their bodies plowing a shallow trench in the gravel. Junior felt a hot spike of pain in his shoulder and clenched his teeth, refusing to cry out. Verris twisted around underneath him, grabbed him, and dug his thumb into the wound.

He flung himself away from Verris, who was on him immediately, trying to grab his shoulder again. Junior heaved him off, rolled away, and started to push himself to his feet when his side exploded in an agony that made the world disappear in a momentary whiteout. For a second, he thought his father had used a cattle prod on him, then realized it had actually been a hard punch to the kidney.

Junior fell over and Verris gouged his injured shoulder with his thumb again. Blood saturated the bandage and soaked through his shirt as the wound opened a little more but Junior still refused to cry out. He hit the back of Verris's elbow, forcing him to straighten his arm and let go. Junior grabbed for him, intending to put his arm in a bone-breaker, but Verris's other hand came up and threw a handful of gravel and dirt in his face.

Rubbing his eyes frantically, Junior kicked out with both feet at where he thought Verris was and connected only with air. Ignoring another bolt of pain in his shoulder, he rolled away and started to get up, only to have Verris horse-collar him again. His head hit the gravel, which broke the skin in several different places. Junior sat up, blood running down the back of his neck. Verris elbowed him in the face and everything went black as his jaw slid sideways.

When his vision cleared he was flat on his back and his dedicated, loving father was present on his chest, punching his face into mincemeat. "—trying—" *punch* "—to make you—" *punch* "—a *man*—"

Father of the year, Junior thought, and dug deep for the strength he needed to show Verris he'd already done that himself.

Junior brought his legs up, twisted the right one around Verris's neck and torqued him away. Scrambling to his feet, Junior saw the assault rifle he'd dropped earlier. In one continuous motion, he swept it up, pivoted on the ball of his foot and met Verris's lunge by planting the butt end squarely in the middle of his grinning face.

Verris staggered back, wobbled, but stayed upright. Junior flipped the rifle and pointed the business end at him.

"Well?" Verris said. "Go ahead. You've got your target in your crosshairs! *Do it!*"

He deserved it, Junior thought. Hell, Verris was *literally* asking for it—and yet he couldn't.

Why the hell not? What the hell was stopping him?

Screw it. Junior flipped the rifle and slammed the butt into Verris's face again. Verris crumpled to the gravel without a sound. Junior slung the rifle, sprinted for the edge of the roof and parkoured down to street level.

* * *

As soon as the kid was gone, Verris pushed himself to his feet. That last blow had stunned him a little but it hadn't been full force. Right before impact, Junior pulled his punch. The kid couldn't even hit him with all his strength, let alone shoot him. Obviously his duties as a father weren't finished.

Verris turned to his left. Another Gemini soldier stood alone on a neighboring roof. He was dressed in a full-body suit made of next-generation Kevlar, his face covered by a more compact version of Junior's night-vision gas mask. Here was the soldier that military commanders dreamed of but never imagined could actually exist—the perfect fighter. And this was the perfect time to turn him loose. Verris nodded, then jerked his head toward the street.

The masked soldier hopped over the edge of the roof and bounded down the wall as easily as an athlete might have sprinted along a road. He hit the street and kept going, his strides so long that he hardly seemed to touch the ground. When he came to the hardware store, he ran up the outside to the roof without breaking stride.

Verris smiled. Everybody was going to learn—or, in Junior's case, relearn—a lesson tonight. It remained to be seen who would live through it.

For a small town, Glennville had one hell of a big hardware store, Henry thought as he finished Danny's tourniquet. It was makeshift—a ripped-up apron with a screwdriver for a windlass, secured with a piece of rope. A store of this size probably had a first-aid kit with a commercially made tourniquet but there was no time to look for it.

He got Danny on her feet and helped her limp away from the exit and farther into the store. There was at least one more rear exit as well as a loading dock—more than the two of them could defend. They had to find a place to hole up until he could get Danny to a hospital. That was assuming they got out of here alive, of course, something Henry had categorized as extremely difficult but still possible. Then Danny had been shot in the thigh and that changed everything.

Henry sneaked a look at her; he knew from experience that a tourniquet hurt like hell but she didn't make a sound except for an occasional short intake of breath.

At the end of a long shelf of flowerpots and bags of soil, Henry spotted a step stool on wheels. "Take a break," Henry said. He eased her down onto it, then crouched low to peer left and right along the wide aisle running crosswise in front of them. The store seemed empty—he didn't see or hear anything to indicate otherwise—but Henry was sure they weren't alone. If he'd been in command, he'd have stationed a couple of guys here. He and Danny hadn't exactly sneaked in without a sound so whoever was in here probably had a fairly good idea of their locations. Dammit.

Could he and Danny get to the firearms department before the Gemini guys caught up with them? There wouldn't be any sophisticated military weapons but kneecapping someone with a shotgun was an effective defense, if rather messy. He might make it alone—

No. A much better idea was getting them both out of here. Danny was more likely to survive escaping than last stand at the Remington counter.

"We should keep moving," Danny said and started to get up.

"Stay there," Henry told her. "I walk, you roll." He held her shoulders to steer her across the aisle.

"Maybe we should find a shopping cart," she said with a small, trembly laugh.

"No way," Henry replied. "I always get the one with the wobbly wheel. Drives me nuts."

She gave another shaky laugh as they came to another cross-aisle and stopped again while Henry checked it out. Still nothing. They crossed the aisle into wiring and electricals. A plastic sign on the shelf showed a smiling cartoon light bulb with a word balloon that said: *Always Stay Grounded!*

"How zen," Danny said between clenched teeth.

"If you say so." Henry brought her to a stop in the middle of the row when they both heard a very faint squeak, the sound of a rubber sole on clean floor tiles.

Henry pushed Danny's head down so she was bent double and fired through the shelf beside them. Plastic and rubber fragments flew in all directions as the shelving collapsed and he heard two bodies hit the floor. He peered through the wreckage of the shelves; they were gone. He'd gotten them before they could even fire a shot—that was the good news. The bad news: he had just let everyone in the immediate vicinity know where he and Danny were.

Danny tried to stand up but Henry pushed her down again, this time more gently. "Did you hear them come in?" she asked. He shook his head. "Maybe they were already here, waiting."

"Then why didn't they take us out sooner?" Henry said.

Danny shrugged. "Not enough of a challenge?"

Henry's blood turned to ice water. That might not have been as absurd as Danny had meant it to sound. Nobody outside Gemini knew what Verris was really up to, what he was doing with the soldiers under his command. Making a better soldier was a lot different than making a better mousetrap, and how Verris was going to accomplish that wouldn't be pretty.

"Henry?" Danny's eyes were wide and worried, more concerned for him than the wound in her thigh. Her face was paler and she was sagging on the step stool. If she didn't get medical attention soon, he was going to lose her, and she knew it as well as he did. She had to be pretty scared but she was still toughing it out, playing the badass.

He could have used a partner like her, Henry thought. Monroe was good—*had* been good, he corrected himself with a pang—but Danny Zakarewski was a WMD.

"How many rounds have you got left?" Henry asked her.

She looked apologetic. "Five or six."

"Okay, here's what we're going to do," Henry said briskly, and rolled her to the end of the shelf, where she had a view of the next cross-aisle through a rack of fuses. "You hold here and watch the choke point. I'm going to find a way out for us—"

Danny caught his arm in a grip that was unexpectedly strong. "Sorry, but you're not going *anywhere* unless I go, too." She unslung her rifle, put it down on the floor, and drew her sidearm. "I'm *not* letting you die out there alone."

Henry felt a rush of affection for her. She was really something—a fucking lion.

"But you can check my tourniquet again. That would be okay," she added.

He did so. It was still secure. She wasn't losing any more blood but it wouldn't be getting any less painful. They had to get out of here before the pain became too much for her.

"Danny, I'm sorry," he said suddenly.

"For what?" she asked him, surprised.

"For dragging you into all this."

"*I* was the one surveilling *you*," she said with a small shaky laugh.

If she hadn't been injured, he would have pulled her into a bear hug. "Anyway, sorry," he said, looking down at her wound.

"*I* don't regret it," she told him.

Now it was Henry's turn to be surprised. "Seriously? Come on, if you had to do it over again and we were back on that dock, and I asked you to meet me at Pelican Point, you'd still say yes?"

"Hell no," Danny said with another shaky laugh. "I'm not an idiot. I'm just not sorry that I did, that's all." She laughed again. "Now let's shoot our way out of this so we can go get a drink."

Henry's grin was fleeting—he heard a door open at the rear of the store, although he wasn't sure whether it was the one they'd come in through or another one, the one he might have found if Danny had let him go. He gave her hand a squeeze and she squeezed back. He listened closely and heard the very faint noise of four or five soldiers fanning out. Danny yanked hard on his arm and mouthed, *Down*, then rolled off the stool onto the floor just as they opened fire from three separate positions.

Merchandise exploded, shelves burst into fragments, collapsed, toppled over, caved in—today was definitely a bad day for retail in Glennville. Henry rolled Danny backwards with him; she was having trouble keeping her bad leg from dragging on the floor. There were five shooters and they kept coming, spraying everything in front of them with automatic weapons fire. The noise itself was punishing, beating his ears, his head, his whole body as the three shooters converged on him and Danny. He had to get her out of this, he thought desperately as they returned fire; he had to get her to a hospital before she passed out, before the goddam tourniquet wrecked her leg so bad they had to amputate.

Unfortunately, he had just fired his next-to-last bullet.

Suddenly one of the Gemini soldiers went down, blood spurting from his neck. *Good one, Danny,* he thought, and shifted to line up two of the remaining shooters in front of him. If he only had one bullet left, he was going to make it count double. Henry took aim; his last bullet went through the eye of one Gemini soldier and kept going through the eye of the one behind him. And now both his and Danny's weapons were going *click-click-click*.

Henry took a breath. "You were a great partner, Danny."

She nodded, then her face twisted in pain. Her hand found his and they held onto each other, watching the remaining two soldiers advancing on them. They had stopped firing for the moment but their rifles were up and ready. Were they just saving ammo now that he and Danny were out? Or were they supposed to hold them until Verris got there?

Danny deserved a lot better than this, Henry thought. If there was any justice in the world at all, her life wouldn't be ending before it had even really begun—

Abruptly, there were two new bursts of machine-gun fire from *behind* the Gemini guys. Henry's jaw fell open as they dropped to the ground so fast they probably didn't know they were dead yet. But it was another couple of seconds before it registered on him that it was Junior who had taken the Gemini soldiers out, Junior coming over to him and Danny where they had just been waiting to die amidst hardware wreckage, handing them fresh ammunition.

Henry's hands automatically reloaded his weapon with no help from his brain; good thing— he was too boggled to think. He'd watched his own death come at him and then veer away more than once, and it always left him shaken.

"Uh... thank you," he told Junior after a bit.

"What he said," Danny added, sounding equally blown out.

Junior grimaced. "Sorry I ran."

"It's been a tough night." Henry laughed weakly. "Where's—"

"You okay?" Junior asked Danny, looking at her leg.

"Still kickin'," she said. "With my *other* foot."

Henry felt his heart rate come down and his breathing slow. He had a job to do and someone to protect. "How many more are out there?"

"I don't know," Junior said.

"What about Verris?"

"Out of commission."

"But alive?" Henry asked.

Junior nodded, looking ashamed.

"Okay," Henry said. "There'll be more coming. Help me get her up—"

Danny put up both hands and shook her head emphatically. "*No*. I can't run any more. Can *you*?" She drew her combat knife from its ankle sheath.

Henry looked at Junior, who nodded. They picked up their rifles and got down on their bellies, Henry facing the back of the store, Junior watching their six, and Danny keeping an eye on their three and nine. In the brief moment of quiet, Henry tapped his rifle stock twice just as Junior tapped his own three times. Then they looked at each other, surprised.

Danny smacked both their backs and gestured at the store around them: *Pay attention*. Henry smiled briefly, bracing himself for whatever was coming up next.

As it turned out, the attack came *down*.

There was a crash followed by a shower of broken glass. Shielding his face with one hand, Henry looked up to see a dark figure descending on a line, firing as he did. Henry,

Danny, and Junior scattered in three different directions; Henry glimpsed the soles of Danny's boots as she dived behind a rack of tools but Junior had disappeared completely. Junior was most likely to come out of this alive, Henry thought. Danny might make it out with Junior's help, but even if she did, the hole in her leg might kill her anyway.

Meanwhile, the new attacker was only going after him.

Bullets chased him up one aisle and around the end of a long set of shelves, where he stopped short, watching as the guy shot through the shelves in case Henry was panicky-stupid enough to run down the other side. Then the killer stomped over the wreckage, firing in a wide arc around himself. Henry took advantage of the noise to get behind him unnoticed and fired a short burst at his back.

The killer jerked slightly, whirled on Henry, and returned the favor several times over. Henry ran up the aisle, vaulted over the wreckage of another set of shelves; his feet came down on some plastic fragments and skidded out from under him. As he fell forward, Henry tucked and rolled head over heels in a series of rapid tumbles while bullets kicked up chips of concrete under the floor covering.

The weapons fire cut off and Henry heard him drop the rifle. In the brief pause before the shooter switched to a sidearm, Henry bounced to his feet and found himself in varnishes and paints. He grabbed up some small cans and hurled them at the guy as he ran. Despite the accuracy of Henry's aim, however, it seemed as if his attacker barely noticed them bouncing off his shoulders, his chest, even his head.

Henry tried sweeping a whole lot of cans off a shelf hoping to trip him but the guy just tromped over them, kicking them aside.

I'm gonna need a bigger can, Henry thought as he reached a shelf of gallon containers. But they were a lot harder to throw and the guy kept firing as he batted them away. Abruptly, there was a different burst of machine-gun fire, coming from behind the shooter. He broke stride, staggered a bit, then turned to fire at Junior, trading bursts with him until they both ran out.

Okay, buddy, Henry thought, *let's see if your only talent is firing a weapon you don't even have to aim.*

He ran back to varnishes in time to see the guy had found Junior and was using his head to make a dent in a five-gallon can of weatherproofing. Henry took a running jump and launched himself at the guy feet first, the same move he'd used to steal the motorcycle in Cartagena. Except the guy bent his knees and leaned back at an angle that should have been impossible for anyone to maintain without falling over. But somehow he did. Henry sailed past him and landed on Junior.

Henry rolled away from him but not quickly enough. A hard kick missed his head but caught his shoulder blade; Henry winced, feeling something crack as he went sprawling on his belly. He scrambled up, rotated his shoulders to see if anything major was broken. Mobility wasn't impaired but it hurt like hell. *Everything* hurt like hell hurt right now, but at least it all hurt the same, nothing worse than anything else. The good news was, it would all hurt a hell of a lot more tomorrow.

If he lasted that long.

Henry drew his knife, and in the corner of his eye he saw Junior do the same. The masked soldier made a quick motion and produced knives in both hands. That goddam mask; when you couldn't see your opponent's face, you were fighting half-blind. He had to get close enough to tear the fucker's mask off. It looked like a more compact version of Junior's night-vision gas mask. The night vision he could understand but had the guy really expected to get tear-gassed?

He feinted to one side, then the other, making little slashes in the air. Junior feigned a lunge, stamped his foot in an old fencing move meant to distract an opponent; their masked opponent didn't fall for it. Facing two guys with knives didn't seem to faze him at all—his posture showed no defensive tension, no stiffness. It was as if he were sure Henry and Junior were holding rubber knives. Henry decided to disabuse him of that notion.

He backed up, then took a few running steps forward. He could see the masked guy steady himself, still holding Junior off while he prepared to bury his knife in Henry's throat. At the last moment, however, Henry dropped to his knees and slid under his arm. It was something he'd secretly wanted to try ever since he'd seen someone do it in a movie.

There was no tiling on the floor here, just cement treated with some kind of sealant—not an ideal surface for a flashy slide. Henry felt the cement scrape through his trousers and sand off some skin. But then, it wasn't exactly classic fighting technique—a Krav Maga instructor probably wouldn't have approved—but he managed to slash the masked killer's thigh without getting slashed himself.

To Henry's surprise, the guy didn't make a sound as he looked down at the gash in his leg—no cry of pain, not so much as a gasp or a grunt; the injury could have been on someone else's leg for all that it affected him. A chill ran down Henry's spine, more intense than a mere goose walking over his grave. Who the hell had trained this guy, the Manchurian Candidate? The Terminator?

Junior took advantage of the attacker's momentary lapse of attention to circle around behind him. Realizing what Junior was going to do, Henry pushed himself to a standing position and tried to keep the guy focused on himself while Junior vaulted the ruins of a shelf for a flying kick with both feet. But unbelievably, half a second before Junior would have hit him, the guy *ducked*. As Junior sailed over him, the guy's leg shot out—his *wounded* leg— and kicked Junior hard in the lower back.

Henry shook his head slightly, unsure if he had really just seen that. Junior rolled over as the masked fighter came towards him, and somehow heaved himself into a backwards roll, barely escaping a driving punch to his crotch.

Oh, so it's that *kind of fight,* Henry thought; as if there were any other kind. That slash to the thigh still wasn't slowing the guy down. He'd also lost one of his knives, but Henry didn't count on that giving him or Junior any sort of advantage. Junior sprang to his feet and immediately charged the guy with his tackling move. The guy raised one leg and instead of taking him down, Junior hit his knee face first.

Henry launched himself forward to slide again, this time baseball-style, intending to sweep the guy's legs out from under him. But before Henry reached him, the guy *flipped* over his head, tumbling in midair in a way that somehow managed to be more casual than showy. He came down behind Henry and kicked his shoulder blade again.

For a few seconds, the world turned blinding white while the nerve in his upper back shrieked in a way that sounded a lot like a human voice. *Shut the hell up,* Henry ordered it and struggled to his feet. So much for paints, varnish, and weatherproofing, he thought; maybe he'd have better luck in power tools. If he could find them.

He pushed himself into a stumbling run. Up ahead, he saw a rack of circular saw blades. *Let's see if he can catch a Frisbee,* Henry thought, as a nasty grin spread over his face.

Then something large and hard glanced off the top of his head and he was sprawling on the cement, scraping his palms and knees. What the *fuck*—

Henry twisted around to see the guy heaving another gallon of paint at him and rolled out of the way before it could smash his face in. And *still* the guy kept on coming at him, like killing Henry Brogan was the one and only thing he had been put on this earth to do.

Junior's words came back to him: *My orders are to kill you.*

Did Clay Verris have a whole platoon of guys dedicated—no, *programmed*—to kill him? Then, as if things had to be even more absurd, he looked up and saw Danny almost directly above him on a mezzanine. He hadn't even noticed there *was* an upstairs—and how the hell had she made it up there with her leg? Her face was shiny and paler than he'd ever seen. Was she crazy from blood loss? What the hell did she think she was doing?

As if on cue, she heaved a gas canister over the railing, straight at the killer. Just as it hit him, she fired. The canister exploded, engulfing the killer in flames.

That's for Baron, you bastard, Henry thought as the sprinkler system went off.

But instead of falling down and dying like a normal assassin, the masked guy actually *walked out* of the flames, still hell-bent on killing anyone and everyone.

Henry's jaw dropped and his heart went into overdrive as he looked around desperately. He was in an enormous hardware store and he had somehow managed to end up against the back wall, empty-handed and unable to get to any of a thousand things he could use as a weapon.

Yeah, it was *definitely* time to retire. Except it didn't look like he was going to live long enough—

His gaze fell on a fire extinguisher. Oh, great—that would be a big help. Just not for him.

But the thing next to it might be.

Or it might not, but he pushed the thought aside. This was what he had—a moment ago, he'd had nothing. He grabbed it and flattened himself against the wall. The gas canister had been a good gambit, clever as hell, and if they'd been fighting any other killer, it would have worked. Henry decided he was going to find out why it hadn't, even if it killed him.

Oh, God, that smell, *that fucking smell*; his stomach twisted like a corkscrew and he tasted bile in the back of his throat. He had reached his limit for that fucking smell; if the killer didn't get him, he might puke himself to death.

No, he didn't smell *anything*, he told himself as he stepped away from the wall and swung the fire axe as hard as he could, burying it in the killer's chest.

The guy's legs flew out from under him and he crashed to the floor on his back. Somehow Danny was downstairs again, gliding over to Henry on her stool just as Junior appeared. That fucking smell was even stronger, even though the man on the floor was no longer burning. He was struggling to breathe, but bizarrely there was no moaning, no crying. He wasn't even writhing in pain.

The indoor rain shower petered out. Henry looked from him to Junior. "I'll say this for your old man. He knows how to train a soldier." He crouched down and pulled off the guy's mask.

Everything stopped.

The guy on the floor gazed up at them, his expression dazed, like he was seeing something beyond his understanding. There were probably lots of things he didn't understand, Henry thought; concepts and realities that a person had to grow into, situations that only someone with many years of experience could make sense of. This guy was just too young. Danny and Junior were kids to Henry but this guy was a *real* kid—he couldn't have been any older than eighteen. Only it was himself, Henry Brogan, at eighteen. Or Junior at eighteen. Or both.

Henry had been sure Verris wouldn't stop at one clone but it gave him no pleasure to be right. Junior looked like he'd just taken a hard blow to the head with a sledgehammer. It was one thing to know something in the abstract but quite another to see the proof lying on the floor with a fucking axe in his chest.

Welcome to my world, Junior, Henry said silently. *It only gets weirder from here.*

Suddenly, an intense protectiveness toward Junior and Danny swept over him, followed by guilt for failing to keep them safe. Henry wondered if this was how parents felt when they were driving their kids to the emergency room after they'd fallen down and broken their arms.

Or maybe it was more like what his mother had been feeling when she'd jumped into the Philadelphia municipal pool to save him from drowning.

She hadn't seen his father every time she looked at him, Henry realized suddenly—*he* had. And his mother hadn't been able to save him from his own wrong-headed thinking like she'd saved him from drowning. That had always been up to him, and it still was.

All of this passed through his mind in a heartbeat. A shrink might have called it a great breakthrough but he wasn't in a shrink's office, he was in a shot-up hardware store with two clones, one of whom had burned alive and was now dying with an axe in his chest, and an agent about to go into shock from a gunshot wound.

Damn, this had to be some kind of record for the most simultaneous crises during the first week of retirement.

Danny was bent over the dying clone looking at all his injuries in horrified incredulity. Ms. First Aid, Henry thought; even if she'd still had her burn bag with her, she wouldn't have found anything in it to help him.

"Don't you feel *pain*?" she asked the clone.

The dying clone looked from Danny to Henry with a puzzled frown, and then to Junior. Obviously Verris hadn't let him in on the family secret. Henry wondered what Verris had called him—Junior 2.0? The Next Big Thing?

And what had he called himself?

Well, they would never know. The clone's eyes fell closed and his breathing simply stopped. As if he'd died peacefully at home in bed, not in the wreckage of a hardware store with burns all over his body and an axe in his chest.

For a long moment, they were all silent. He had to take care of them, Henry thought, looking at Danny and Junior's shell-shocked faces. It was up to him to help them get through this and then put it behind them, although he had no idea how. Nowhere in any of his training, formal or informal, had there ever been anything about what to do when your clone tried to kill you but you killed him first.

"I don't know why you're so angry with me. You were the inspiration for all of this."

Junior turned from the dead clone on the floor to see his dedicated, loving, *present* father ambling toward them in an easy, casual way. He looked like he had dropped in to pick up some tools for his latest project and he just happened to have a semi-automatic weapon with him.

"You okay, son?" Verris asked Junior.

Junior blinked at him. What the hell did Verris expect him to say to that—*Sure, Dad, but I think I need a hug?*

But Verris had already turned to Henry. "Know where I got the idea?" he said. "It was in Khafji." Verris was actually smiling as he set his weapon down on a nearby shelf, one of the few that were still standing. "Watching you go house to house, wishing I had a whole *division* of soldiers as good as you, wondering if that could be possible. You should be flattered."

Henry gave a single, humorless laugh. "*You* should be *dead*."

Verris chuckled, as if Henry had said something witty. "You saw what I saw over there: friends being sent home in pine boxes or struggling with life-changing injuries. And the atrocities. Why should we accept that if there's a better way?"

Keeping his eyes on Henry, he moved closer to Junior. "And look what we created." He gestured at Junior, like a game-show host showing off the grand prize; it made Junior want to slap his face until his head fell off. "He's got *both* of us in him. Don't you think your country *deserves* a perfect version of you?"

"There *is* no perfect version of me," Henry snapped. "Or *him*—" he nodded at Junior. "Or *anybody*."

"No?" Verris looked down at the dead clone, his face sad. "*He* was on his way to Yemen—the perfect soldier for the job. Instead, thanks to you, his place will be taken by someone with *parents*. Someone who feels pain and fear— which we had edited *out* of this soldier—someone with just as many weaknesses as the terrorists we're trying to kill. You're going to tell me that's better?"

Junior's own words came back to him: *You made a person out of another person.*

Except a *person* had parents. A *person* felt pain and fear. If Verris had edited those things out of this soldier, what was left that made him a *person*?

"You're talking about *people*, Clay," Henry was saying. "Screwing with their humanity to make them into your idea of the perfect soldier."

Verris nodded as if he thought Henry was finally getting it. "Why not? Think how many American families we could spare. Nobody's son or daughter would ever have to die. Vets wouldn't ever come home with PTSD and kill themselves. We could keep the whole world safe without any actual grief. So who would I be hurting?"

"You hurt *him*," Henry said, gesturing at the dead man on the floor. "Like you hurt Junior. Like you hurt *me*. You can't just *use* people and throw them away—suck them dry, take their *humanity*, leave them with nothing—"

"Henry..." Verris shook his head, looking disappointed that the source material for his magnificent clone project didn't understand after all. "This is the most *humane* thing we've ever done."

Junior had had enough. "How many more of me are running around out there?" he demanded.

"*None*." Verris seemed surprised by the question. "There's only *one* you, Junior."

Junior and Henry looked at each other; he gave Henry a barely perceptible nod to let him know he wasn't buying it and Henry did the same.

"*He* was just a weapon," Verris made a dismissive gesture at the dead man. "*You* are my *son*—and I love you as much as any father ever loved any kid."

Henry was right, Junior thought as he drew his Glock; Verris *should* be dead. "I didn't have a father," he told Verris. "Goodbye, Clay—"

Like that, Henry's hand was on his, his touch gentle but strong, making him lower the gun. Junior stared at him in amazement. Henry shook his head.

"So what the hell *do* we do with him—turn him in?" Junior felt as if he were boiling with rage inside, on the verge of exploding. "You know they're not going to try him and they sure won't shut down his lab. We have to end this right now!"

"Look at me," Henry said.

He didn't want to, didn't want to look at anything. The only thing he wanted to see was Clay Verris's face when he pulled the trigger.

"*Look at me.*" Henry's voice was calm, even tender, and Junior obeyed. "You pull that trigger and you're going to break something inside of yourself that will never get fixed."

Junior gazed into Henry's eyes; they were so much like his own and yet Henry had seen so much more, *knew* so much more. He was only starting to understand how much he *didn't* know. But one thing he knew for certain: Henry had never lied to him. Clay Verris, however, had lied about everything, even about who he really was.

"Don't," Henry said. "Let it go. Give it to me."

Henry's hand was still pressing down on his, steadily but gently, not trying to overpower him but to show him, help him. All the resistance drained out of Junior and he lowered the gun.

"You don't want those ghosts," Henry said as he took the Glock from him. "Trust me."

Then he turned to Verris and shot him.

Verris dropped with a neat hole just above his eyebrows and a much larger, messier wound in the back of his head, where the bullet had exited with most of his brains and half his skull.

Junior gaped at Henry, wide-eyed, unable to move or speak.

But speaking wasn't necessary. Henry jerked a thumb at the back door. Junior nodded and they carried Danny out between them.

CHAPTER 20

Standing at the Copper Ground counter, Janet Lassiter was beyond pissed off and on the fast track to meltdown.

Every day there was another crisis she had to deal with, another five-alarm fire the agency and/or Clay Fucking Verris expected her to put out with nothing more than a squirt gun and half a pail of sand—and more often than not, the squirt gun was loaded with gasoline and the sand was actually gunpowder.

Yet somehow she always figured out how to pull it all together and keep the whole goddam shit-show ticking right along when she could have called in sick. Or suddenly decided to take all sixty-four weeks of vacation time she had built up. She could have even quit outright, walked away and never looked back. Talk about AMF! That would do it for the whole sorry bunch of them, Gemini included. But no, she kept coming in every day without fail. Good old dependable Janet Lassiter, lifeguard at the covert intelligence swimming pool, where there was no shallow end and everyone was always in over their heads.

And did anyone appreciate it? Did they *hell*. The whole time she'd been in this job, the closest thing she'd ever gotten to a thank you was—well, she couldn't remember any more. The job had eaten her life and rewarded her with constipation, gingivitis, and high blood pressure, not to mention the never-ending joys of working in a boys' club, with Clay Verris as the head boy.

So with all she had to put up with, was a goddam latte every morning *really* too much to ask? Ten minutes she'd been waiting for her soy latte—*ten minutes*, which put her behind schedule. She'd already paid but it wouldn't ruin her if she just walked out and went somewhere else. The stupid barista would probably call her name three times, then drink it herself.

But dammit she didn't *want* to go somewhere else. Copper Ground was a goddam hipster hangout but she didn't mind too much because the coffee was actually good, they never ran out of soy milk, and, most importantly, the place was closer and more convenient to her office than any other coffee shop. But this was the third day in a row they'd kept her waiting so long she was running late.

When she'd complained, they'd said they were working shorthanded, very sorry for the inconvenience. The *inconvenience*? They had no idea what inconvenience really was. Dammit, this was *coffee*. She *needed* coffee to help her face another day full of things that everyone said couldn't get worse actually getting worse. What the hell was so goddam hard about making a cup of goddam coffee? It wasn't goddam rocket science. Hell, it wasn't even *government admin*.

"Hey!" she said finally as the barista got started on yet another order that wasn't hers.

"Yes?" The woman looked up with a perfect corporate smile.

"My *coffee*?"

"Coming right up!" the barista said with perfect corporate cheer as she handed a cup to someone else. *Again*.

"Yeah? *When*?" Lassiter demanded.

The barista's corporate smile faltered slightly. "Just a few folks ahead of you, then I'll be happy to—"

"Jesus," Lassiter turned away, fuming. This was hopeless, she thought; if she had to wait, she might as well do it sitting down. She took a step toward her usual table, then froze.

Some woman—some *bitch* was sitting in *her* chair, at *her* window, looking at *her* lousy view of downtown Savannah. All the morning regulars knew that was *her* place. Who the hell did this bitch think she was?

Then she turned around and Lassiter found out.

"Surprise—I survived." Agent Zakarewski gave her the thousand-watt smile of someone who didn't suffer from gingivitis, constipation or high blood pressure. "Sorry."

In Del Patterson's opinion, the best thing about DC bars was how perceptive the bartenders were. They knew when you didn't want to talk about the game or complain about your kids or your ex or the job (which he couldn't even admit to having). They just served you drinks, made sure you didn't run dry, and let you go to hell in your own way. Going to hell was a very lengthy process and DC bartenders knew better than to interrupt you while you were building up momentum.

When the can of Coca-Cola appeared on the bar in front of him, Patterson thought he had to be seeing things—a pesky hallucination from a guilty conscience, which always picked the goddamnedest times to wake up and tug his sleeve. He closed his eyes. *You're a day late and a dollar short,* he told his conscience. *Now get lost and don't come back without a warrant.*

But when he opened his eyes, the can was still there, and none other than Henry Brogan was sitting on the stool next to him. This was no hallucination—as guilty as Patterson's conscience was, it didn't have this degree of wattage.

"You know better," Henry said, sliding the glass of whiskey over to himself.

Patterson gave a short, humorless laugh. "Surprised you give a shit."

"Well, a bunch of assassins *did* try to kill me on your watch," Henry said, chuckling. "But that doesn't mean I want to see you drink yourself to death."

Yeah, that was Henry, Patterson thought, feeling worse. The man was full of integrity and decency, qualities Patterson was pretty sure were innate. He had no idea how the DIA had managed to get their hooks into someone like Henry but he was pretty sure everyone involved would burn in hell for it, himself included.

"The Gemini lab's been dismantled," Patterson said. "The cloning program is history."

"And Junior?" Henry asked. His voice was light but with an undertone that let Patterson know there was a lot riding on whether he liked the answer.

"Junior's untouchable," Patterson said. "No one will bother him, ever. And we checked— there are no more clones."

Henry nodded. "What about you?"

Patterson dipped his head noncommittally, suppressing the urge to tell him to stop being so goddam decent. "Internal Affairs called. I'm looking at charges. But if I bury Janet, I can make a deal."

"She earned it," Henry said.

Patterson nodded glumly. He started to say something, thought better of it, tried to say something else and still couldn't find the words. He took another breath.

"I'm really sorry, Henry," he said finally, and winced at how utterly lame that sounded.

But to his surprise, Henry offered his hand and said, "Take care, Del."

Goddammit, Henry was going to beat him to death with decency, Del thought as he took it. "You too." He placed his other hand briefly over Henry's. "And, uh, happy retirement."

CHAPTER 21

Sitting on a bench in the middle of the City College campus, Henry thought, *What a difference six months makes.*

Not a phrase from which songs were made—it was too sensible, too realistic, lacking in lyrical drama. But people didn't live in songs. It took time to recover, for bones to knit and wounds to heal, for bruises to fade and fears to subside. Twenty-four little hours couldn't possibly cut it. Even six months might not be quite long enough to recuperate completely but it was a pretty good start.

Another good start was the name on the passport he was holding: Jackson Verris. Henry had initially been surprised the kid had decided to keep the surname. But after a little more thought, he realized it wasn't all that surprising. Having a lousy father wasn't a rare thing. Personally, Henry figured the lousy-father rate at fifty percent, give or take, and hoped he wasn't underestimating. He had firsthand knowledge about lousy fathers and he'd still been Henry Brogan all his life. You were who you were. He wasn't his father and Jackson Verris wasn't his.

Like the man said, what's in a name? Probably the same as what was in life—whatever you put into it.

Okay, he was getting *way* too heavy now, Henry thought, and slipped the passport back into the manila envelope with the rest of the paperwork. Maybe it was the environment influencing him to get cerebral, although City College wasn't exactly an ivory tower. Ever since Budapest, however, Henry had acquired a more conscious respect for higher education; it was something he wanted for Junior. Correction: Jackson.

"Hey," said a familiar voice behind him.

"Hey, yourself," Henry said as Danny sat down beside him. "Good to see you. Congrats on the promotion. I hear the DIA's got big plans for you. Think you're up to it?"

"After you?" Danny laughed. "I'm pretty sure I can handle anything."

There were a few more lines around her eyes, Henry noticed; some from laughing, more from worry, reminding him of Jack Willis. Although he was sure things would come out a lot better for her.

"How about you?" Danny asked. "How have *you* been?"

"Just got back from Cartagena," he said. "Settled Baron's estate, scattered his ashes in the Caribbean. All I want to do now is put some good in the world, you know? I've just got to figure out how."

Danny patted his arm. "You'll get there. How are you sleeping these days?" She was still smiling but her voice had turned serious; it went with her smile-worry lines.

"Better," Henry said truthfully.

"No ghosts?"

"Not for a while," he said. "I've stopped avoiding mirrors, too." He was starting to feel a little uncomfortable now. Danny would have told him that after all they'd been through together, neither of them had anything to feel ill at ease about. No doubt she was right about that but he still found it difficult to talk about certain things and no matter how close they were, he probably always would.

But before he got stuck trying to find a way to change the subject, the subject changed itself. "Speaking of mirrors," he said, looking past her with a grin.

Danny turned to see Junior—ahem, Jackson—coming toward them with some friends, a guy and two young women. The other three seemed to be on their way to somewhere else; they paused and had a quick discussion, probably about where they'd meet up later. The utter normalcy of it made Henry's throat tighten and his eyes start to fill. He didn't care to talk about his emotions but he sure had a lot of them lately. Most were good but even those weren't always easy to cope with.

When they were especially intense, the memory of flailing his arms and kicking his legs in the deep end of the pool would suddenly pop into his head. His father had thrown him in because water was simple and simple was all his father knew. If the man had been immersed in what Henry was feeling, *he'd* have drowned.

Junior—no, *Jackson*, Henry had to remember he was *Jackson* now—told his friends he'd see them later and waved goodbye as he came toward Henry and Danny. As soon as Henry got to his feet, the kid wrapped him up in a big, enthusiastic hug, then did the same to Danny, his movements easy and casual without any awkwardness at all. Henry waited till he was done hugging, then held up the manila envelope.

"What's this?" Jackson asked.

"'This' is you," Henry told him. "Birth certificate, Social Security card, passport. Also, your credit report. Turns out you've got a pretty good credit rating. And I like the name you chose."

"Thanks. Jackson was my mom's name," the kid informed him, as if he didn't know.

"I'll have you know she was *my* mom first," Henry retorted.

The kid rolled his eyes. "Yeah, yeah."

Henry puffed himself up in faux outrage. "Don't you 'yeah, yeah' me, young man. Not when I'm about to show you a great place for lunch." He began to usher them in the direction of his favorite deli. "Only half a block off-campus; you'll love it."

The newly minted Jackson Verris felt as if his head was spinning. Going on missions was easy compared to this. It seemed like he had to juggle a hundred different things in his mind—he had to remember where to meet his friends later, how to sign up for the classes he wanted, where all his classes were on campus, what days, and what time, where he had put the list of textbooks he had to buy, and now he had a manila envelope full of information all about himself.

How did people keep track of everything? Maybe that's what they did with their phones; they put all the stuff they had to think about on them, which was why they were always looking at them. But how did they remember to carry their phones around with them in the first place or remember where they put them? He wasn't sure he would ever get the hang of this so-called normal life. Sometimes it was all he could do to remember his own name was Jackson Verris now, not Junior.

"So," Danny said, nudging his ribs with her elbow, "have you settled on a major yet?"

At last, a question he could answer. "I'm leaning toward engineering."

"Engineering?" Danny looked at him as if she'd never heard of anything so crazy.

"I know, right?" Henry said, then turned to him with the same look. "*Listen* to her. If *I* were you—which I am, sort of—I'd do computer science."

"Oh, *hell* no," Danny said, doing her best impression of Henry. "Save that for grad school. You want to start in the humanities—"

"No, wait—don't listen to *her*," Henry said.

"No, don't listen to *him*," Danny said quickly. "You need a grounding in the classics—"

This was getting out of hand. "Uh, guys…" he said.

"Excuse *me*," Henry said to Danny. "I'm trying to talk to myself here—"

"Yeah, you're talking to yourself, all right," Danny replied. "But you're sure not talking to *him*—"

"*Guys*," he tried again.

"I made a lot of mistakes when I was young," Henry was saying.

"And now you need to let him make his *own* mistakes," Danny said evenly.

Jackson stopped where he was. It took a couple of seconds before either Danny or Henry noticed. They turned to look at him, bewildered.

"Everyone chill the hell out!" he ordered them. Their expressions said they hadn't seen that coming. "I'm going to be okay," he added, a bit more quietly.

A broad grin spread across Henry's face. "Well, if *you're* okay, *I'm* okay."

Danny made the 'okay' sign with both hands and they all laughed. But even as he was laughing, he wanted to hug Henry, tell him he'd just said the one thing he wanted—*needed*—to hear and he hadn't known it until that very moment.

How had Henry managed that? Maybe it was just because he and Henry were so much a part of each other.

But it could also have been because they were family. A family consisted of people who cared about each other, helped each other—not because one of them wanted something but because people needed to care for each other, to help each other, love each other.

For a moment, he had an almost irresistible urge to tell Henry all of this and how Henry had given him everything he'd always wanted before he had even known what that was. But he knew Henry wasn't comfortable talking about emotions, not because he was repressed or shut down but simply because he was Henry. Talking about his feelings just wasn't his thing and never would be. Not in so many words, anyway.

But that was all right. Recent events had convinced him to be wary of anyone who constantly had to tell you how much they loved you. There really was such a thing as protesting too much.

Now he smiled at Henry, then sighed and shook his head.

"What?" Henry asked him.

He sighed again. "I can't believe that in thirty years I'm going to look like—" he gestured at Henry. "*You.*"

"Are you *kidding?*" Henry stuck his fists on his hips in mock indignation. "You should be so lucky, young man! You should be so *lucky!*"

All three of them cracked up as they started walking again.

"Now, first of all," Henry said in an exaggerated, lecturing tone. "I work out every day—*every day.* Yeah, go ahead and laugh—wait till you're fifty and we'll see if you're dragging your lazy ass around the track—"

"You mean fifty-one," Danny put in.

"Don't interrupt, young lady, or you'll be grounded," Henry said, shaking a finger at her. "Okay, secondly—

and pay attention, this is *extremely* important—I brush, I floss, I rinse, and my teeth are *spotless*. Seriously, I got *zero* cavities, baby. *Zero*."

Yeah, Jackson Verris thought, this new life was going to take some getting used to but he had no doubt at all it would be worth it.

END

For more fantastic fiction, author events,
exclusive excerpts, competitions, limited editions and more

VISIT OUR WEBSITE
titanbooks.com

LIKE US ON FACEBOOK
facebook.com/titanbooks

FOLLOW US ON TWITTER AND INSTAGRAM
@TitanBooks

EMAIL US
readerfeedback@titanemail.com